Love's Affliction

A novel

Fidelis O. Mkparu

Harvard Square Editions
New York
2015

Dedicated to

Oby, Ifeoma, Nky, and Junior

Firefly

Your light guides and abandons me

And when I hold on to your illusion,

It deceives my trusting soul, and leaves me

Feeling my way through the dark alone.

Your spark shows me the path

But you forsake me along the way.

When I reach out for your glimmer,

I find only darkness.

Chapter 1

MY FATHER ONCE TOLD ME that I have a special gift. My propensity for spiritual insight was a sign that I could have been a shaman. He claimed that I came from a paternal lineage bequeathed with enviable natural healing powers, and encouraged me to attend medical school. He had guessed my plan.

A pogrom, and the ensuing ethnic civil war in my country, accentuated my ethnic minority group's despair. The vanquishers destroyed our schools. The future of young Nigerians like me looked bleak. However, we would never surrender mentally. I followed my calling on a six thousand mile journey across the ocean and beyond to the 'free' world.

I searched for the moon my first night in America and fell asleep dreaming of home. Waking to the silence of my room at midnight, I resolved that other dreamers may waste their time searching for illusions, but my quest would be different. At sunrise of my first day on campus in the August of 1977, all my dreams crystallized. I paced around my small dormitory room reciting my future plans. Yes, I did. In those formative days, I used to orate on how I'd conquer the world of science and become famous. Hearing my own voice gave me courage. It was not delusion, but elation that ruled that morning.

At noon, from my dormitory window, I could see the alluring sun. My body needed a caress from the North Carolina midday sunshine. I unpacked my long-sleeve shirt and wool slacks, an outfit my Nigerian boarding school had described as 'proper attire' for young men. It was hard to temper my exuberance as a young college freshman.

Trying to exit my dormitory through the side door, I grabbed the brass doorknob and flinched. Who would have figured that a knob would be warm enough to inflict pain? There were so many new things to learn. Would it take pain to learn those lessons?

I followed a long path that led to the administration building. Walking briskly down the concrete trail, the sun stung my skin, and the stifling heat bathed my lungs with every breath I took. I looked up to the sky and wondered if it was the same sun that had gently darkened my skin for seventeen years of my life, in Nigeria. I ascended a small hill in my sweat-soaked, long-sleeve shirt and wool slacks. My pace decreased due to exhaustion. In desperation, I turned to look in the direction of my dormitory, and inadvertently tilted my head up to the sky. The sun nearly blinded me, but it did not deter me. I squinted on my second try. Unfortunately, the second look did not change the fact that I was farther away from my dormitory than I had expected. I sighed deeply. "I'm in trouble." What else could I have said? Only a fool would not have understood my precarious situation.

Undeterred by the hardship I faced, I walked on, until I reached my destination. The administration building.

I followed the signs to the international students' office. I scanned the crowded room for someone to talk to about class registration, but no one seemed to notice me. Several groups of students, some in short pants and casual tops, carried on with their conversations. Not only did I stand out in the way I was dressed, but my natural tan was the darkest in the room. And I was sweating profusely. "Clean up first," I muttered to myself. I tried to leave the office in search of a bathroom, but more students walked in.

"You need help?" came from behind me in a captivating Carolina drawl, immediately arresting my retreat. I turned around fast, and I almost fell over. Standing next to me was a stunning girl with dimples, alabaster skin, and long golden hair. My eyes travelled from her red blouse to her white shorts. She watched me with a smile, but I could not stop my unauthorized visual inspection. I was so enthralled by her beauty and elegance that I was speechless. In a trance.

"Hi. May I help you?" she asked me with a bit of formality. It was a needed change because I came back to my senses. I felt giddy when she lifted her hand to shake my sweaty palm. Was sun struck?

"I'm Wendy Crane. I help foreign students." Her southern twang, completely new to me, made her words sound fascinating. Even with all my boarding school etiquette, watching her lips move, made me forget to introduce myself.

"Thank you," came out of my mouth when I probably meant to compliment her beauty. It's a good thing I did not have the courage.

While I struggled to compose myself, which felt like eternity, she said, "What you need, Hon?" She had the most relaxed demeanor I had ever encountered in my life. What a life I'd had: proper attire, measured speech, chaperoned boarding school dances, mandatory siesta, and everything else that could bore me to death.

"I'm Joseph Fafa. I need help with my registration."
Amazing how my tongue loosened up in her aura.

Of her own initiative, Wendy Crane walked with me to the
registrar's office where I enrolled as a student. I learned that
molecular biology was one of the required courses for
freshmen biochemistry majors, and as a sophomore biology
major, she was required to take the same course.

"Would you like to join us for dinner at five at the school
cafeteria?" she asked.

I didn't hesitate to say yes. Only a dead man would have
said no to such a beautiful girl, and from the feelings cooking
inside me, I knew I was not dead.

I walked on air back to my dormitory, hardly noticing the
heat. I cannot recall if I walked, or ran. No sun could have
slowed me down after meeting Wendy. "Dinner at five," I
mumbled to myself several times on my way back to Chelsea
hall.

It dawned on me that I did not know anything about
American girls. "Uh-oh, I'm in trouble!" I am not sure if I said
it aloud.

At dinner that evening, she introduced me to her friends,
then to cheeseburgers and fries. Initially, I tried to use my
cutleries on the cheeseburger, but she gently took them away
from me. My 'foreign' ways entertained them for the evening,
and Wendy's gregarious friend, Lisa, laughed throughout
dinner at my expense. Although my comedy session was
unrehearsed, judging by their laughter, it must have been
punchy. I knew it was not a date, but she did tell me, "You're
nice," before I left.

From that first day, Wendy and I were inseparable. We
studied together, and dined together most of the time. One

week into our friendship, while she was teaching me the fundamentals of the piano keyboard in our school music room, our hands met midway. We turned toward each other and kissed. "I'm glad we got it over with," she said. I had no clue what she meant, but I kissed her more. Our tongues wandered. What a kiss!

Two days after our first kiss, Wendy invited me to a 'Campus Crusade' meeting at the student center. I accepted warily. For a young man coming from a war-ravaged country, I had a different understanding of the word 'crusade'. The meeting started. They shouted words like "You're my savior, my light, and all I need." The wailing annoyed me, but I persevered. Wendy wanted to talk to their leader after the event.

After a long wait, a young man, probably thirty, with a trimmed beard, and long blond hair, approached us. He did not shake my hand, nor did he smile. "Are you a Christian?" the fiery-eyed man asked me.

"I'm a Catholic," I answered.

"Leave CC girls alone," he said.

"What?" I asked, not sure if I heard him right.

"Greg, he's a good boy," Wendy said.

"He defiles you, and you say he's good?" Greg said.

"Wait a minute, sir. I didn't defile anyone," I yelled at him. Wendy grabbed me by the hand and we walked away. She told me how she joined the group because of her fundamental Christian values. We had a lot to sort out if there were going to be more kisses between us.

Someone passed a note under my door: "Looking for a runaway African Monkey, please call the local zoo if found." I took it to the 'Dean of Men'. He felt that it was "a misguided joke" and should be ignored.

Wendy and I faced a daily barrage of insults from fellow students, which affected Wendy tremendously. That was how my friendship with Wendy progressed, until the day I was physically injured by a group of four boys during a concert. One of the boys had called Wendy, "A disgrace to White race," for attending the concert with me. I asked them to stop calling her names. They responded to my verbal request with punches. I left the concert with a black eye.

When Wendy ran off to France, on the verge of mental breakdown, I was devastated. I spent the next year afflicted with the pain of lost love. I devoted all my time to my schoolwork. Although I excelled academically, a loneliness unlike anything I'd ever known before crept into my life and refused to vacate.

After one year in France, Wendy came back to North Carolina. I was surprised that she wanted to revive our friendship.

It is true that things like mores may change over time, but love remains the same. Love has no dimension, or ethnicity. It remains what it has always been for eternity, love. And the ones who yearn for it the most are the afflicted.

Chapter 2

WENDY WAS BACK! I spent memorable spring mornings frolicking with Wendy until it became difficult for us to be apart. She would rush over to my place after her morning shower with dripping hair, and always had the same excuse: "Couldn't wait to see you, Hon." It made me feel special that I was important to her. I wondered what she saw in me.

I asked several times, "Why me Wendy?" She smiled instead of answering my questions. I came home one day and found a sealed envelope under my door. I tore the envelope open. A handwritten note from Wendy.

Hi Joseph!

You asked me what it was about you that drove me to get to know you.

Where should I begin?

Your gorgeous smile that warms up a room

Your soft-spoken caring voice that stopped me dead in my tracks

Your subtle accent that made me hot

Your tall, trim physique that shows you take pride in yourself

Your classy, stunning looks that provoked me to say "yum" under my breath

That sophisticated, intelligent way that you carry yourself that makes most people insecure. <u>NOT</u> *me!*

The package made my heart pound. But these things were just the beginning. They were before I even began to know the "real" you. Now it's so much more than those superficial things. You make me feel special, like no other boy ever has. You make me feel whole when we are together, and incomplete when we are apart. I

never dreamt that I could feel as I do when I'm with you. I cannot
live without you in my life. I love you.

    Wendy.

    I saved Wendy's note in my suitcase. I read it almost every
day.

    On a spring Saturday morning in 1979, Wendy and I were
eager to spend time together, so we ignored the swirling dark
clouds that hovered above us. We had stopped at a small lake
to watch mating frogs perched on water lilies when the rain
began to fall. It was the first major rainfall of that year, and it
started as a torrential downpour, which was uncharacteristic of
early spring in North Carolina. I held Wendy's hand as we ran
for shelter in the expansive college botanical garden. We
stopped at the ornate arch-entrance, where the overhead
massive concrete beam partially sheltered us from the lashing
rain. As the splattering rain soaked our feet, we shivered and
huddled together.

    The shuddering of Wendy's jaw became uncontrollable. I
ran my hand down her wet golden hair and kissed her
quivering lips. It was our first public kiss, and even the rain
could not dampen the warm feeling inside me. With her head
tilted, she looked deep in my eyes. Her magnificence held me
spellbound. For a moment, her jaw stopped trembling.

    "Wow! I'm tingling all over. Good kiss, Hon. I love the
tongue thingy," Wendy said. She sighed as she slowly
disengaged from our embrace and looked at me intently. I
smiled as she continued effusively. "You look good, you kiss
well. What can't you do? Poor me." She wiped her lipstick off
my lips and hugged me. Her fingers ran through my Afro,

which I'd spent a great deal of time putting together, before the rain soaked it wet.

We were still holding each other when I whispered in her ear, "What a relief. I'm glad you didn't slap me for kissing you out here." As I spoke, partial darkness engulfed us. I looked up at the sky. Dark, low-hanging clouds gathered barely above the tree level. "I'm worried about this crazy weather. We should head to the amphitheater," I said.

"Take me anywhere, Hon. I'll always follow you," she said. For a moment, I wondered what she meant, but multiple lightning strikes unnerved me. There was no time to probe her statement. We ran to the nearby amphitheater and climbed to the stage to take shelter under its retractable canopy. We held each other to keep warm, and her warm breath titillated my neck every few seconds. There was nothing I could have said that would be enough to express my feelings. Our silence deepened my emotional bond with her.

She looked into my eyes, and, as if reading my mind, said, "Being with you feels so good. I'm sorry I ever left you. Thanks for taking me to my favorite place in the world, for just you and me. Nothing else matters now." Tears rolled down her cheeks.

"Did you think about me in France? I mean, did you miss me?" I asked.

"I thought of you many times, but I was confused. I missed my friend and lover," she said, smiling.

"I'm glad you did," I said.

"I want to go back with you and experience so many things together. Well, there's still plenty of time to enjoy each other before we graduate," she said. Her hand rested on my cheek as she kissed me. A quick peck, for reassurance. I pulled her closer to me and gave her a real kiss.

"You're a bad, bad, boy," she drawled.

"Being bad is good for us. You said so, when we met," I said with a smile, but her countenance changed.

"I wonder what our lives would be like now if we'd continued our friendship a year ago. Tell me Hon; are we good for each other?" She was solemn as she spoke.

"If I could take away every bad experience you had with me, I would say that I'm good for you, but since they still hurl ugly words at us, I wonder if you're not better off without me," I said.

My disillusionment from all the racism only further exposed my vulnerability. I bit back the tears in front of the girl who meant the world to me. "I have toughened up since I came here, because I have no other choice, but you can avoid the abuse by walking away from our friendship."

She looked at me intently before she spoke. "I can't walk away from you after all we've been through together," she said.

"Maybe that's the best thing for you to do," I suggested. It was the fear of falling deeply in love with her that caused this insincere suggestion. Losing control of my emotions scared me more than the racial affront I had to deal with, because once I unlocked my vulnerability, there was no way to regain control.

"You don't mean that. I'll never leave you again. I need you," she sobbed. I wiped her eyes with my wet hand, but her tears flowed more.

"You told me your father doesn't approve of our friendship. What do you think he'll do when he finds out that we're more than study buddies?" I asked. A lightning flash followed by loud rumbling noises interrupted our conversation.

As we watched a barrage of pelting hail, I pulled her closer and kissed her. Booming thunder continued in rapid succession until it all fused together. The phenomenal downpour that followed, rapidly saturated the ground. Small puddles coalesced into flowing streams as the rain continued. We ran for it. By the time the rain stopped, our clothes were drenched, our jaws shuddering more intensely.

I took Wendy back to her dormitory soaking wet, and apologized for choosing the wrong venue for our date. Some of the students in her dormitory lobby whispered among themselves when we walked in with our drenched clothes and unmitigated exuberance. We stood by the elevator door and looked at each other sanguinely without saying much. Even in my wet clothes, I did not want to leave her. Finally, the elevator came for her, and as she walked in, I said, "I had fun with you today." The elevator door closed before she could say anything.

I stood and watched the elevator panel light up with successive numbers until it reached 12. When the number remained unchanged for more than one minute, I left the building. The temperamental rainfall lashed my body with torrents of hail as I ran to my apartment.

* * *

By mid-afternoon that Saturday, the dark clouds dissipated, and the sun came out. Since the school cafeteria had closed, I stopped by a local diner across from the college chapel for a quick lunch, before my study period with Wendy and Lisa. As soon as I walked into the diner, the owner, a burly middle-aged man, who stood by the landing, said, "Joseph Fafa! How are you my friend?"

I smiled. "Not bad at all." He shook my hand and squeezed my shoulder. It felt like he was rearranging my joint. He was a good-humored fellow, so I did not complain.

"Hey, you owe me for saving your rear. Without me, those knuckleheads would have rearranged your face." He chuckled and then added, "Where's the cutie you almost gave up your life trying to impress?"

"That was months ago, Mr. Eagan." I looked behind me before I added, "Francesca finished college last year and is now a swimsuit model. I guess I wasn't good enough for her after she made it big."

"Has it been that long? Well, I can't forget the cuts on your face. Look, you never stop a punch that way. You duck, and punch back." I could not help but laugh watching his oversized belly jiggle as he demonstrated the boxing moves.

"I didn't want to fight those boys in the first place," I said.

"You were fearless taking punches from them. A true African warrior," he said with seriousness.

I laughed. If only he knew that I grew up in a bustling commercial city and never saw, or even heard of an African warrior. I stopped laughing when his facial expression changed to a puzzled look. "I tried my best, sir, but there were five of them, and only one of me. Unless you count Francesca," I said with a smile.

"Not after what you just told me."

It was hard to forget what befell me that day when I went to the diner with Francesca. Five boys crouched like monkeys and called me an "African ape." I called one of the boys "an idiot" and he threw a punch at me. I tried to walk away, but another boy kicked my leg. He instantly received the brunt of my anger. My punch to his face knocked him down. The other boys came to his rescue and threw several punches at me when I tried to stop him from getting up. It felt as if I was on my way to hell after I saw so many stars from their blows to my face. I was lucky that Mr. Eagan effectively intervened. One of the boys threatened to shoot my "black ass." The local police responded promptly to Francesca's urgent call.

"By the way," he said, "I saw a picture of you in *The Courant* receiving awards. I hung it on the wall for weeks. I'm glad you stayed to get your education. We're slowly changing around here. Good luck to you," He shook my hand as he spoke.

* * *

Wendy was in our study cubicle when I arrived. She was wearing a tight-fitting navy blue dress with gold trimming and a pair of blue pumps. Her gold earrings, studded with exquisite gems, matched her intricate necklace. Even more than her *haute couture*, her smile overwhelmed me.

"All dressed up for me, or do you have another date?" I asked jokingly.

"You're a class act. You think there's someone else? I just shared the most romantic morning of my life with you. I can't even get the taste of you out of my mouth," she said.

"What can I say? I have never seen you dress up to study." I walked around to look at the back of her dress.

"You could've said I looked nice, instead of being mean. My dad is coming back from South America. Mom wants me to meet her at the airport at around seven p.m.," she said.

"So, you're wearing airport attire for the Cranes?" I asked.

"It depends on the situation. He's flying back with some executives and wants to show off his family, like he always does," she said with a smile. While I was still admiring her dress, she asked, "You want to keep me company?" Lisa walked over to our table and briefly interrupted our conversation.

"Going to church, Wendy?" Lisa asked. Wendy looked at her and frowned, but Lisa laughed.

"As if you don't know we're in the library," Wendy whispered. Control yourself before they kick us out."

"We're wasting time we don't have," I said. We were studying for our medical school admission examination. I looked at Wendy, and added, "I'd be happy to go with you to the airport, but I'll stay away from your father." We sat down and gazed at each other.

"What's going on here?" Lisa demanded. "You keep on staring at each other. Acting like you're up to no good." Lisa didn't stop her harangue until Wendy and I opened our books to study.

We had a great deal of work to do before the admission exam, but Wendy kept staring at me. Occasionally, I glanced at her and smiled. However, I had to be tactful because Lisa noticed everything we did. Each time I smiled, Lisa looked at Wendy's face. It appeared that our mode of non-verbal communication captivated Lisa. I felt that from the limited amount of time Lisa spent turning the pages of her book, she did not accomplish much. Even with all the distractions, I managed to achieve most of my goals, but my reading efficiency plummeted. Reading several paragraphs twice worried me, so I left our study room for a break outside the library.

Immersed in the frightening thought of failing my medical school admission examination, I walked to the soccer field. I was worried that my budding romance with Wendy could unravel all the efforts I had made to be an honors student. Every time I tried to think of something other than Wendy, she came drifting back to me. The fun we had earlier that day in the botanical garden held my brain captive. My heart raced as I contemplated what would become of my future if I did not get a good score on the exam.

Standing in the middle of the soccer field alone, I felt my anxiety increase. I ran back to the library so fast that I was gasping for air. Wendy and Lisa stared at me as I approached our study cubicle. Still panting, I picked up a notebook to fan my face, but sweat continued to drip from my forehead. Wendy came over to my side of the desk and sat down. She gently wiped the sweat off my face with tissue paper and kissed me. It was our second public kiss.

Lisa looked at us in disbelief but did not say anything. She tried to concentrate on what she was reading, but she could not keep her eyes off us.

"What happened to you out there?" Wendy asked, and put her arm around me before she added, "Are you worried about us? I'm scared too, but we can make it work."

"I'm concerned about how little I have accomplished today," I said. She removed her arm from my shoulder and smiled.

"That's good to know because I thought you were having regrets about us," Wendy said, as Lisa stared at us more. Lisa cleared her throat, but we ignored her.

"You need to tell me what's going on here," Lisa said, as she stood up. A bewildered look had replaced her usual smile.

"You really want to know? Well, Joseph kissed me this morning, and it set my body on fire," Wendy said with interspersed chuckles.

"Oh! Volcano Joe. I should've known better than to trust this fake . . . whatever," Lisa quipped, which made Wendy laugh.

"Volcano Joe? What's that, Lisa?" I naively asked.

"Go ahead, pretend you're an ignorant foreigner, as you always do. You think you can fool everybody. Academic awards here, scholarships there. You don't fool me." Lisa would have gone on forever if I did not interrupt.

"Since you asked, we went out this morning, and during the rainfall, yes, our lips touched," I enunciated every word slowly. Lisa initially appeared irritated by my antics, but Wendy smiled.

"You're a smart Alec. I hope that's what you gonna tell Papa Bear when he finds out you kissed his daughter," Lisa said with a smile on her face.

"Thanks for the compliment, Lisa," I said, "if that's what you intend, but I have one correction: I didn't violate anybody's daughter."

Wendy listened without saying anything, intermittently looking at her watch. As Lisa and I continued bantering.

"You lied to me, Wendy. For the past two years, you claimed to have no romantic interest in him. What happened to you? I'm supposed to be your best friend, but you've been lying to me," Lisa said.

"Let's just get to the airport," Wendy said.

Lisa looked at me and shook her head. It was supposed to be Wendy and me spending time together, but Lisa invited herself.

Wendy, smiled and said, "I've got to go. You mind driving, Lisa?"

"Somebody's got to drive the lovebirds to the airport," Lisa said.

"Now we're lovebirds?" Wendy said.

"Just teasing you two," Lisa said.

We scooped up our books and left the library, Lisa walking ahead of us. I held Wendy's hand, and when Lisa turned around, we disengaged our hands. The event repeated several times. Lisa was taunting us for fun.

*　*　*

The regional airport was almost empty. In the arrival lounge, a woman and two young girls huddled together. They looked at us quizzically as we walked by. The young girls continued to stare at us after we sat down.

Wendy kept busy rummaging through her purse, while Lisa read a magazine. I leaned back and stretched my legs. After sitting idly for more than ten minutes, I left the girls and walked around the empty airport arrival lounge. I checked the arrival board, but could not find any commercial flight that was to arrive within the hour, so I went back to my chair.

I watched time pass by until rhythmic tapping sounds from high heel shoes punctuated the stillness of the lounge. Eager to know whose noisy shoes interrupted my concentration, I turned around and saw Wendy's mother walking toward us in her dainty pumps as if floating on air. Her gold necklace studded with large Tanzanite gemstones glistened in the ambient light. She glanced in our direction and smiled. Wendy, filled with excitement, sprang to her feet, and hugged her mother. They inspected each other's outfits and nodded in unison.

"Mom, you remember Joseph?" Wendy asked, as she pulled me up from my chair.

"Of course, I do. How can I forget that smiley face?" Wendy's mother said as we shook hands. "How's school this semester?" she added.

"So far, I'm doing well in all my classes, but I'm ready to end this semester and start my final year. I can't wait to graduate," I said. As I spoke to her, she inspected me from my head down to my feet and back to my head. I had on a decent white shirt and a pair of light blue wool slacks, but I wondered if they met with her approval.

"That's great, Joseph," Wendy's mother said before she turned to Lisa who stood next to me.

Usually, Lisa was the chatterbox of the group and had a carefree essence, but she had been quiet since we left the school library. Wendy's mother finally succeeded in engaging her on equestrian issues. Lisa regained her ebullient spirit talking about horses. For more than fifteen minutes, they exchanged ideas on caring for show-horses. After listening to their endless tales of the best horses for competition and championship meets, I walked away. At the information desk, I busied myself with pamphlets on interesting places around town displayed on a wooden cabinet. I kept two pamphlets, which I felt might help me in planning my next date with Wendy. I tried to pick up more pamphlets, but I jumped when a pair of hands squeezed my buttocks. Before I could turn around, I heard Wendy giggle. She had no interest in horses either and was probably bored of her mother's discussions with Lisa.

"Hold my hand. I feel so much better at the slightest touch from you. It's amazing." She closed her eyes. "I forgot to tell you. My parents are going to France in two weeks. We were to travel together during spring break, but I changed my mind this morning. I told my mother I'm staying in school, and she wasn't happy with my decision," Wendy said.

"Why did you change your mind?" I asked.

"Pretend you don't know. I don't enjoy missing you. Is it wrong that I want to be with you?" she said as she walked to my side to hold my hand.

"That's nice to hear. I want to spend time with you too, but your family comes first," I said. I would have given up anything at that moment to be with my own family, but my father wanted me to stay in school and finish my education.

"Go ahead, ruin it for me. That wasn't what I expected from you. You could've faked some excitement, even if you didn't feel it," she said. Without hesitation, she disengaged her hand from mine.

"I'm sorry, Wendy, but I feel your family should take priority over me, however much I would love to spend spring break with you," I said.

She ignored me and looked away. "My dad is here," Wendy shouted. I turned to watch Wendy run with her high heel shoes on the highly polished airport floor, which caused me anguish. I took a deep breath and held it until she reached her father without any mishap.

My heart fluttered. I refocused my attention on the pamphlet display case. I had barely picked up a pamphlet on Wilmington, North Carolina, when I heard the *click, clack* of high-heel shoes approaching.

"Joseph, come over here and say hello to my father."

I dropped the pamphlets in my hand and walked over to greet Mr. Crane. Mrs. Crane's left hand clasped her husband's right hand, while her right hand held on to Wendy's hand. Lisa stood by the side of the Cranes and watched me with an uncharacteristic simper. Closer to the wall, two men in blue suits stood and watched us.

Even though Wendy's family formality overwhelmed me, I mustered enough courage to say, "Hello Mister Crane. I hope you had a nice flight?" The impassive man towered over me, and made me feel small, even at six feet tall. Instead of a firm handshake, his hand gripped mine like a vise. I was in pain until he let go of my hand. "The flight was flawless. My pilot is probably the best in the country." He then turned to Lisa and asked, "Y'all here to see me?"

"We finished our studies early and came to be with Wendy," I said before Lisa could answer him. After the handshake from Mr. Crane, I could not let Lisa decide my fate.

"Don't you have a girlfriend? You could've spent all this time with her, rather than waste it at the airport," Mr. Crane said. Wendy froze. A void opened up around us. Lisa, Wendy's mother, and the two men standing by the wall, walked toward the private luggage retrieval area. Their sudden departure distracted me, but I regained my composure quickly.

"Wendy and I enjoy spending time together. She asked me to be with her," I said. When I turned to Wendy for support, she was wearing a frown and did not say anything.

Mr. Crane let out a loud sigh as his face turned red. His bulging eyes virtually looked through me, and fixed me at the spot where I stood. "Listen, you bastard, stay away from my daughter. I don't want her confused. I'll make this request only once." He moved closer to me as he spoke, but I stood my ground. "Find another girl. Your kind. And leave my daughter alone," he continued, shaking his finger in my face. He turned to Wendy and said, "You're going home with me. I don't want you around this fool."

Wendy stared straight ahead in shock.

After his edict to Wendy, he walked away from us. It was the first time I regretted obeying my parents' instruction to 'respect my elders.'

Wendy stood where her father left us and cried. I reached out to hug her, but she wiped her tears and walked away from me . Lisa rejoined me while I stood there contemplating what to do. She smiled and leaned her head toward me as if she was searching for something on my face. Her action gave me an eerie feeling.

"It looks like I'm taking you home alone, Loverboy," Lisa mocked me. "Papa Bear said you should find your own type. Hmm, I wonder what he means?" she continued.

"I don't care about what the old man said. My only concern is Wendy. I hope she's OK," I said.

"Wendy must be in love with you to stomach all the bad names she's been called on campus since you landed here like a bad hurricane. Two freaking years of torture. That's it! Hurricane Joe!"

"Will you stop playing around, Lisa? This is serious. The old man warned me to stay away from his daughter, but what hurts me more is that Wendy did not defend me. I thought she cared about me," I said.

"She does. Look at the way she looks at you. Don't tell me you don't notice what she does. The only problem is her father. I'm sure the two of you will find a way to be together," Lisa said. Her statement surprised me because it was the first time she said anything that suggested her concern for my happiness. "Let's get out of here," she said. It took Lisa two years to show me her sensitive side. I was at a loss for words. My suspicion that she harbored ethnic, prejudicial tendencies ended that night.

I sat in the passenger's seat of Lisa's car and looked out of the window as she drove through the deserted regional airport road. Darkness had fallen, and there was no moon, or stars, to offer even a glimpse of light. My mind drifted to Wendy, and the first day we met. I was so worried that the fear of losing her again shutdown all my senses. Even if Lisa spoke to me, I would not have heard it. I was lost in myself. When Lisa dropped me off, I sat on the steps in front of my dormitory for at least an hour, and supported my head with my cupped hands. I was expecting Wendy to stop by, but she didn't come that night.

On Monday afternoon, after Wendy failed to show up for our regular lunch meeting in the school cafeteria, I visited her dormitory, but she didn't answer. I was devastated. On Tuesday afternoon, I had a similar fate.

On Wednesday, I visited Lisa's sorority house. It was an old English Tudor on the sorority and fraternity row. Wendy had taken me there once, when we first met, to introduce me to Lisa, who had been her best friend since they were five. Most of the girls living in the house were unfriendly, and it took a lot of courage for me to return alone to such a prissy place.

I stood by the door for a long time and considered what I had to say before I rang the doorbell. When Lisa answered the door, I was delighted to see a familiar face,. "Where's Wendy?" I asked. She stared at me vacuously and sighed. We stood there in silence, looking at each other until she muttered incomprehensibly.

Stepping out, Lisa closed the door behind her, and looked in all directions before she said, "She's set you free. Free from all the freaking racial insults you take because of her." I stood there dumbfounded and wondered why Wendy had to set me free, now that the racial tension that gripped the campus when I arrived two years before had abated. Lisa's statement did not make any sense to me, but I could not argue with the messenger. I turned away from her and painstakingly walked down the steps. She closed the squeaky door.

I waited to cross the street and heard the door open. Impulsively, I turned around and saw Lisa beckoning to me to come back. She walked down the steps to meet me halfway. "Be careful with Wendy's father," Lisa said in a hushed voice. Lisa's behavior bordered on paranoia, and I looked at her with incredulity.

"What are you saying?" I asked.

"You need to be careful. That's all I have to say for now," she said, and then ran up the steps without looking back.

Although I felt that Wendy's father was not a delightful man when we first met, he did not display any outward hostility toward me. Powerful men like James Crane dealt only with important people in commerce and industry. However, I was worried enough about what she said that I resolved to avoid courting any danger.

Chapter 3

MY OUTLOOK ON SPRING had changed by the time the pre-med society banquet came around. For medical doctor wannabes, this was the main event of the year. Whispers of the event permeated every science classroom, and unabashed critics gave opinions on their rivals' dresses before even seeing them. I had to contend with my indifference toward social events before I asked a first-year law student who participated in a campus demonstration I organized for the anti-apartheid movement to be my date for the banquet. Apart from campus activism, I felt that I did not have much in common with Lily.

That changed after Lily accepted my invitation. The more we talked, the more I appreciated that she was a New Yorker with an attitude. I realized the locals talked about her accent as much as they talked about mine. They disparaged her Jewish ethnicity almost to the same level as they did my Nigerian heritage. Suddenly, I had a perfect companion for the event.

I had to wait for Lily to finish dressing after I arrived at the house she rented one block away from the college. She kept me waiting for more than ten restless minutes and finally walked into her small living room. I could not recognize her in her body-hugging white dress. It was better than most of the dresses I had seen so-called movie stars wear on Oscar night. She strutted around her living room for me and I gloated about my knack for attracting beautiful girls. I heard myself repeating, "Nice dress," several times. Even though I felt privileged to be with Lily, I closed my eyes and imagined that I was with

Wendy. Fortunately, my reverie was so brief that she did not seem to notice my absence.

*   *   *

The banquet hall was full by the time we arrived. We made our way through the crowd in the hall. Crystal-studded chandeliers reflected mesmerizing colors of light on the ceiling. The reverberating sound of excited students made the hall seem bigger than it was.

Lily and I found a table with two empty seats and sat down. Two of the girls at our table whispered to each other and laughed as we greeted everyone. Even though I overhead them say, "Mandingo searching for white girls," I ignored them. However, as they continued to enunciate their feelings aloud, even calling Lily "an overdone rag doll with a funny nose," she took notice.

"You clowns have something to say?" Lily asked.

"Do I even frigging know you?" one of the girls asked Lily with an angry tone of voice. To my delight, Lily ignored the girl and her question.

The two girls carried on with deplorable racial invective as if we were not there. "What a pair of losers: Blackie and the Jew," the shorter, fiery girl said. I was about to get up, when the announcements began.

A cheery Wendy Crane made the welcoming statement from the podium. "Ladies and gentlemen, we're gathered here today, as every year, to celebrate our achievements, and to give our beloved senior students a well-deserved send off to various medical schools across the country." It was the first time I had seen or heard her voice since the unfortunate encounter with her father at the airport a few weeks before. "Dinner will be served first before the awards ceremony," she added, before she put the microphone down and walked to her table. I could not identify the other occupants of her table, apart from Lisa. I thought about going over to say hello, but I could not find the courage to do so. And I did not want to offend Lily.

As if hypnotized, I could not keep my eyes away from Wendy's table. Lily soon caught on. "Is there something wrong? You act as though your mind is somewhere else." It took her intuitive question to bring me back to her.

"I'm OK. But, it's amazing how students don't value true friendship," I said.

"I'm not sure what you mean. I value your friendship," Lily said.

"Not you. I was just thinking aloud. I'm very sorry," I replied. She smiled and then flipped through the event program. Occasionally, she looked at me and smiled. If things were different in my life, I would have enjoyed being with her.

When my mind drifted back to Wendy's table, my real date for the night, Lily Levenstein, pulled her chair closer and said, "Since you invited me to an event with dancing on the program, you'll have to show me how to boogie." She smiled radiantly and reached for my hand. I could not tell how her hand felt. Wendy had rendered me emotionally empty.

I couldn't ignore Lily after such a direct hint, so I said, "Me dance? What makes you think I can?" Lily looked at me with wide eyes, which prompted me to qualify what I said. "I'm not sure what type of songs they'll play tonight. Honky-tonk music isn't my style. Dancing depends on what they play." She laughed when I gave multiple conditions that would influence my dancing with her. Lily laughed loudly. Fortunately, the hall was so noisy that no one else cared about Lily's distinct contribution to the high decibels of the gathering.

As soon as the first song came on, Lily said, "There's no excuse for you now. I love this song. Let's go and boogie."

My heart pounded to the slow beat, but I could not say no to her. "Of course. We can dance to your song and any other song they play tonight," I said as I stood up from my chair. I held her hand and led her toward the dance floor. We passed by Wendy's table before we made it to the hardwood. Wendy stood up as I walked by, but I ignored her and walked on. Lisa smiled and waved at us.

Bill Withers song '*Lovely day*' transforms dreary times into groovy moments. By the time we arrived at the dance floor, the music had possessed me. I closed my eyes and imagined I was in paradise. There was no inhibition left in me at that moment. Lily rested her hands on my shoulders, but I pulled her closer by placing my hands on her buttocks. Her head found a comfortable place on my shoulder as we moved our hips in circular motion. "You're a naughty boy," Lily whispered in my ear.

"I know," I replied. She lifted her head up and smiled as we continued with our sensual display on the dance floor. Like everything else in life, the song ended, and I escorted her back to our table.

I had barely sat down when I heard, "How could you? Disgracing yourself out there on the dance floor with that disgusting sexual display." I turned around and found an angry

Wendy. Lily looked at me as if waiting for an explanation. I felt uneasy and tried to suppress a smile.

"Why worry yourself about my dancing? I was dancing with Lily, not you. She didn't complain, why should you?" I asked. Lily, who initially ignored my exchanges with Wendy, stood up after our voices became louder and said, "Let's be civil kids." To my dismay, Wendy angrily wagged her finger at Lily.

"Who's this floozy with you, Joseph? Go ahead, tell me any lies you want. You squeezed her fat ass like she was a cheap whore." Wendy's voice echoed with rage as she spoke.

"I'm not responding to your trash, fool," Lily said. I held Lily's hand to prevent her from using it accidentally.

"Lily is a good friend. She left her studies tonight to attend this stupid event with me. I wish you would be civil to her. It's not like you to be so mean to people." Wendy's engorged eyes spilled her tears. I picked up my napkin from the table to wipe her tears, but she knocked it out of my hand.

"You're mine. I won't let you disgrace me in front of my friends. Go ahead, tell your Lily about us," Wendy said. I looked around the hall with concern that we might be attracting more attention from the crowd, but most of the students were still on the dance floor.

"There's nothing to tell her about us except that you left me because of your father, and I haven't heard from you in weeks. For someone who claims to care about me, you have a funny way of showing it." I tried to control my anger as I spoke but it was difficult to do so. "What else do you want me to tell Lily about us?" I asked in a harsh tone. I waited for an answer, but she ignored me. Instead, she looked at Lily with disdain.

"Your ex-girlfriend acts as if she's about to attack me." Lily said as Wendy continued to stare at her. "Why don't you take me home?"

"Go ahead, Joseph, take her home. You can finish what you started on the dance floor," Wendy said. As we walked away from her, she added, "If you leave with her, just forget about us." I ignored her threat because I felt that I could not lose what I did not have.

Once outside the hall and away from the noise, I apologized profusely to Lily. "That's a crazy bitch," Lily jokingly said.

"Wendy is usually reasonable," I said. I was relieved that she found the dire situation funny, but offended that she used a derogatory word to describe Wendy.

*   *   *

Although our evening came to a sudden end, Lily stated that she had fun with me. Before I left her for the night, she said, "Let me tell you something, Loverboy, this is the last time I end a fun date with you because of your jealous ex-girlfriend." I thought about what she said and wondered why she would want to go out with me again after such a disastrous night.

"I'm very sorry about tonight. Maybe someday I'll make it up to you," I said.

I drove back to my apartment alone with conflicted feelings. I should have taken Lily somewhere else to spend the rest of the evening together.

Wendy was sitting in her car in front of my apartment. Before I could turn off my car engine, she hurried out of her car and walked over to me. She looked in the front passenger seat and then opened the back door.

"Did you forget something in my car?" I asked her sarcastically. She ignored me and continued with her thorough check of the inside of my car. She glanced at me briefly before she walked to her car and drove off.

Over the two years I had known Wendy, she had reacted inconsistently to several issues. However, I had expected her to be more circumspect at the banquet, but, to my disappointment, she let her emotions rule her actions. Even though Wendy displayed unnecessary possessiveness at a public function, my strong feelings for her remained unabated. Like a typical narcissistic male, a part of me was happy that she felt jealous. I reflected on the events surrounding her outburst, and I wondered if I subconsciously baited her to react negatively to my dancing. Since I could not reliably probe my subconscious, I had to let things stand the way they happened.

* * *

I had drifted in and out of sleep several times when I heard a loud knock on my door. Initially, it felt as though the knocks were part of my dream, so I did not get up. The knocking became louder. I put on my robe and walked into my living room. "Who's it?" I asked angrily.

"It's me, Wendy," she retorted loudly. I opened the door and found her shivering. It was common in North Carolina early spring, to have some teeth-chattering cold nights. I grabbed her hand and gently pulled her inside. It was a few minutes after two a.m.

Once my kitchen lights illuminated Wendy's face, I realized that her eyes were still red and swollen. I hugged and held her for as long as she would let me. Foolishly, I felt that it was the best way to tender my apology for the evening that I had inadvertently ruined for her. However, after I thought about it critically, my action was illogical. She ruined the evening for me, so she should be the one apologizing. The hug felt good. "Screw the logic," I muttered under my breath.

Wendy lifted her head from my shoulder. "What did you say?"

I released her from my grip. "It's not about you, love. I was thinking aloud." She smiled and walked to the couch.

"Hold my hand again, Joseph."

I reached out and held her hand. It was still cold, so I rubbed it with my two hands until it felt warm.

"Amazing." She smiled and put her head on my shoulder. In a barely audible voice, she said, "I love you, Joseph. I don't want to lose you again." I could hear her breathing, which sounded more like bursts of sighs. She lifted her head, looked in my eyes, and added, "You promised to take me away from here a year ago. I wonder if you ever will."

"I went through a rough time last year, and I wanted to run away. Regardless of the bigotry and harassment, I feel that we shouldn't run away from our problems. Our best bet is to stay in school and face the haters." She looked at me attentively and smiled occasionally. "I believe our friendship will be stronger if we're honest with each other. However, every time you shut me out of your life, it hurts more than all the insensitive names they call me around here. You're the only person that can hurt me more, with your disappearing acts." Before I could finish, she hugged me. We stretched out on the couch and held each other until the jolting train horn from the nearby train tracks woke us up at five a.m.

Chapter 4

THE TWO YEARS OF CAUSTIC BIGOTED ALLUSIONS had wounded my soul. I survived in North Carolina and even excelled in the midst of unwitting fools who routinely engaged in racial diatribes instead of scholarly discourse from my first day in the small college town. Unprepared for the racial tension that engulfed the area in the mid to late 1970s, I was grateful that it was limited to verbal attacks, initially.

Wendy developed a habit of driving to my dormitory on Friday nights. We sat by the side entrance steps and talked until late. Sometimes we gazed at the sky in search of bright stars. She loved the stars that stood out from the rest, and I preferred full moon nights, because they made her face more radiant. Her companionship made my suffering less painful.

Occasionally, we heard racial slurs from the second floor windows, but we ignored it. One evening, two football players yelled from the third floor window, "She wants his Bojangles." I looked at Wendy and laughed.

"What the heck is Bojangles?" I asked.

"Bojangles, well, ehm, I think, I'm not sure, but," Wendy rambled on. She knew, but could not tell, she was too shy to tell me, or she had no clue what it meant. Southern colloquialism sometimes leaves one confused.

On another Friday evening, two months into my second month in college, it rained heavily while I was studying. It was cloudy when I left the library, but the rain had abated. Walking along the path to my dormitory, I whistled to some birds I could not see. Anticipation of an evening with Wendy reduced me to a hopeless romantic. My mind focused on only one thing; gazing at stars. The joy we shared, when dark clouds cleared briefly to allow us a peek at our favorite stars, were momentous. I expected such an evening when I saw 'our step' from a short distance. The golden sun had dropped out of the sky. Subdued streetlights were coming on. I climbed the first step.

A cold liquid dripped on my head, and when I looked up, it covered my face. My eyes stung. I could not see, so I yelled for help. No help came, so I felt my way into the building. It was obvious to me that some boys passed me because I heard their laughter. My curses rained on them. I rued the day I left my country to become a caricature for these depraved schoolboys who would never become men.

"Stop defacing the walls with white paint!" It was a female voice I recognized. Our dormitory manager. "What prank are you pulling, fool?"

"I need help Mrs. Barnes. Someone poured paint on me as I was coming in," I said. More laughter from the boys punctuated our exchange.

Some types of humiliation make you feel worthless, because there is nothing you can do. I felt worse than that.

I reported the incident to the 'Dean of Men' the same day. He promised to look into it, but I never heard back from him. I felt humiliated.

As weeks passed, my dormitory life returned to normal, until a dozen notes that said, "Looking for a six-foot-tall African Negro to hang," appeared all over my dormitory floor.

I ran to the 'Dean of Men' office with one of the notes. "Dean, I'm afraid for my life," I said to the man responsible for protecting my wellbeing on campus. He laughed, and threw the flyer in the waste bin.

"They won't hurt you. Just silly boys, horsing around," he said.

I left his office and reported the incident to the international students' office. Before the sun set that day, they placed me in the graduate student housing complex. I believe that I could have been physically harmed if I had remained in the dormitory because of the level of ignorance of some of the students living there.

Through it all, Wendy was my solace and reliable companion, but her equivocation during her father's tirade at the airport left me discontented. She did come back after the banquet fiasco more attuned to my emotional needs. We dined together and explored the expansive college botanical gardens whenever we needed an escape from the daily grind of pre-med demands.

*   *   *

On one beautiful spring day, Wendy and I found a secluded manicured patch overlooking a small stream to spend the sunny afternoon. We ascended to a small ridge with enough space to accommodate our quilt, and nestled comfortably. Apart from bullfrogs with their intermittent sounds, the place was desolate. Suddenly, the cacophony of sounds from the bullfrogs subsided, and we felt a sense of oneness with our serene environment. Intoxicated with

Wendy's sensuous aura, I stripped down to my underwear and surrendered my body to the Carolina sun. My mental exhilaration put me in a state I liked to call 'my inner paradise'.

"Lie close to me, Hon. I want to feel your body next to mine. Your touch is so soothing," she said, stretching out her hand to touch me.

"I'm already close, unless you want me on top of you," I said. She laughed at my suggestion.

"You'd crush me. All I need is you nearer to me, Hon, but you complain," she said. I tried to pull her closer, but she resisted. "I want you to come to me. Show me you want to be close to me," she added.

She wasn't making any sense, but I moved closer. "What difference does it make who moves?" I said, but she ignored me.

The North Carolina sky hovered over us with its majestic blue color as the sun caressed our skin. Her beautiful tanned body kept my eyes captive, and my hands trembled as I turned her perspiration mixed with sun tan oil into a glistening emulsion. She moaned as I applied more pressure to sensitive parts of her body. I held my hands up at that point since going further would have violated a gentleman's code of conduct in that part of Dixie. She smiled mischievously and encircled my body with her arms. We held on tight to each other, as the heat of our love blended with the sun, to ignite a disreputable passion. I do not remember how we managed to let go of each other.

I stood up to walk around and Wendy stood up too, but did not follow me.

"Where do you think you're going? I need you right here, next to me," she demanded. It was not typical of Wendy to make so many demands, so I turned around and walked back to her. She sat down on the quilt with her legs stretched forward as soon as I returned. "Where were you going?" she asked, as she stretched her two hands forward to grab my legs.

"I guess you won't allow me to stretch my legs," I said as I sat down next to her.

Wendy looked at me with the most enticing smile on her face and tossed her long golden hair to the side. She flipped her hair again, and it lashed the left side of my face. I held her hand to stop her from playing with her hair, and she let out the most interesting giggle. "That serves you right for leaving me," she said, as she loosened my grip and removed her hair from my face. She rubbed my forearm and stopped midway to look at my face intently.

"Look at me! I'm tired of my skin looking pale. I hope the sun turns it bronze like yours," she said, as she nestled her head on my shoulder. I held on to her, but could not find the right thing to say to a beautiful woman who was unhappy with herself. She turned and looked at me several times, but all I could offer was a smile. After a protracted silence, she scooted away from me, and sprawled across the quilt.

"Hey, sun goddess! You need more sun tan lotion before the sun roasts your back," I said. She looked at me attentively as I spoke, but did not say anything. She turned away from me, and I added, "I love you just the way you are." She looked at me and sighed. I wondered why she sighed, but did not ask her. Instead, I continued, "I love you Wendy. No. Not only love, I need you."

"That's sweet, Joseph, but why did it take you so long to tell me? It took you forever, but I'm still glad you love me and my pale skin." She gently punched me on the side and added, "That's for keeping a girl waiting to hear sweet words from you."

"You know how I feel about you, so stop overexposing your skin to the sun," I said.

"For you, I'll stop, my jungle bunny," She said it with an adequate dose of sarcasm and unblemished flair so that it sounded sexy. Her comedic delivery was impeccable, as she turned socially forbidden words into flattery. There was something different about her that day, but I could not find the reason for her sudden change. The easiness she had with words enticed me, and I felt that we had moved into a new comfort zone with each other. It was apparent that her jocularity added more spice to our sizzling relationship.

I realized that Wendy had verbally outwitted me, so I took our silliness further by tickling her until she lost control of herself. She pleaded for mercy, but I only stopped after she lost control, laughing and farting at the same time. I declared myself the winner of our comedic interlude. She did not fret, and carried on as if nothing had happened.

For hours, we exposed our bodies to the titillating effect of the spring sun. Several times, she rubbed my skin as if she was tending to a delicate object with enthralling features. Occasionally, she placed her forearm next to mine, but when I became aware of what she was doing, she complained loudly about my insensitivity to her plight. As her skin tanned, so did mine, which made it impossible for her to catch up.

"Pay attention for a minute. Our inimitable relationship has other profound reasons for its success, unrelated to matching tans." The words came out of nowhere, as it often did when I became enthralled with loquacious nonsense. What do you expect from a young man who spent his formative years at an exclusive boarding school learning so-called proper social skills?

Wendy became openly annoyed with me after my statement, and when I reached out to hold her hand, she moved away from me.

"What do you know about how I feel?" she finally asked.

"I never said I'm privy to your inner thoughts," I said.

"For once, talk American English. I'm getting tired of your formal gibberish," she said.

I let her brood undisturbed for as long as she fancied. Even when she looked at me occasionally and sighed, I remained silent.

My thoughts wandered back to what just happened between us. Did she really believe that tanning her skin could end all the unmitigated provocation and racial misrepresentations we faced on campus daily? How one-dimensional her obsession with tanning was. It could not change her golden hair and green eyes. Her progressiveness and temperance were more important to me than her outward beauty. Simply stated, her physical beauty merely accentuated her inner goodness. That enviable quality of moral goodness that she possessed helped me navigate through the throes of a small town's racial bigotry.

After we had been silent for a long time, she said, "I'm sorry. Do you hate me?"

"You're asking silly questions just so you can hold my hand," I retorted.

"I'm not being silly. Your mind wanders off a lot. What's going on with you?" she asked, looking at me pointedly.

"Just thinking about all the trouble I've put you through for being my friend since I came to this stupid small town," I said as I rubbed my forehead with the palm of my hand.

"Have I ever complained? You're a worrywart, Joe," she said as she straddled me.

"The name is Joseph. Call me Joe again, and I'll call you Wen," I said as she lowered her body and rolled around with me.

"Who, what, Wen, Joe?" she asked.

"I guess we're now Joe and Wen," I replied.

"Follow your daydream back to Nigeria, Joe. I'll stay here and wait for you to come back," she said. I couldn't tell if she was truly angry.

"Why don't we focus on what makes us happy. I feel best when I'm with you. Isn't that what love is all about?" I asked.

"I feel the same way about you. In France, I named a park bench Joseph. You can't imagine how many conversations I had with you daily sitting on that bench. I hope you understand why I feel lonely when you take your mental trips to places you refuse to share with me," she said solemnly. The tears that followed made her statement even more distressing.

"Some things are hard to put into words. Most of the time, I don't feel it's fair to share my mental pain with you. How could you understand my state of mind when fellow students make mockery of my heritage? You only witness a portion of what I deal with every day. I think about how things could have been for me, if I had stayed at home for my education. Coming back from my daydream, and finding you lying next to me, makes me happy," I said.

Wendy hugged and held on to me. My heart was beating fast.

* * *

I met Wendy and Lisa at the student center bowling alley. The place was bustling, not typical for a Saturday night on campus after most of the local students had gone home for the weekend. I hugged Wendy and pulled out a chair for her to sit down. Lisa complained that I did not give her a hug. I laughed it off. Lisa was always clowning around.

Two girls with their male companions walked over to our table as we waited for a bowling lane. The girls exchanged pleasantries, and then introduced their male friends.

Wendy pulled me up from my chair and said, "Girls, meet my friend Joseph."

I shook their hands. "It's nice to meet you," I said.

One of the boys was about my size. Six feet tall and of medium build. His handshake was not as firm as I had expected from a young college boy. He also avoided eye contact. I attributed his quirks to shyness. His girlfriend was vivacious and inquisitive., One question stood out from all the puzzling questions she asked me. "Are you going back home when you finish school?"

"I'll make that decision after I finish medical school," I said.

I walked over to the last boy and shook his hand. "Nice to meet you," I said, but instead of moving on, I asked him, "Are you a soccer player?"

His answer was quick and tart: "I'm not." A conversation stopper. He was of medium build, and probably five feet six inches tall, which was a perfect size for a good center forward in a soccer team.

The girls talked and laughed, while the boys avoided speaking to each other. They remained despondent. We had to wait longer than expected for a lane.

Finally, a group of students left their lane, so I went to the attendant's window to sign up for it.

On my return to our table, Wendy's friend asked, "Can we join you guys?" I looked at the girl and smiled.

"Of course you can," Wendy replied. "We have all night to bowl." Wendy turned to me and asked, "I hope you're OK with them joining us?"

"Why should I mind, after all, we're here to have fun," I told Wendy.

Wendy bowled first and made a perfect score. She held her breath when I rolled the ball down the lane. She crossed her fingers and watched all the pins fall. As if it was the greatest achievement of my life, she hugged and kissed me several times. I was not good at bowling and wondered how I managed to bowl so well in my first attempt that night. "More bowling, more hugs for me," I said.

On their first attempts, the two boys made less-than-perfect scores, and their faces became sullen.

Sitting next to Wendy, I felt her energy and joy, which affected me. Her turn to bowl. She picked up her ball, walked back to me, and said, "Kiss me and my ball for good luck?"

I smiled and said, "I'll never turn down an offer to kiss the most beautiful girl on campus."

She hugged and kissed me passionately. Holding me, she said, "We make a good couple, don't we?"

"We're a couple? I thought we were just fooling around," I said with a smile.

"You're a spoiled brat," she said as she gently twisted my arm.

I retrieved my arm from Wendy, hugged her, and lifted her off the floor. Wendy's feet were barely back on the floor when one of the boys said, "Look at that stupid coon messing around right in front of us." Sudden rage took over. I grabbed him by the shirt collar.

Wendy reached out, and held my hand. "Joseph, let go of his shirt," she shouted.

I released his shirt collar.

The other boy approached us. "Are you that stupid, boy?" His question riled me, but I held my tongue. Wendy pulled me aside, but the boys followed us. Their girlfriends sprang up from their chairs and held them back. Other bowlers gawked.

The two boys left, but their girls stayed. "I'm very sorry about the ugly situation tonight," One said.

"I'm ashamed of our friends," the other added. "Please, accept my apology."

"You haven't done anything. There's no need to apologize," I said.

Wendy sat on her chair and looked away from me. As much as I tried, I could not get her attention.

"You don't need to feel bad. It's not your fault they're ignorant. We've been through this before. I'm OK," I said. Wendy still ignored me. She excused herself for the night.

"Let me walk you back to your dormitory," I said.

"I don't need more aggravation tonight," Wendy said angrily, and walked away. I watched her leave the Student center and felt disappointed with myself for being so impulsive.

"I'm sorry Joseph, but I have to stick by my friend," Lisa said. She walked out with the girls.

I watched the other students' bowling balls roll down the lanes and things became clearer to me. You throw a ball to knock down pins. Sometimes you succeed fully, or partially. You may even fail to knock any pin down, but the ball always comes back to you, no matter the outcome, to give you another chance. Is that not what we get in life, a chance to try again when we fail? I left that issue alone. There was no philosophical treatise there. Only the reasoning of a confused fellow.

*   *   *

Early Sunday morning, I went through the breakfast line and took my tray to the table by the entrance of the cafeteria. I waited for almost an hour, but Wendy did not show up for breakfast.

On my way back to my apartment, I stopped by Wendy's dormitory and found the door to the lobby unlocked. I entered the building without calling her room. The lobby was empty, but an early Sunday morning religious program on TV was making a lot of noise. Although no one was listening to the preacher in the lobby, his loud castigation of evil doers filled a void.

At my push of the button, the elevator door opened instantly. A deserted lobby, and an empty elevator, were normal for a Sunday morning in the dormitory, but the unlocked entrance? It felt eerie. I ignored my feeling and ascended to Wendy's floor. I stood by her door for a while, because I was unsure of what to say to her. Then, I knocked. Wendy opened her door wearing a dazzling white chiffon dress and a white chapeau tilted to the side. Her beautiful smile, and perfect set of teeth, added an immaculate air to her persona. I ventured into her room without an invitation from her.

Her room was uncluttered, and on a bulletin board by the side of her window was my photograph. Below the photograph was a handwritten note, "Never let me fall for you," and the date, October 15, 1977. I walked closer to her display, but she interposed her body between the wall and me. I tried to nudge her to the side, but she resisted, saying, "It's too late to change anything. I've already fallen for you."

I stood there looking at her. "I hope you know I have always loved you."

She smiled as we looked at the picture together.

"You're not curious about the date?" she asked.

"Of course I'm curious, but I'm ashamed I don't remember anything about that day," I said.

"You should be ashamed. How could you forget the day I picked you up at your dorm and took you home to meet my mother? It was a special day for me. I wanted to kiss you in my room. Remember how my mother came in with an African tapestry and disrupted everything," she said. She'd picked me up with her red Fiat sports car and drove so fast that I almost wet my pants. Her father was in Europe at the time, so we had a chance to spend time with her mother. She was a good hostess, and acted as though she cared about my welfare. She offered us breakfast in their palatial mansion and gave me a tour of their expansive horse stable.

Wendy walked to her open window to peer outside. Wind blew through it, carrying her captivating perfume my way. "Why did you leave so suddenly last night?" I asked.

"I was disappointed with your reaction to that guy, but I understand how you must have felt listening to his trash," she said.

"You're wearing white today. As a peace offering for your unreasonable admonition of my reaction last night?" I asked jokingly.

"Why can't you speak plain American English?" she said.

"What's wrong with the way I speak?" I asked.

"I told you before that you use too many unnecessary big words," she said.

"Let's get back to my question," I said.

"I hate to disappoint you, but I have a Christian revival meeting at my church. I have to pick up my mother." She held on to me. "We can meet at your place this evening. Maybe listen to some jazz?"

"That sounds like a good plan."

Chapter 5

AS THE END OF THE ACADEMIC YEAR APPROACHED, I had limited time to decide what to do for the summer session. Going home to my parents was not an option. I had to use the summer session to accumulate academic credit hours so I could finish college in three years and graduate with Wendy. Wendy and I had talked about attending the same medical school so that we could be together. We were dependent on each other emotionally, to the extent that sometimes I wondered, how we'd survived apart before we met.

I could not find anything nice enough to give Wendy on her birthday that I could afford. "You give me the special gift of love," Wendy said. It was two days before the feast of Pentecost. It was time to reassess my faltering Catholic faith. In so many ways, she influenced me positively without knowing her contribution to my spiritual maturity. Without her gift of the Holy Bible to remind me of her one request, "forgive those that offend you," I probably would have developed unrestricted resentment toward the local population.

On a perfect spring day in April, Wendy walked into one of my classes a few minutes before the class ended. She sat next to me as the professor was concluding his lecture on thermodynamics. Her titillating perfume caused a unidirectional turning of heads as the scent permeated the entire room. She extended her hand to me in the midst of a thought-provoking assertion from our young professor, but I ignored the gesture. However, when the professor turned to the blackboard to illustrate the point he made, I turned to Wendy and accepted her hand.

Her short white dress, which exposed two beautiful long legs up to her mid thighs, distracted me the most. I could not focus, as my eyes darted from the blackboard to her bodice, and down to her legs. It was the longest ten minutes that I could remember.

The Professor walked over to Wendy after he concluded, and said, "Hello Miss Wendy. What brings you to my classroom?"

"My friend here needs some time away from his studies for his own good," Wendy said, pointing at me.

"I hope you enjoyed my lecture as much as Joseph Fafa usually does," he said.

"I was late, and lost with all the calculations," Wendy replied.

"A neutral answer, but I'll accept it as positive." He smiled as he added, "Say hello to your parents for me."

Wendy shook his hand, and said, "I will. You and Aunt Gloria visiting soon?"

The professor walked ahead of us as we exited the classroom, but once outside, he turned around and said, "Maybe when the semester is over. I would love to play croquet with your dad." He paused and then continued. "By the way, how did you meet Joseph Fafa? I thought his only interest was getting A's."

"We've known each other since he came to America in 1977. He may deny it, but he's my boyfriend. Well, my parents don't know we're dating. Don't tell my dad about us," Wendy said as we reached the professor's office. He smiled and leaned against his office doorframe. "Take care, you two," he said as we left the building.

Wendy's response to the professor puzzled me. My concerns about our status as a couple dissipated as I looked at her long, ballerina's legs strutting in her short dress. Along the way, she interwove her fingers with mine, and adjusted her pace several times to synchronize our walk. The gentle spring sun and dry air made it a delightful day.

Close to the cafeteria, she stopped briefly to say hello to a group of students as I continued to walk. Wendy could not catch up with me, so she yelled, "Slow down, Joseph. You walk too fast." Instead of slowing down, I stopped until she caught up with me.

"I'm sorry for forgetting you're a lady," I said.

"I bet you're preoccupied again," she said teasingly.

"How did you know? I'm preoccupied with my new fling, summer school. It's around the corner," I said.

"Stop clowning around for a second. You talked about going home for the summer. Did you change your mind?" she asked.

"I need to graduate with you. Summer school is the only option," I said.

"You rush through everything," she said, and then hesitated before she continued. "I hate to ask a personal question. You know I'm here for you, if you need my help in any way. Sometimes I wonder if you have enough money to live on." The way she said it made me feel that she was genuinely concerned about my wellbeing.

"It's not about money. My father has been paying my school fees without any difficulty," I said.

"What's the issue then?" she asked.

"I really don't know. I just want to finish school as soon as possible," I said. I looked at her with admiration, and continued, "Maybe I don't want to be here without you."

"You're a tease, but that's a good answer," she said as she grabbed my shirt collar. "Have you talked to your academic adviser about this?" she asked.

"I discussed available options with him. He wants me to work in his research lab this summer. That's six credit hours, but I have to add another course to make it nine." She listened attentively as I discussed all the courses I had as options.

"I'm taking experimental psychology for the summer. Why don't we take it together?" she said.

"What's experimental psychology?" I asked.

"Come on! You're one of the brightest students I've ever met, and you don't know about experimental psychology? Tell me a believable lie," she said.

"I took general psychology," I said, but she ignored me.

We were standing by the cafeteria door talking and forgot to go in for lunch. I looked at my watch and realized that we'd spent our lunchtime on trivial issues. My next class was a laboratory session, and setting up the station for my experiments would take at least ten minutes.

Wendy watched curiously. My eyes darted from my watch to her every five seconds. I began to pace around, but she ignored my childish display of impatience. Maybe out of compassion, she said, "I know you're ready to leave, but do you want to meet for dinner tonight?"

"You're so kind. I can't believe you want to spend more time with me. Fancy dinner? Like your Chez-bistro, or not so fancy, like my place, the school cafeteria?" I said.

"I'll do anything you desire, Hon," she said. She tried to suppress it, but laughter overpowered her. "Cafeteria is your place? I love your playful side, but you don't show it often," she added. What she said was not funny, but her snorting laughter was.

We left the cafeteria with several issues unresolved, but I knew that attending summer school, and graduating the following year with Wendy was nonnegotiable for me.

"I'll pick you up at 5:00," I said as I kissed her cheek. She grabbed my hands and pulled me toward her for a real kiss. She watched me wipe my lips, and said, "You should be proud to show my lipstick on your lips, you silly boy."

I hurriedly ascended the slight elevated walkway, while Wendy walked a few yards behind. There was still ample time to make it to my laboratory early.

I passed a group of four students walking in the opposite direction. One stopped, and said, "Hello Joseph. Where have you been?" I looked at her closely. She was a girl from my English communication class a year before. Her physical attributes had changed significantly in one year, making it difficult to recognize her. She appeared taller and slimmer than the last time I saw her. Her mocha skin complexion appeared to have lightened.

"Hello Doreen," I said to my own bewilderment, because I was not sure how I remembered her name.

"Wow!" she exclaimed. Her excitement puzzled me too. "I thought you went back to your country to finish college," she said after looking me over.

"I never planned to leave Central North Carolina. The academic experience I have had so far has been rewarding," I said.

"And you love being here with me," Wendy added, to my surprise. Wendy stood by my side and put her arm around my waist. Doreen looked on as Wendy pulled me toward her. I stood there speechless for a second, but it felt like eternity.

"Are you going to introduce your friend?" Doreen asked.

"This is Wendy," I said.

"Hi Wendy, nice to see such close friends," Doreen said.

"We're not close friends. I'm his girlfriend," Wendy said with unabashed emphasis, and a forced smile. Her assertiveness, although tempered with civility, surprised me.

"Joseph was so nice to me in English class. I would love to have him audition for our summer production, *Romeo and Juliet*. He's tall, well built, and handsome. Audience would love him. Convince him to expand his horizon in dramatic art." Doreen was still talking when Wendy cut her off.

"He's busy this summer taking experimental psychology with me," Wendy said.

I was unhappy with Wendy's overprotectiveness, so I excused myself from the girls and ran toward the chemistry building. I looked back midway, and they were still standing where I had left them.

* * *

On my way to pick Wendy up for dinner, I anticipated all the questions she would ask me about Doreen, and it made my palms sweat. On reaching Wendy's dormitory, I found her standing by the door waiting for me. Although she seemed pleasant, I was still apprehensive.

"You finally made it," she said, as I walked into her dormitory lobby.

"I'm sorry for being a tad late," I said.

"You probably stopped somewhere, to talk to some girl, on your way here," she said sardonically. I ignored her statement. "Nothing to say, Loverboy?" she asked, as we left the lobby.

I opened the car door for her without saying anything, and she reciprocated by ignoring me. Surprisingly, she adjusted my shirt collar several times after I sat down, as if there was something wrong with it. She stopped fidgeting, and stared at me unabashedly.

"You're going to tell me about Doreen, right?" she asked. Without giving me the chance to answer her, she added, "I'm sure you prayed I would forget about your friend, the way you forgot your lab session talking to her."

"There isn't much to tell. We took a communication class together last year. That's all," I said with the meekest voice I could muster.

"I guess you're a saint, so I have to believe everything you tell me," she said.

"I don't know where you're trying to go with this," I said.

"You do, Hon. I saw the way you stared at her dark skin. I know she's beautiful, but you didn't have to stand there absorbed," she retorted.

I knew that it was not the right time to smile, but I could not keep myself from laughing.

"Did you go out with her?" she asked angrily.

"No, I didn't. I don't really know her well. I know a little about her. She has a Brazilian mother, and her dad is American. I think a diplomat, somewhere in South America," I said. As much as I wanted to ignore Wendy's silliness, I felt that the best thing to do was to be candid with her.

"Why did she ask you to be her *Romeo*?" she asked.

"She asked me to audition for a part in a play. She didn't say what part. You were there and heard it," I said. She kept silent until we arrived at the restaurant.

I hurried out of the car and walked to the passenger's side. "Please don't get the door for me," she requested, but I ignored her. "Thank you for holding the door for me," she added.

We had reached an impasse. I was unequivocally innocent, but suspected of being guilty of an amorous dalliance with someone I barely knew. Regardless of the accusation, I knew that if I had continued to expend unwarranted energy trying to extricate myself, I would sound guilty, so I kept quiet.

* * *

The maître d' said, "I have the best seat in the house for Miss Crane," which made her blush. The relaxed atmosphere inside the restaurant made it difficult to discuss serious matters, but before our meals arrived, she brought up Doreen again.

"I'm not sure why you mention Doreen's dark skin," I said.

"Just a thought I had. You may prefer such girls," she said without equivocation.

"Are you serious?" I asked.

"I have seen you staring at them lately," she said.

"Staring at who?" I asked.

"Your skin-type girls," she said.

"You make me laugh. I don't remember staring at any girl but you," I said with a smile. She annoyed me with her statement, but I tried to find humor in her accusation.

"You can't deny it," she said with a seriousness that baffled me more.

"I like you because of who you are, not your skin color," I said, but quickly added, "I mean, I love you for being beautiful inside."

"You really love me?" she asked.

"Of course, I love you," I said as I pulled my chair closer to her. She reached out and held my hand. The warmth of her touch took me back to the first time we met and how good things were between us. I was daydreaming again.

"Where's your mind?" she said in a deep Southern drawl delivering a light punch to my side. Her light punch usually signaled the end of hostilities between us, but I was unsure of her action this time.

"I don't speak hillbilly," I said, and she laughed. I worried my statement was offensive, but her laughter put me at ease. "Why do you always have to punch me?" I protested.

"You deserve a punch once in a while, for turning me into a nervous wreck," she said gleefully.

"You may not believe this, but I was thinking about the time you left me for your French adventure," I said.

"The truth is, my father made me go. He said it would be a good experience," she said unapologetically.

"Yep. I heard that before. You left me to the wolves, and I was devoured by Francesca," I said.

"It was your fault. You didn't even fight for me, instead, you found someone else. Why didn't you come to France, if you really wanted me?" she asked.

"How could I? You never gave me a chance. Left no address, or phone number. Blamed your father for our plight, and then blamed campus racial intolerance. I'm not really sure why you left," I said.

"I made a big mistake, but of all the girls on campus, why did you settle for Francesca?" she asked.

"I didn't settle for her. You asked me to help her with physics," I said.

"Help her I said, but not to fall in love," she retorted.

"Well, she used me and dumped me like a tool. She's out there parading herself as a supermodel. A real deal Southern belle. Every time I read those magazine articles about her, I feel like throwing up. They should ask me about the 'Jezebel' who put a knife through my heart and twisted it to her delight," I said.

"You said you were over her," she teased.

"I'm sorry, Wendy, but she's a sore subject. I really need to forget what she did to me."

"It's OK. I shouldn't have left you the way I did." Her voice quavered as she continued, "I'm glad we're back together."

"Tell me you're not anticipating another jaunt to France, because I don't have the money to travel the world looking for you," I said while she squeezed my hand.

"We're wasting time talking about the past. Finish your meal, Hon. Let's get out of here," she said.

"I'm ready to go right now," I said.

"Hot stuff, I need more kisses. Plant one on me right now. I love when you kiss me," she said with a smirk. I walked ahead to hold the door, but she pulled me back and kissed me. Well, she tried to. We had enough evil eyes on us that my legs wobbled out of fear. I was not ashamed to admit that I walked without grace.

Wendy confused me more every day. The open affection outside the college campus was something new. I had to toughen up to meet her needs.

Chapter 6

PEERING ACROSS THE ENORMOUS ENCLAVE of the botanical garden on a Saturday morning, I fully appreciated the local saying that God blessed the Carolinas. Lush, green vegetation abounded in every corner, and unmistakably heralded a rebirth after an unusually cold winter. A rhapsody of bird song pervaded the tranquil natural reserve and added to the earthy feeling of rejuvenation of life. Enthralled by the cascades of golden morning sunrays that pierced through the imperfect shade of the tall trees, Wendy and I walked into the garden.

We came to a wild area with a small hill hidden by a thick growth of shrubs and small trees. We walked briskly up the hill until we came to a cleared path. I made it up the hill first and rejoiced as the winner of the undeclared race. Wendy ignored me and walked on.

Ahead of us was a tall, black rectangular polished stone that reflected the morning sun. I started to run toward the object, but had to stop because Wendy was still breathing heavily from our short race up the hill. She eventually caught up with me.

We reached the base of the black polished stone with ornate calligraphic inscriptions, which attracted my attention. Wendy put her arms around me while I read the inscriptions aloud.

"Love is the second greatest gift from God, next only to life itself."

"You said you love me, but are you ready to surrender your heart to me?" Wendy asked, interrupting my reading, after I had barely finished the first line of the inscription.

How did one surrender his heart? I pondered over what she meant, and came up with what I felt was an appropriate answer to her question. "Love is a gift from God, mortals don't give love, they share it. I already share abundant love with you." I felt elated with what I felt was a profound answer to her question.

"You're spoiling my morning with your philosophy. Why do you always show off? Just answer the question," she said.

I was not sure what to say, so I held her very close and whispered in her ear, "You already know I'm devoted to you." She let her hands go from my waist, and stared at me. I stuttered in an attempt to say something more reassuring, but she walked to the other side of the monument.

Unrelenting, I went to her, and put my arms around her waist. She let me hold her while I read the rest of the inscriptions. From the opposite side of the track, an older couple walked to the base of the monument, touched the black stone, and kissed. They stood there holding each other for a long time. Wendy looked on, and smiled.

"Did you see what they did? That's what we're supposed to do to commit to each other," Wendy said.

Not deterred by Wendy's demand, I kissed her and said, "I'm committed to our love."

"Stop joking around, Joseph. We're supposed to touch the stone before the kiss."

"Come on, Wendy, are we really going to participate in a medieval rite for lovers?"

"For your information, you medieval Catholic boy, this place where we stand, is called 'lovers point.' It was here that a boy, probably nicer than you, who was going off to the Civil War, secretly met his girl for the last time, because they hid their love affair from her rich parents. Unfortunately, he never returned from the war. His girl came to this place daily searching for him after the war ended. Some people say she ran around in circles because she heard his voice calling her. She never married, and died at the age of eighty." Wendy wept as she narrated the story.

"It sounds very touching, but it's probably not a true story," I said with a touch of sarcasm, which made her wriggle out of my embrace.

"Why won't you do this one thing for me?" she pleaded.

I looked in her teary eyes, and my sense of reasoning left me. Surrendering my love unconditionally to her was the only way to get out of that morning's quagmire. As I reflected on why she left me for France, and reached out to hold her, my heart fluttered.

Holding her hand, I walked closer to the black stone, and touched the stone. I pulled Wendy close to me and held on to her. Our lips met, and our tongues caressed with delight. For a moment, we forgot that we were in a public place. An eerie silence overtook my senses, as we stood there expressing our raw feelings.

In my elated state, it felt as if we had triumphed over all the bigots with their wanton opinions. Out there that beautiful morning, we stood there kissing until it became Wendy's and Joseph's lovers' point.

A man, probably in his sixties, walked closer to us, and said, "Stupid kids don't respect sacred grounds anymore. This place was erected for real lovers, not for freak shows." We ignored his comment and carried on. Words were not enough to extricate me from Wendy, as my heart pounded in sheer ecstasy and my legs trembled. Only when my right hand inadvertently travelled up Wendy's shirt did I disengage from her, because I realized that we had lost every inhibition we had.

"Why did you stop kissing me?" Wendy asked.

I looked at Wendy raptly from her head to her delicate feet, admiring her long golden hair, dimples that accentuated her beautiful face, two beautiful mounds on her chest, curvy waistline, and her dainty feet. It was unequivocally obvious to me why I stopped kissing her, because we had almost crossed over to what the locals called 'public indecency'.

I turned away as my yearning for her intensified. To hide my aroused state, I walked to the opposite side of the monument and refocused on the inscriptions. She followed me, and asked, "Are you OK?"

"I'm trying to read the inscription on this side of the wall," I said.

"You should be looking at me, and not the wall," she said.

"To preserve our way of life, we the Carolina Confederate soldiers join our brothers-in-arms against the tyranny of our broken union." I read the first line of the inscription to Wendy and then stopped.

"What's wrong with you again?" she inquired.

"What can be more ridiculous than making out with you in front of a Confederate monument?" I said.

"That was a long time ago. It's now a place for lovers like us," she said.

"What a twit I am," I mumbled to myself. For a moment, I deluded myself into thinking that I heard those despicable words, "Uncle Tom," from nowhere. It had been twelve months since an irate black female student called me that name when I was walking to the library with Wendy. The unfortunate thing was the embarrassing fact that mastery of the English language did not guarantee my mastery of colloquialisms, in Central North Carolina. Wendy had to explain to me what "Uncle Tom" meant in their local parlance. It was an awkward moment for her explaining to me bigotry as practiced by people of my own race.

"I'm ready to leave this place. I can't hang around here and be laughed at," I said.

"I didn't mean to embarrass you, if that's how you feel about this special place of ours," she said. "My great grandfather fought for the Confederacy because he thought it was the right thing to do. I'm sure most young men from this part of the country felt the same way. His military service did not make all his descendant bigots," she continued.

"I didn't know your great grandfather fought for the Confederacy," I said.

"Does it change anything between us?" she asked somberly.

"Not at all. How can it change how I feel about you? You've been good to me," I said.

She walked to the foot of the monument and sat down. I stood there looking at her without saying a word. The unfortunate division between us left me confused. As the morning sun shone directly on her face, I worried that her fair, freckled skin might get sunburned. I extended my hand to her, and she took it without hesitation. On the spot where she sat, was an inscription, "Funded by Dedicated Daughters of the Confederacy (DDC)."

"Who are these daughters of the Confederacy?" I asked.

"It's just a social organization started as a support group for the descendants of Confederate soldiers. All the women in my family are members. I became a member after my sweet sixteen," she said.

"There's so much to learn about your North Carolina. I'm very sorry about my ignorance and insensitivity to your heritage," I said.

"I feel the same way about your heritage, Joseph. Maybe someday you'll tell me more about Nigeria," she said.

We walked down the hill. I contemplated the events of the morning as we left the garden.

Chapter 7

MY FATHER ONCE SAID TO ME, "My son, always know what you want in every situation." His argument was that only people who were sure of what they wanted, could without equivocation, say what they could not accept. I thought about his advice when I walked into Professor Nancy Crane's office on Monday morning to get her permission to register for the summer experimental psychology class. Although I received an A+ in general psychology, I was unsure of my readiness to delve into an advanced course in human behavior. My inclination had been the physical sciences, which I believed were easier to master.

Before then, I had never compromised in my quest for academic excellence. I was concerned about my limited interest in experimental human behavioral science, and wondered how I would benefit from a course that was, in my opinion, in a muddled academic area. The brochure I'd read stated, "A research class in extrasensory perception with a special emphasis on telepathy and hypnosis." It surprised me that I had let Wendy talk me into an academic area in perpetual darkness. I worried that Professor Crane would hypnotize me to render me ignorant. After all, she might be prejudiced.

Professor Crane's secretary was on the telephone when I walked into her office. She acknowledged my presence by a mere wave of a hand in the direction of an empty chair. I sat down at the far corner of the room. There were no pictures or certificates on the walls, and the rug on the floor was threadbare. It was not what I had envisioned for a departmental chairperson's office.

"Sorry to keep you waiting. You're here to see Professor Crane?" the secretary finally asked.

"I need authorization to register for the summer session of the experimental psychology class," I said.

"I'll let her know you're here. She's answering a call," she said.

Waiting for Professor Crane, I stared at the barren walls. The room was so quiet that I became sleepy after ten minutes of inertia. The sounds that emanated from the secretary's typewriter finally brought me back to life.

"Professor Crane will be off the phone soon," the secretary said, as if she knew what I was thinking. I simply smiled.

I nearly fell asleep again when two students walked in and sat down across from me. I resumed my ardent activity of staring at the blank office walls, but persistent sneaky drowsiness forced me to rub my eyes several times.

Eventually, Professor Crane came out of her office, and saved me from the embarrassment of falling into a deep sleep. She was a very tall, athletically built, middle-aged woman with graying hair. She was wearing an undersized, open-toed pair of brown sandals and a long white coat with several coffee stains. I could not help but wonder why a college professor dressed so shabbily.

"Who's first?" Professor Crane asked us directly, ignoring her secretary who could have provided that information.

"I was here first," I said. She walked closer, and towered over me. Looking up to her while seated made me feel subservient, so I stood up. She stepped back a little because we were too close to each other.

"What can I do for you?" Professor Crane asked.

"I'm here to get approval for summer experimental psychology class," I said.

"I don't know you. Are you a psychology major?" she asked.

"No, ma'am. I'm a biochem major," I said.

"Interesting. Come into my office. Tell me why you need my class for biochemistry."

We walked into her inner office. It had minimal decoration except for her doctoral degree certificate, which was on the wall behind her desk. Several academic journals were scattered all over her desk. I gave her my registration card, which she looked at briefly before placing it on top of one of her journal piles. "Have a seat," she said as she walked over to her chair.

"You're aware the class is a summer research project for senior psychology majors?" she asked.

"I heard non-psychology majors can take it with your permission," I replied.

"That's true, if you had more than an introductory psychology class. I rarely deviate from that rule." She picked up my registration card from her desk and looked it over again.

I sat there ignoring her disorganized desk and wondered why she needed a second look at the registration card. The only information on my card was my name, birthdate, and student identification number. I left my class standing blank because I would become a senior at the conclusion of the academic year in two weeks.

"What do you know about extrasensory perception?" she asked, still holding my registration card.

"From what I learned in general psychology, it's the ability to perceive what others may not," I said with some hesitation. Although I had a basic understanding of extrasensory perception, I was unsure of my choice of words.

"You're partially right. There's more to what I do here at the college. My research requires a great deal of concentration and intuition. Let me test your level of situational awareness. Tell me what you noticed about the two students across from you in the outer office. Maybe, the color of their shirts," Professor Crane said.

"I'm sorry, Professor Crane. I didn't pay attention to their shirts," I said.

"I like your honesty. Good quality, but you're not ready for my class. A senior biochemistry major? Well, I'll give you a second chance. You have two days to develop, and present to me, a technique to enhance your situational awareness," she said.

I felt warm inside, and my palms began to sweat as I considered what the professor thought about my academic readiness for her class. Making excuses to myself that the social sciences were not on the same par as empirical physical sciences could not erase the feeling of inadequacy that overwhelmed me. I should have seen the opportunity to get out of taking the class, but I became obsessed with my unpardonable ineptitude as I anticipated the best remedy for my lackluster performance. I was trapped.

I had walked into Professor Crane's office ethereally clothed in all the accolades the college had bestowed on me, and I left there stripped naked by a simple instinctual question. It was a humbling experience. My swagger refused to leave the office with me, so I stumbled out of the psychology department. Memories of bygone academic awards flashed before my eyes. I thought I heard a voice that said, "Joseph is the best student of the year." Was it my own whisper, or a voice in my head? The voice scared me more than my failure to remember shirt colors. "I have to regain my credibility, and my sanity," I whispered to myself.

* * *

The last week of the semester was memorable in so many ways, but saying goodbye to some of my friends who were graduating felt like the end of everything that mattered. I had an A+ average in all of my classes, therefore final examinations were not compulsory for me. It was not playtime yet, though. Class attendance was mandatory until the last day of lectures.

During biochemistry that Monday morning, I could not concentrate. I was thinking about the assignment Professor Crane had given. Mere completion of the assignment was not good enough. I felt that my presentation had to be outstanding in order to redeem my wounded ego.

On Tuesday morning, less than twenty-four hours after disgracing myself, I waited outside the psychology office until the secretary arrived. She ignored me, and unlocked the door to her office. I walked in with her and sat down in the same chair I had occupied the day before.

"Weren't you here yesterday?" she finally asked.

"Yes, I was, but I'm here again today to present my proposal to Professor Crane."

"I don't have it in the books. What time did she tell you to come?" she asked.

"She just asked me to come back when I was ready," I said.

"There's a departmental meeting at nine. I'm not sure when she'll be in," she said as she flipped through her agenda.

"I'll wait for her, if you don't mind," I said.

"I'll be setting up the conference room for their meeting. You can stay here," she said.

Instead of staring at the walls this time, I took a mental picture of everything in the outer office. I even noted the type and color of the secretary's headband. I was still taking stock of everything when Professor Crane walked in. She smiled when our eyes met, which put me at ease.

"You again. Forgot something in my office?" Professor Crane inquired.

"No, Professor. I'm ready to present my concentration technique," I said with the most unassuming tone.

"Have you come up with a technique already? I hope it's not a long one. I have a meeting in fifteen minutes," she said as she walked toward her inner office. I followed her, but she stopped and asked me to wait in the office conference room.

The conference room contained a long rectangular table, plain oak chairs, and a projector. The walls in the room were as barren as the departmental office. I walked around the room and noted the model of the projector. I even lifted the slide carousel in case there was something hidden there that I should find. Professor Crane walked in while I was still holding the carousel in my hand. She barely looked at me before she sat down.

"Before you start, I need to let you know that I spoke to your academic adviser, Professor Ezir. He wasn't aware you wanted to take my class. Lucky for you, he had no objection." She looked at me as if she expected me to say something, but I kept quiet. She then added, "Go ahead, let me hear it."

"Professor Crane, I apologize for my inadequacy yesterday. Music helped me in the past to concentrate, so I spent several hours yesterday in the music listening room. I listened to the operas of Antonio Vivaldi, and was able to recreate mentally the events of the previous day in detail. While the music played, I closed my eyes, and remembered details of the two boys who walked in. One boy had on a white T-shirt with country music singer Don Williams's photo on it. The second boy had a plain red T-shirt."

"I don't need the information about yesterday. I need details of your technique," she said impatiently.

I regretted showing off with my detailed description. "I closed my eyes and focused on the music for two minutes. I could hear all the components of the ensemble that I did not appreciate initially. After five minutes of maximum concentration, I explored events in my past that came to mind. It took several tries before I could recreate the details of those events in my mind." I knew that she had limited time so I tried to be as succinct as possible. However, I was concerned that I might have left out important details about the technique.

"I've heard enough for now. See you in my lab this summer. You'll present details of your technique on the first day of class. My colleague, Dr. Claris Ayer, who has an interest in psychoanalysis, will join us," she said.

"Thank you, Professor Crane. I'll see you in two weeks," I said with the utmost gratitude. She asked me to pick up my registration card from her secretary.

I still had doubts about my readiness to take an advanced course in psychology. I was concerned because a poor grade could ruin my chances of getting into medical school. Outside the psychology building, I wondered why she wanted to invite someone else to listen to my presentation. In my opinion, my technique was not interesting enough to warrant the presence of a psychoanalyst. I was unsure of what a psychoanalyst did, but I had assumed that a psychoanalyst was someone who dealt with the mentally ill, because deranged people were called psychos.

* * *

It had been more than twenty-four hours since I last saw Wendy. It was too late to start looking for her before my first class. I walked briskly to the Mathematics department and was surprised to see Wendy sitting alone in the back row of the classroom. There were ten students registered for the class, but only two were present. I wondered how she knew where to find me, and why the professor let her stay. Wendy stood up when I walked in, and hugged me.

"I was looking for you everywhere. Where have you been? I called your apartment last night, you didn't answer, so I went there this morning, but you were gone," Wendy said frantically.

"I'm very sorry, ma'am, but Professor Crane gave me an assignment before letting me into the class. I spent most of yesterday doing it," I said with a smile.

"Crazy Nigerian. Don't call me 'ma'am', sir," she teased. "Well, sir, you could've told Nancy that you're my sweetie. She would have signed your registration card without any hassle," she said.

"Who's Nancy?" I inquired.

"Have you already forgotten Professor Crane's first name?" Wendy asked.

"I didn't know you were on first name basis," I said.

"She's my aunt, silly," she retorted. "Who do you think is funding her crazy research? My daddy's corporation and our family foundation pay all the bills for her department," she said.

I froze. "Does she know about us?" Registering Professor Crane's class was a mistake. What if she was prejudiced and didn't approve of my relationship with her niece?

"Not yet," she said.

"Should I ignore you when we're in her class?" I said.

"Do whatever is suitable for you as long as you don't look at other girls," she giggled. "I'll see you in the cafeteria at lunch. In case you decide to go back to your apartment, ignore the nasty note I left on your door." She hurried out of the classroom, as the teacher was about to start the lecture.

Chapter 8

SLEEP ABANDONED ME that Tuesday night, three days before the end of the spring semester. Too many things plagued my mind, and as much as I tried, I could not lay them to rest. My feelings for Wendy had grown, but I was more afraid of losing her than ever. Every day we spent together made me yearn for her companionship more. I was an emotional mess.

I became frustrated after several failed attempts to fall asleep. Close to midnight, I phoned Gina, who had been my student mentor my first year in college. She was a beautiful, well proportioned, six-foot tall, mixed-race girl, with long curly black hair. The first time I met her family, she said with a smile, "I adopted Joseph for us," and her father, a tall black American, comically added, "Welcome home son," as he hugged me. During supper, she asked me to taste her mother's pie, and for some strange reason, I said, "I will, Sis." She playfully remained my sister from that day. She said it was a Southern ethnic thing that some people could not fully appreciate. Apart from Gina's academic successes, she had common sense and patience. Moving to Florida to attend medical school did not stop her from keeping up with my school activities. It felt natural to call her that night, even though it was late.

Gina was too sleepy to hold a coherent conversation, and kept on mumbling, "Things are good in Florida. You should come and visit." Still talking about my visit to Florida, she fell asleep. Yelling on the phone didn't wake her up, so I hung up.

Thirty minutes after midnight, I called Wendy. She had once told me to call her any time I needed her, so I did not feel guilty making such a late night call for a frivolous reason.

The phone rang several times. "Hello, who's this?" Wendy asked.

"I'm sorry for calling you so late, but I need your input," I said.

"Are you OK, Joseph?" she asked.

"Yeah. I just have many things on my mind and need to talk to you about them," I said.

"It's late, and I'm asleep," she said.

"I have a lot of decisions to make by tomorrow. I called Gina, but she fell asleep on me," I said.

"Gina? What does she have to do with it? I'll be over right now." She hung up before I could explain to her why I called Gina. Wendy's wrath would be one more thing I would have to deal with that night.

I lived in the college apartment complex, which was across the street from Wendy's high-rise dormitory. I was concerned about her safety at that odd hour, so I stood outside my apartment door waiting for her. Instead of walking over to my apartment, she drove. She stepped out of the car in an untied robe, and it was evident that she only had her panties on. She did not fret about her partial nudity as she walked past me. It was difficult to decipher if she was angry with me, or just trying to hurry inside my apartment because of her partial nudity. She did not acknowledge my presence at the door.

She slumped on my davenport with a sigh. I inspected her nude body, and then sat down next to her. "Are we OK?" I asked her as usual, but she ignored me. I used that phrase so frequently with Wendy that I probably said it in my sleep.

My hand conveniently wandered to her thigh, and travelled to her legs. She continued to ignore me, and acted as if she had fallen asleep. Her silence did not deter my wandering hand. Probably satisfied with the dose of silent treatment she delivered to me, she looked at me with sullen eyes, and pulled me down to her recumbent position.

We held on tight to each other with our noses rubbing together, our arms wrapped around each other. She said, "Hi." I waited for her questions about the conversation I'd had with Gina, but none came. As time passed, with Wendy drifting in and out of sleep, I concentrated on the asynchronous sounds of our heartbeats. Under their hypnotic rhythm, I briefly yielded to the harbinger of dreams. I woke up and found Wendy's lips resting on mine, and drifted back to sleep.

In my dream state, I felt Wendy trying to reposition herself. Her robe parted in the middle and revealed two perfectly erect nipples. I rubbed my eyes several times to see if I was awake, but I was still staring at her ample bosom.

"Do you like my boobies?" she asked. I sighed because I felt it was a setup. My head nodded in the affirmative without further hesitation. What other answer could I have given when I was staring at two perfect mounds, punctuated by two perfect, erect nipples? Maybe she did not know how good they looked. Impossible. "Go ahead, Joseph. Touch them. I know you want to," she said as she lifted my hand to her chest.

I obliged her request as if I was doing her a favor. Touching them was not good enough, so I massaged her nipples and watched as they hardened. I heard a voice that said, "Wendy, where are you?" The same voice I'd heard in Dr. Crane's office. I woke up and realized that I had had an erotic dream. Although I became despondent because it was just a dream, sleep, the ultimate tease, took me back to my fantasy.

"Joseph, wake up. Stop talking in your sleep," Wendy said, shaking my body. I had been drifting away again to my Carolina paradise. I rubbed my eyes and wondered if we had achieved synchronicity in the course of our dreams because when she turned to make more room for me, my dream became a reality.

"We could've talked on the phone. No urgent need for you to come over tonight," I lied as my hand travelled all over her body. Her presence made me forget everything that had been weighing me down. I felt rejuvenated.

"So you're not happy to see me? Even if you pretend to be unhappy with me, we're still going to talk about your fake sister Gina tonight," she said. She sat up and exposed more of her body.

"I'm disappointed in you," I said. "Gina was the only one I could count on when you ran off to France, and your friend Francesca tore my heart into shreds. By the way, I saw her in a TV interview the other day. She called herself a born-again Christian." I quelled the anger in my voice and continued with alacrity. "Who was there to lift me up? It was Gina, of course. She has been the one constant good thing in my life, and has always treated me like a little brother. I know she's very protective of me, but she means well."

"You went on vacation with Gina and her family last year, but refused to go to the south of France with me, and I met you before you even knew Gina existed. The way she claimed you as the brother she had always wanted is strange. She was only supposed to be your student mentor, and not your fake sister."

"You're talking about two different situations. France is very far away. I don't have the money to travel that far," I said.

"You always have excuses for everything. We could have taken my dad's jet, and stayed in our chalet. My mother and Scott were the only ones there. Dad left France yesterday. He may not have warmed up to you, but my mother adores you," she said.

She looked at me with sad eyes that made me reach out to caress her cheeks. Tears rolled down as she put her head on my shoulder

"I don't think your father would put up with your expensive plan. He ordered you to stay away from me." I lifted her head from my shoulder and looking at her directly, added, "What makes you think he has changed his mind?"

"My mother accepted you, and I'm sure my father will eventually get used to you," she said as she put her head back on my shoulder.

"Before we get too deep into this discussion, you need to know I'm going to Florida this weekend to visit Gina's medical school. She feels that I may like Florida better than North Carolina."

"Are you serious? I thought we agreed to be together in medical school, here in North Carolina?" she asked angrily.

"I'm only going to Florida for a short visit, not moving away. The other issue is Professor Ezir's suggestion. He wants me to apply to the new six-year MD-PhD program here. I could do research with him during medical school. His offer of a full-tuition scholarship and a monthly stipend was hard to resist, but I'd have to be admitted to medical school first." I paused and waited for her reaction but when she did not say anything, I continued. "According to him, the application process is only a formality because I've met all the admissions requirements. He's served on the admissions committee in the past, and knows the process."

"So, why go to Florida? To be with Gina? When we can spend that time together until summer school starts? Do you really know what you want from her? Sometimes, I wonder." Wendy looked at me with a cold stare. "Am I ever going to be the only girl that you need?" Her southern drawl deepened with anger.

"Stop saying silly things. You know I'm happy with you. Gina is like a sister to me, and nothing more," I said. Looking at her, I wondered if she knew how disappointed accusations and questions were making me.

"If you're telling the truth, you won't mind going together," she said.

It was a valid argument. "All right."

We spent the rest of the night talking about our future. The excitement in her voice as she talked about the two of us going through medical school together was clear. She even suggested that we live together, which I called a trial marriage. I smiled, hearing about our future together, so she went on to suggest buying a five-bedroom mansion surrounded by acres of woodland close to the medical center. It was only when she got to house furnishings and playroom provisions that I started worrying. Not sure how serious she was, I asked, "How would we afford such a place without full-time jobs?"

She eagerly answered, "My trust fund."

We had known each other for two years but had never talked seriously about our future together. I was petrified that she might start making elaborate plans without my consent. It was all about what she wanted, and I felt that she was in a hurry to tie me down. Merciful sleep finally took me away from a situation that was ripe for a major disagreement.

*   *   *

Professor Ezir was on the telephone when I arrived for our meeting in his office on Wednesday morning. His secretary requested that I wait in the conference room for him. I had expected an informal meeting to discuss my progress in school and my summer research project, but this venue troubled me. I was tempted to ask the secretary why he chose the conference room, but I did not give in to my curiosity. Instead, I proceeded to the room we fondly called, 'the graduate student execution chamber'. It was the very room where PhD students defended their dissertations.

Inside the conference room, bound biochemistry journals impeccably collated by month and year in built-in bookshelves made from highly polished natural wood gave a distinctive look to the walls. I sat patiently waiting for Professor Ezir, but, after a while, I stood up and wandered around the room. A large plaque on one of the walls caught my attention. I ambled over for a closer inspection. On the undergraduate section of the plaque, I found 'Joseph Fafa' listed for 1978 and 1979 'Exceptional Chemistry Student Award recipient' in gold letters. Displayed on a separate plaque with an inscription, '1979 ASC scholarship recipient', was my photograph.

My initial apprehension dissipated as I stood in front of the plaque, staring at my name. For a brief moment, it felt as if I were looking at the name of a stranger. I must have been so awe-stricken looking at my own name that I did not notice when Professor Ezir walked into the room. I had won several special awards before, but I didn't know I'd made the department's honors listing. Most of the time, only graduating seniors and graduate students received such recognition.

"Nice, isn't it? You should be proud of yourself," he said. He was smoking a cigar.

"Thank you, Professor Ezir. I feel overwhelmed," I stuttered.

"Hard work and dedication earned you the privilege. Be proud of your accomplishments," he said.

"I'll continue to do my best, sir," I said with a subdued voice.

He walked closer to the wall and read the names listed on the plaque with occasional editorial comments about their accomplishments after they left the institution. The only name I recognized was Gina McRee, whose name appeared twice, in 1975 and 1976. She was the only female student listed on the plaque, and Professor Ezir had a lot to say about her. At the end of his long discourse, he said, "Gina was the best student this department produced until you came along." I conveniently ignored his comparative editorial statement, and, fortunately, he did not elaborate. The most gratifying thing to me at that moment was the apparent fairness in recognizing the department's academic accomplishments.

Professor Ezir put out his cigar and sat down. While he looked through his papers, my eyes wandered back to the plaque. He cleared his throat.

"Have you thought about the MD-PhD program?" he asked, after he closed his folder. The tone of his voice was comforting, not like an executioner's.

"Yes, Professor Ezir. I was up last night thinking about all the options. The new program sounds good. It will help me bridge medical research with clinical medicine." Halfway through my answer, I gulped air anxiously, which attracted his attention. My anxiety manifested as a loud sigh, but I continued with my protracted answer. "I'm aware the MD-PhD program demands more time, but I'm ready to do the work needed." My sigh was inadvertent, and I realized that it could convey the wrong connotation. I tried to sound more enthusiastic.

"I'm waiting for approval from the Dean before I present my offer officially to you. The medical school admissions committee will interview you as a formality. Your admission is practically guaranteed, unless you're found to be psychologically unsound." He smiled as he made the last statement. It was the first time I had seen Professor Ezir in a light mood since I joined his department. I wondered if he would be as supportive of me when I returned to the same conference room to defend my PhD dissertation.

Professor Ezir was in a cheerful mood, but he used the opportunity to admonish me about getting into another situation like I had with Francesca. "Stay away from showoffs who don't deserve your company, even if they're supermodels." He told me how the press hounded him for personal information on me, when Francesca made the front cover of a national sports magazine barely clad in a swimsuit. Conservative residents in the area, including Professor Ezir, hated the behavior of young girls 'flaunting their bodies' for financial gain.

At the conclusion of our meeting, he cautioned that I should be careful with my choice of friends, so that I would avoid unnecessary scrutiny from reporters in the future. I apologized to him profusely for bringing unsolicited publicity to the department. During my apology, I inadvertently said, "I didn't know she would become famous when we met." The old man just looked at me and smiled.

*   *   *

I turned in all my class assignments before five p.m. on Wednesday, which meant that the spring semester was officially over for me. The serene college campus during final examinations did not deter me from a mission to find available students at the center willing to play table tennis. I deluded myself into believing that my game was at the collegiate competition level, and the unpopularity of the game in America helped me propagate that false notion. I played the role of a table tennis instructor most of the time, but my mission that evening was to find competent players. I was on an ego trip after this apparent validation by Professor Ezir.

Halfway to the student center, I ran into Doreen and two other students. Doreen was wearing a pair of snug bell-bottoms, a departure from her usual loose summer dresses. In my euphoric state, I could not control my eyes darting from her revealing top, to her seductively contoured jeans. I tried to convince myself that I was merely admiring her without any lustful desires.

"There you are, my young *Romeo*. Are you ready to accept your destiny?" Doreen said, running the palms of her hand down the sides of her waistline. I followed her hands until they stopped at her mid-thighs and imagined her trying to put those tight pants on. I was young and impressionable.

"Hello, Doreen," was all I could say.

Doreen was probably aware of my distraction, and when I failed to respond adequately to her initial comment, she said, "I'm excited to see you again, Joseph. Have you changed your mind about my proposal?" Her two female companions watched our exchange briefly and walked on.

"It's nice to see you too, but unfortunately, I won't have the time to audition for you," I said with a yawn.

"Are you all right?" she asked.

"I was up all night, and I'm paying the price now," I said.

"Studying for your finals?" she inquired.

"Not really. I'm done with all my classes because my professors excused me from finals. I had a lot on my mind about life decisions, and people I could hurt with those decisions," I said.

"Since you're free, would you like to stop by my apartment on Friday?" she asked.

"I would have loved to, but I'm flying to Florida on Friday."

"Florida? Going for fun?" she asked.

"I hope so." My answer was unexpected, but I tried to make the best of it. "It's probably good for me to get away from here, even for only a few days, before summer school starts."

My palms began to sweat, and I felt dizzy as we carried on with our conversation. Beads of sweat rolled down my face, and as much as I tried to conceal my symptoms, it took control of my body. Doreen stepped closer to me, and wiped the sweat off my face with her handkerchief. Her perfume might have smelled better than Wendy's. The beautiful ones always smell good, lure you in, and break your heart. What a twisted world.

"It looks like you're getting sick. Should I take you to the health center?" she said. Her concern sounded genuine, so I stopped imagining what she wanted from me.

"I haven't eaten much today because of all the things I had to do. My sugar level is probably low," I said. She felt my forehead, as if it would refute what I claimed to be my problem.

"I'll walk with you to the cafeteria, if you don't mind?" she asked.

I appreciated her concern, but she was overbearing. It would not be healthy for me to have another woman in my life.

"Thank you. I can make it without assistance," I said. The way I looked at her waistline made me wonder about my sincerity, and my devotion to Wendy.

"Do you have any medical problems?" she asked. The level of concern she showed for my wellbeing surprised me because we did not know each other very well.

"Not really," I answered with hesitation, and then added, "I didn't know you were a doctor too."

"My grandmother had all kinds of health problems. I used to help her with her medications. She used to sweat when her blood sugar was low," she said.

"I appreciate your offer, but your final exams are more important than taking care of me," I said.

She put her arm around my waist and said, "Let's go and get you some food. Sorry, I meant to say, some grub," she chuckled, but I did not find her manly imitation funny. How ironic it was that her mockery of what she felt was a manly expression was alien to me. Not even once in my life, had I used the word grub. However, I succumbed to the expected polite protocol in such situations, and gracefully smiled.

"You win. I'll go with you,' I said.

She walked with me to the cafeteria, and took her arm off my waist at the door. I looked around for girls that knew Wendy, but found none. It was a needed relief when she found an empty table and sat down. Instead of heading immediately to the food line, as I had wanted, I stopped and asked, "What can I get for you?"

She promptly said, "Thank you, but I'm OK."

There was no shame in making a strident effort to eliminate any immediate threat to one's life. Hunger was the only threat I faced that evening, so I stacked my food tray to address all my nutritional needs. When my tray was half-empty, I looked up for the first time. Doreen was immersed in a book. To a casual observer, we probably looked like a soulfully disconnected couple. However, before I finished my meal, she stood up, and with her characteristic ebullient charm, tendered an apology for leaving. Her compassion made me feel guilty about not auditioning for the summer play, but I knew that I could not risk the anger of a jealous girlfriend.

Chapter 9

WITH LOTS OF TIME on our hands, Wendy and I spent Thursday night at a local bistro playing with our food more than eating. Just to be together and unhurried was utterly fulfilling, so much so that our waiter had to rewarm my food twice. While I waited for my rewarmed food the second time, Wendy pulled her chair closer to me, and placed her left leg across my lap. I impulsively caressed her leg as she deliberately moved closer to me until her inner thigh welcomed my wandering hand. She looked at me with yearning eyes, and our heads only travelled a short distance before our lips touched. Our waiter never returned with my steak, so we paid our bill and left the bistro.

We strolled around our tranquil college campus aimlessly, and passed only two groups of students coming out of the library.

"What a beautiful night. If I could have my wish, I would spend evenings like this with you for the rest of my life," Wendy said as we approached the walkway in front of my former dormitory. This was where she'd visited me in 1977, a few days after we met. A bold move on her part considering the racial tension.

"That sounds good to me. I hope medical school will allow us enough time to enjoy a carefree life, at least once in a while," I said, as we hugged under a streetlight. She stepped back and leaned against the lamppost. I encircled her and the lamppost.

"You're a crazy foreigner, Joseph. Are you hugging me, or the lamppost?" I laughed, but she quieted my lips with a kiss. It was obvious that Wendy was happy with me that night. I wish we could have stayed that way forever. We stood by the light looking at each other as students passed by, mumbling unintelligibly.

Without discussion, we found our way to my apartment. Wendy's presence always brought verve to my abode, but that night was exceptional. We listened to an assortment of jazz and danced until very late.

* * *

I was not sure if Wendy told her parents about our upcoming trip to Florida. Even though I felt that she should let them know where she would be for five days, I avoided bringing it up. I knew being with her would elevate my spirit, so I was not eager to jeopardize our trip by insisting on informing her parents beforehand. It was selfish, but I did not regret it. To make things worse, I also did not inform Gina that Wendy was coming. Wendy and I took an early flight to Florida on Friday morning.

Once we boarded, it dawned on me that we were travelling as a couple. We took our first unprepared leap into the commitment without realizing the magnitude of what we were doing. For the first time, I thought about what my parents' reaction would be if they found out about such an unvirtuous romantic exploit. My mother would have disowned me if she knew that I went on a vacation with my girlfriend. She was the one that routinely defined our family virtues when I was growing up, and her ideas were conservative.

As more passengers boarded the aircraft, my heart rate accelerated, and a damp warmness gripped my body. I closed my eyes, probably to dissociate myself from my immediate location, and I felt remorseful about some of my actions, which were contrary to my conservative Catholic upbringing. My feeling of guilt was so overwhelming that I considered praying, but when I opened my eyes and looked at Wendy's beautiful face, my yearning for her returned. She glanced at me and smiled, as if she knew what was troubling me. My journey to righteousness would have to wait for another day. I wouldn't give her up for anything.

"Do you think Gina will be upset that I came?" Wendy asked.

I welcomed the question. It broke the deafening silence. "Probably, but I'm sure she'll get over it. She's really a considerate person, and fun to be with, once you get to know her."

"I hope she isn't the type that hates to change her plans," she said with a concerned look on her face. For a moment, she sounded sincere.

"How hard could it be to add an extra dinner plate?" I asked.

"That's reassuring, but I still have my worries," she said as she squeezed my hand, and held on to it.

An elderly white female walked to our row and requested a passage to the window seat. We stood up to let her in. She sat down, looked at Wendy, and said, "Hi young lady. You look as beautiful as my granddaughter."

"Thank you, ma'am." Wendy said. The elderly woman glanced at me and smiled, but did not say anything. Wendy placed her head on my shoulder, and closed her eyes. The elderly woman stopped fidgeting with her seat belt, and looked at us with a befuddled facial expression.

"Hello young man, are you Cuban?" the woman asked me.

"No, ma'am," I answered emphatically.

"I thought you were. You have their build, and lots of Cubans in Florida openly accept mixed-race relationships," she said callously. Her comment sounded ignorant, so I snubbed her, and turned to Wendy.

Wendy looked at me, and shook her head in disbelief. "Ignore her," she said.

"I did," I said.

It was difficult to ascertain if the elderly woman had a problem with our open affection, or if she was just curious about us. She must have felt better after she spoke to us because she opened her Bible to read, and left us alone.

Once we took off, Wendy fell asleep with her head on my shoulder. I stared at the glaring 'fasten seat belt' sign, until I drifted into protracted introspection.

*   *   *

Our bumpy flight finally landed with a loud thud. Wendy slept through the rattle and bump that followed our landing. I used the ends of her hair to tickle her ear. She woke up and gently slapped her ear, which made me laugh.

We meandered through a surging crowd in the airport terminal walkway. Wendy handed her bag over to me, and darted into the bathroom. I waited outside the bathroom door feeling elated that I would be spending so much time with the girl I was in love with. The moral issues I'd had earlier about our escapade, dissipated. Mired in euphoria, I did not notice when Wendy emerged from the bathroom, until she took her bag from me. She flung it over her shoulder, and reached out to hold my hand. Rather than walk, she playfully pranced down the airport concourse until we reached the baggage claim area. It felt good to be young and carefree, for a change.

Standing with exasperated travelers at the baggage depot were Gina and a remarkably tanned young female. Once Gina saw me, she smiled and walked toward us. I tried to walk faster toward Gina, but Wendy put her left arm around my waist and kept me from dashing away from her.

"Oh, you're with her," Gina said in a subdued voice as she put her arm around my shoulder and tried to pry me away from Wendy.

"I told you we're back together," I said. Gina tried unsuccessfully to relieve me from Wendy's grip. I could have twisted away from Wendy, but I did not.

"Yea, Wendy again. I didn't believe it when you told me. I kind of wished it wasn't true. I guess you forgot how downtrodden you felt when she left you. I was there to pick up the pieces of your broken heart, but now she's back to complete what she didn't accomplish then," Gina said angrily, and left off trying to retrieve me from Wendy.

"Gina, I love Joseph. I never intended to hurt him," Wendy said, still holding onto my waist. She looked triumphant. Gina retreated.

"Remember me, people," Gina's friend chided us. Gina sighed, and pulled me by the hand toward her friend, with Wendy in tow.

"Marianna, here's my adopted brother who used to be an innocent boy. Now he's wayward from the look of things," Gina said. Wendy loosened her tight grip on me and turned her back on Gina. Gina had failed to free me from Wendy's grip by physical means but managed to achieve her goal with derisive words.

My negligence to inform Gina about my travel companion had created more tension than expected. The worst I'd anticipated was a simple rebuke, nothing more.

"Ignore what Gina says about me. I'm not wayward," I said with a smile, and Marianna smiled back. "It's nice to meet you," I said as I extended my hand to her.

Marianna prattled inaudibly as she shook my hand. Her action was more consistent with that of a shy grade school girl.

I hugged Gina. A smile twinkled on her face. The warm hug with Gina elevated my spirit, and I felt confident that I had doused the fire that was raging inside her.

I held Wendy's hand, and said, "Marianna, this is my girlfriend, Wendy."

"So you are really serious again?" Gina interrupted me. She waited for an answer, but I ignored her question. Gina was still angry. "Francesca just used you up, and left you. Seems like these two friends are passing you back and forth.".

Gina seemed determined to air all the bad things that had happened to me. Her castigation of my naïveté right in front of everyone at the airport shocked me. Maybe I was not adept at relationships in 1977 when I was seventeen years old, but two years had passed, and I had learnt from my mistakes.

"Don't put down my relationship with Joseph," Wendy said firmly. "I love him. Accept it, or leave us alone. You claim to be his sister, but we've been here for fifteen minutes, and I haven't heard a single expression of love from you. You're angry with me because you brought your friend to meet him. I spoiled your plan, didn't I? Tell your friend to go home. He's mine, and I'm not going to give him up." Wendy's anger was palpable. All the French finishing school training failed her woefully in front of me that day. Gina had managed to unsettle the school's reigning 'Miss Congeniality.'

Gina and Wendy continued bickering while I retrieved our luggage. Away from them, I noticed that they had attracted the attention of more passengers than I had realized. I could only imagine what mordant words Gina hurled at Wendy, because I was not close enough to hear it. Wendy's lips were moving as fast as Gina's.

With two suitcases in both hands, I walked over to Gina and said, "Forgive me. It wasn't intentional." My voice was very low, such that she was the only one that probably heard what I said.

Gina put her arms around my shoulders, and said, "I'm sorry, too, for losing my cool. You need to know that I'm concerned about your wellbeing."

"What plans do you have for us?" I asked Gina. It was a good way to empower her in front of Wendy. She brightened at my gesture.

"Well, on our way to drop off your things at my apartment, I'll show you the medical school first, then, we'll do lunch. We have a newly constructed basic science building with nice research facilities. I can't wait to have you here next year," Gina said, exuding excitement. She was in charge of my life again. She thought.

"Gina, don't kill the messenger, but it appears that Joseph hasn't told you about his plan to attend medical school with me in the Carolinas. He's been offered a spot in the new MD-PhD program," Wendy said gloatingly.

It did not feel good to be in the middle of a tussle between two women trying to control my life. "Why, Wendy? Why start another fight? I was waiting for the right time to tell Gina about the offer. It's not even official. I had planned to discuss things privately with her. I value her opinion very much and need her input before I commit to any school," I said, watching Gina's anger rise.

"I'm always the last to know about your plans, Joseph. I wish I hadn't spoken to some of my professors about you. If I had known you were happy in the Carolinas, I wouldn't have invited you to visit my school," Gina said.

"I'm still looking at all my options. You sound so happy when we talk on the phone, and that's why I'm here. I want to experience the same happiness in medical school, as you do," I said.

"That's why we need to be together. Don't I make you happy?" Wendy asked. It was apparent that I'd made a mess of things with the wrong choice of words. I could not take them back and was not eager to apologize to anyone. It is better to walk away, than to argue about an issue with no winning options. There was no possible way to keep Wendy and Gina happy at the same time in matters relating to me. We had reached an acceptable impasse, so I headed to the exit door. Marianna followed me.

"I'm sorry about the misunderstanding," Marianna said.

Why would she apologize for something she did not cause?

"You seem to be special, and that's probably why everyone wants to help you," she continued.

I was not sure where she was going with her statement, so I said, "I'm not an invalid that needs help." The clamor to help the 'incompetent immigrant' got to me.

Marianna, who probably felt offended, said, "I hope to see you guys later," and walked ahead. We followed her to the parking lot.

*   *   *

On our way to Gina's apartment, Wendy's comments grew more circumspect. What surprised me most was her willingness to let Gina plan our activities, and how pleasant her voice was when she said, "I'm really sorry about what happened between us at the airport. You didn't expect me to be with Joseph. It was my fault. I couldn't bear the thought of being away from him for five days, so I insisted on coming with him." Gina acted as if she didn't hear Wendy and kept on driving. Wendy looked at me with worry, but I could not offer anything to relieve her anxiety.

I was about to say something to Gina, but she trumped my intended intervention saying, "I should've been told you were traveling together. I deserve at least that much respect from the two of you."

"I hope there's enough room for us. If not, we can always check into a hotel," Wendy said.

"I'm worried my apartment may not be good enough for you. My food too," Gina said.

"I'll stay with Joseph, and eat whatever you have," Wendy said.

Gina looked over her shoulder at me, but I looked away. She looked at me one more time, then turned to Wendy, and said, "If I remember things right, you never ate at the school cafeteria. You gave him your meal cards to avoid wasting them. You had your meals delivered." Gina hesitated for a moment, and then added, "I don't expect anything different from the daughter of Mister Crane. Your family owns the biggest company in North Carolina. I'm sure my apartment and my food aren't good enough for you."

Wendy responded angrily, "My father is the owner of the company, not me. I don't expect any special treatment from anyone. For your information, I never demanded any preferential treatment at school, nor did I ever get out of my responsibilities because of being a Crane. Ask Joseph; I work hard for what I get." Her voice rose in crescendo as she spoke. "Joseph, please tell Gina I'm a regular person. I may have my quirks, but I have never felt superior to anyone." She looked at me solemnly, and then added, "Hon, you know me intimately, better than anybody else knows me. Tell Gina I'm a good person." She looked away from me as tears rolled down her cheeks.

Wendy's comment touched me very deeply, and I tried very hard to contain my own tears. I placed my hands on her shoulders, but when I tried to talk, Gina interrupted me with an uncompromising tone of voice. "Wendy, I wonder why you expect me and your professors to treat you the same as every other student? Is your father not the chairman of the board of trustees of the college? I once heard that he even tells the school president how to run the institution. After all, he gives the school and the medical center millions of dollars every year, to allow him to exert his authority over them." She slowed the car down, and looking at Wendy said, "You're privileged, whether you accept it, or not."

"Are you done with your assault on her?" I asked.

"I may have more to say later, but I'm done for now," Gina said.

"Gina, I didn't realize the extent of the Cranes' involvement at school. She's not the type that brags about herself."

"Joseph, she shouldn't have to tell you about her family. You feel the power of the Cranes in North Carolina even when they're not around," Gina said.

"Your speculation is beyond my understanding. Maybe I am just an ignorant foreigner who doesn't understand American ways, but I still feel comfortable with Wendy," I said.

"One day, little brother, you'll feel their power bearing down on you," Gina said.

"I'm not sure what you're talking about, Gina, but go ahead and let your imagination run wild," Wendy said with no hint of her Southern drawl, and launched into a speech worthy of some of the fancy girls I debated in high school. I almost clapped for her.

But when I considered whether I was good enough for Wendy from a socioeconomic perspective, I saw that Gina's assertion's were not as blunt as they could have been. I thought over everything she said and felt suddenly inadequate. As if my self-doubt was not bad enough, my mind wandered to the dream house Wendy wanted for us, and I saw that to live as well as she wanted us to, she would have to support the two of us financially. I was a proud African. The idea of Wendy supporting me was not the future I had envisioned for myself.

Even with my concealed self-doubt, I leaned closer to Wendy and whispered teasingly, "You do know that I love you for you, and not for your money?"

Wendy turned around and kissed me. She then said, "My family's wealth shouldn't affect who I love, and who loves me. I didn't see the need to discuss details of my father's activities with Joseph. He fell in love with me, not with my family. Do you know how many boys I've met spouting corny lines like, 'So you're the daughter of James Crane?' That's a big turn off for me. It was refreshing to meet someone like Joseph who cares about me, not my family's connections."

"Let's stop talking about other people's money. Why don't we talk about the party we're crashing tonight," I said.

"OK, Joseph. Let's stop talking about my family, but crashing a party? I'm not sure," Wendy said.

"We're crashing a party tonight?" Gina asked with a pleasant voice.

"All I want is some fun tonight after all the bickering between you two," I said.

"We're going to the funkiest night club. It's the best party to crash. We're going to boogie until the sun comes up," Gina said snapping her fingers.

Wendy whispered, "I get to dance with my favorite boy. Can't wait for the fun, Hon."

Gina's hostile behavior toward Wendy had worn me down emotionally, but I welcomed her change in attitude, with slight trepidation. The mere suggestion of going out to have fun, turned out to be the buffer we needed to keep the two warring parties from hurling barbed verbiage at each other.

Gina turned the radio volume up, as her car moved slowly on the scorching asphalt. A popular song, "Ain't no stoppin' us now, we are moving on," by McFadden and Whitehead came on, and we tried to sing along. However bad we were, we kept singing and dancing with our upper bodies. It felt so good to hear everyone laugh. The spontaneity continued after we got out of the car. The biggest surprise was that Gina walked up to Wendy and hugged her. She then said, "I'm very sorry for all the mean stuff I said. You seem to care about my little brother. I couldn't imagine a better person than you, for him."

"I'll take good care of him," Wendy said. I still felt slighted because I did not need Wendy to take care of me. However, I concealed my feelings to avoid another conflict.

"I'm starving. I hope there's a plan for lunch soon?" I said.

"Let's go inside, freshen up, and then find a place for lunch," Gina suggested.

"I hope we're going to a nice place, not a cheap taco joint for burritos," I said, but my playful statement failed to elicit any reaction from Gina.

We walked into Gina's townhouse apartment, which was sparsely but tastefully decorated in bright colors. Her rattan furniture accentuated with tropical print fabrics and matching curtains brightened up the sitting area. The kitchen and a small dining section were partially visible from an oblong opening in the wall that partitioned the areas.

We walked over to three pictures on the wall. One was my awards day photograph from 1978. The second was Gina's family portrait, and the third was a young man in military uniform.

I sat down, but Wendy remained staring at the photographs. Gina joined her, and asked, "Is there something wrong with my pictures?"

"Who's the guy in military uniform?" Wendy asked.

"He's my fiancé. Unfortunately, he was transferred to Germany six months ago," Gina said.

"Are you moving to Germany when you finish medical school?" Wendy asked.

"We're not planning to get married soon. I still have to do my residency after medical school. Who knows, he may be back in the States by then," Gina answered.

"Your father looks very tall, like a basketball player."

"He played in college. Also played briefly in the NBA before he was injured," Gina said.

"Looking at the photograph, I couldn't decide on your mom's race," Wendy said.

There was complete silence in the room. The air-conditioner throttled and stopped blowing cold air. It appeared that Gina was not in a hurry to answer Wendy's indirect question, but she eventually said, "My mother is a Lumbee Indian, one of the largest tribes in North Carolina. They have a colorful history."

"It's story time. Too bad we don't have a campfire to make it authentic. Go on Gina, tell us about the Lumbee Indians," I said.

"Not today, but someday I'll tell you about the tribe that adopted you as their own, my little brother," she said.

Wendy laughed. I was not sure what was funny, but the way she said it made me laugh too.

"Gina, I thought Lumbee Indians denied any heritage tied to American blacks," Wendy said. "I remember reading some chronicles in high school about the role Lumbee Indians played in the Confederate army and their disappointing relegation to a colored race after the Civil War. A lot of people felt they were not a true Indian tribe, including the North Carolina Cherokees."

Wendy sounded very authoritative in her assertion about the history of the Lumbee tribe. She went on to narrate several stories about her grandfather's dealings with Lumbee tobacco farmers and the mistrust they had about every other group. Her grandfather said that the Lumbee Indians were Mulattos and not a pure race.

Gina swallowed hard, and sighed several times as Wendy spoke. She frowned when Wendy said that the Lumbee tribe was complicit with the Confederate army during the American Civil War. I felt that Wendy's statements were inappropriate because she was not an expert in American Indian history, and was mostly relating oral history, which was fraught with bias.

"I apparently don't know much about the history of the Lumbee tribe as you do. I'll leave that up to my mother to discuss with you when you get back to North Carolina," Gina said.

"I hope I didn't offend you." Wendy said. "Your parents' mixed marriage interests me. It's funny how there's so much pervasive racial mistrust in this world, but the young ones always fall in love with each other across racial lines." Initially I thought her statement was profound, but the more I thought about what she said, the more confusing it sounded.

"Are you talking about your own interracial love affair?" Gina asked.

"Of course, I'm talking about Joseph and me. There's nobody else that matters as much to me in the world," Wendy retorted.

"My vote is that we should go out to eat, and spend some time exploring the city of Gainesville. We've had enough arguing to last us a long time," I said.

"I totally agree with Joseph. There is a bathroom around the corner, if you need to use it before we leave," Gina said.

Wendy went into the bathroom, and I quietly apologized to Gina about some of the uncomfortable discussions we had had since our arrival. Gina loudly said, "I prefer honest, open discussions rather than trying to figure out what someone believes in." For the first time, I commented on the size of the diamond mounted on her engagement ring, which shifted the discussion to her life in Florida, and her plans for the future. Wendy rejoined us, and we left Gina's apartment without any further rancor.

* * *

We had barely entered the car, when Wendy complained about her uninspiring wardrobe, and requested a quick jaunt to the local mall to buy an outfit. At the mall, Gina decided that she needed an outfit too, but had difficulty finding a dress she liked. I grew tired of sitting around waiting. Wendy eventually bought two outfits muttering the lame excuse that she could not settle on which one she liked best.

I hummed incomprehensible tunes occasionally to mask my rumbling stomach. It was not surprising that after the inordinate amount of time spent shopping for dresses, we had to settle for a takeout lunch-cum-dinner. On our way back to the apartment, we stopped at a store and bought soda pop. At Gina's apartment, all etiquette aside, we descended on our meals. Our voices came back to life, and resonated as before. I was not surprised when the bickering resumed.

*   *   *

I waited patiently as the girls dressed for the evening. Wendy was the first to emerge from the downstairs bathroom, and said, "What do you think?" turning around for me. A tight-fitting cream-colored dress clung to her sculpted ballerina's body, as if the dress was tailor made for her. The low neckline left little to the imagination. But her beauty was not limited to her body shape. Her green eyes glistened in the subdued light, and when she flashed her pearly white teeth at me, I had to gulp for air.

Wendy watched me very closely, aware that she aroused my senses. She turned around, and lifted her braided hair to show me the back of her dress, which was unzipped all the way down to her dainty yellow underwear. My hands trembled as I attempted to zip up her dress, but it did not stop me from reaching inside the garment to feel her naked body. Mindful of the fact that my shenanigans could offend Gina, I retrieved my hands from Wendy's waistline. Afterward, the smell of her perfume lingered on my hands. It reminded me of the lilac field where we had picnics. She looked at me, and asked, "Why did you stop?"

"What did I stop, Wendy?" I asked with faked innocence.

"Come on, Joseph, spare me the altar boy theatrics," Wendy said.

"Look at you. You're so beautiful, and elegant. You can't imagine the happiness your presence brings to me," I said as she reached out and hugged me.

"I love you, Joseph. You're everything I ever wanted, and more," Wendy said.

"I love you too, Wendy," I said.

By the time I realized that Gina had made her way down to the first floor, she was standing next to us and shaking her head. I tried to disengage from the tight embrace, but Wendy held on to me and bit my left ear gently. I tried to turn my left side away from her, but she bit my right ear too, and giggled.

Gina walked slightly away from us, and then said, "Are you kids going to stop mauling each other? We have a town to paint tonight."

"Yes, mother," Wendy and I said in unison.

"I hope you guys don't mind me wearing what I have on," I said. "I don't want to change my clothes just to go out and sweat."

They ignored me. Their silence adequately conveyed their opinion, so I went to the guest room and changed into a white cotton shirt. My white linen pants complemented the shirt well, so I left them on.

I returned to the first floor. Gina greeted me with a smile. "Now you look like our cabana boy. I like it," Gina said.

"You can be my private cabana boy anytime," Wendy said as she winked at me.

"What do I get for my services?" I asked.

Wendy looked at me seductively and smiled. "You can get anything your heart desires, but you already know that. The only thing you have to do is, ask."

"This conversation is getting too deep for me," Gina said.

We followed her out of the apartment.

On our way to the nightclub, we picked up Marianna from her place. Her low-cut red chiffon dress and the glitter sprinkled on her neck glistened under the streetlights. Marianna closed the car door, and greeted us with a sparkling smile, but her perfume almost overpowered me. I rolled down the car window and stuck my head out to breathe some fresh air. Wendy pinched me, and whispered in my ear, "What you're doing is not nice. I'm sure Marianna knows why you rolled down the window." I ignored her, and kept my head partially outside the car.

"It's not nice to whisper when you have other people sitting close to you. I thought you two had better manners," Gina said.

"We're having a private conversation," Wendy snapped back.

"It's my fault, Gina. I rolled down the window because I felt claustrophobic. Wendy was teasing me about it," I said.

"Is it me, or do you guys always act silly?" Marianna asked without addressing anyone in particular.

"Can't you tell they're in love? They're entitled to act silly until they get tired of each other," Gina said.

"Are you jealous of our love, Gina?" Wendy asked, and then added, "I'll never get tired of loving Joseph, if that's what you're waiting for."

"Here we go again. I'm surrounded by bickering women who do not know how to act like ladies. Remind me to stay home next time you go out," I said.

"I'll not go anywhere without you, my love," Wendy said as she kissed my lips.

"Why don't you two spare us your uncontrolled display of lust for each other? In case you need a room, there's a cheap motel around the corner," Gina said. She looked at Wendy briefly, and said, "I'm sorry dear, the place is probably not good enough for you." Gina and Marianna laughed after the comment. Wendy ignored them, and placed her head on my shoulder. No one spoke after that until we reached the nightclub.

* * *

The nightclub had an acclaimed restaurant attached to it. Marianna suggested stopping at the restaurant first where she had a light dinner. Then, we hit the dance floor.

The flashing lights and the reflective disco balls created an enthralling atmosphere in the dance hall. With each flash of light, the silhouettes of dancers appeared, and subsequently disappeared as the lights went off. The thump of the loudspeakers activated the flashing disco lights for a rhythmic mix of sight and sound.

Wendy seemed uncoordinated on the dance floor, even though she was an acclaimed ballerina. Gina was skilled in all the common dance moves, and she strutted all over the dance floor. Marianna had only one dance move for all the songs that played. I danced with the three girls, but when the tempo of the music slowed down, Wendy held me very tight, and moved her hips from side to side. As the music progressed, she placed her head on my shoulder, and our separate steps finally converged into coordinated footwork until Gina asked, "Are you guys making love, or dancing?" Her meddling annoyed me, but I ignored her and danced on. Gina left the dance floor and went back to the table.

Donna Summer's, "Love to Love You Baby," came on with lots of moaning, and took us back to our 'close-body' rhythmic oneness. As I had expected, Gina came back to us and said, "We've danced enough for the night, and I don't want to witness the two of you making love to each other here."

"I'm not sure what you're talking about, Gina, but since you say so, we have no other choice than to leave with you," I said.

Wendy initially refused to leave the dance floor. Gina walked closer to her and said, "I'm not sure when Joseph became naughty. Probably when he was exposed to your friend, Francesca."

"Let's have some fun," Wendy said.

Gina took hold of my hand and pulled me away from the dance floor. Wendy followed us and protesting loudly.

At the bar, Wendy stopped and said, "What we're doing is called being in love. You should watch us, and maybe learn something, so your fiancé doesn't abandon you. I'm sure he's gallivanting all over Europe, and you're here playing our school chaperone. Let us enjoy our vacation."

"Look at this prissy white lily castigating me. Love means more than having your breasts squeezed on the dance floor. It means commitment, and consideration. You haven't shown any of that to the person you claim to love. I'm going to be around as long as Joseph needs protection from phonies like you," Gina said. As Wendy moved closer to Gina, I stepped in to separate them. Marianna, who had joined us at the bar, looked on with a smile, apparently finding the girls entertaining.

"I'm disappointed that the two of you can't get along," I said. I turned to Gina and added, "You talk about me as if I'm a child that needs help. I can take care of myself. I do appreciate your concern about my wellbeing, but give it a break."

"I worry about you all the time. You made a big mistake with Francesca, now you're dating the wonderful tobacco heiress. Only God knows what she has in store for you down the line," Gina said.

"You're nothing but a jealous bitch, Gina," Wendy said.

"It takes one to know one," Gina replied instantly.

"So where do we sleep tonight with all the bickering between the two of you?" I asked.

"We can find a decent hotel," Wendy said.

"That's just an excuse to avoid staying with me. My apartment is not good enough for you," Gina said.

"Do you always have women fight over you, Joseph?" Marianna asked with a taunting smile.

"No one is fighting over me, Marianna. Please, don't make things worse," I said.

"Marianna, I don't know what you're insinuating," Gina said. She turned to me. "We should get out of here because I need some sleep. You can stay in my apartment with your princess as long as she stops calling me a bitch."

We left the nightclub. Gina and Wendy ignored each other.

*   *   *

Just as darkness gave way to early morning sunlight, we dropped Marianna off at her apartment and found our way back to Gina's townhouse. We dragged our weary bodies inside Gina's apartment. Wendy sat next to me on the loveseat, resting her head in my lap. I played with her sprawling hair. Across from us, Gina scowled. When Gina stood up, I thought she was going to bed, but she walked to the kitchen and came back with a glass of milk.

"Is there a place we can go out for breakfast now?" I asked, when Gina finished her glass of milk.

"There's a pancake house not far from here, but it won't be open for another hour. I'm hungry too. The glass of milk didn't help me," Gina said. I wanted to ask her about the choice of a large glass of milk, but could not find the strength to do so. The unimportant issue of the glass of milk stayed on my mind.

Wendy sat up and said, "My honey here is all I need for breakfast."

"Wendy, you talk about your love for this young black brother of mine all the time. If you're so much in love, and can't live without him, why didn't you show him that love a year ago?" Gina asked.

Wendy waited for a long time before she said, "I was younger and naïve then. You can't imagine how I felt when other students called me names. Worst of all, my family almost disowned me. I became unpleasant to be around and felt that Joseph was better off without me, so I left."

"You were the closest friend he had in school, and you found it more appropriate to write him a stupid note, instead of talking to him about what you were going through. I still remember the day you left for France, and how he came to my lab heartbroken. He was too hurt to cry for you, so I cried for him." Gina's voice went up a couple of decibels as she spoke.

"Gina, we had so much fun together tonight, why do you want to mess things up? I'm capable of voicing my opinion about my relationship with Wendy," I said.

"The irony of the whole mess was how Joseph defended all your actions," Gina went on. "That's how people behave when they truly love someone. Would you've done the same thing for him if things were reversed?" Gina asked. "He was so much in love with you, he thought you could never do any wrong."

"I love him too, Gina, and I'll always will." Wendy's voice quavered as she spoke.

"It's pathetic how everyone is always trying to protect me," I said. "I didn't make it this far in life by being stupid. I'm capable of taking care of myself."

Gina interrupted me. "If you're so capable of taking care of yourself, why did you get entangled with Francesca? I guess you couldn't tell she was a gold-digging bitch?"

"Francesca is my sorority sister," Wendy said. "She's not a bitch. I know she's ambitious, and some of her decisions are selfish, but it took the two of them to get involved. I forgave Joseph for his weakness," Wendy said.

"But you were the one that fixed them up so you wouldn't feel guilty when you left him," Gina retorted.

"I didn't fix them up, Gina," Wendy countered loudly. She sighed and then continued, "I only asked Joseph to help her with her classes. I was devastated when I heard they were dating each other. As my sorority sister, I expected she would avoid getting involved with Joseph. She knew I loved him."

"Why don't we stop this conversation before it goes too far? It was my mistake to get involved with Francesca, and I'm not going to blame anybody else. She was good to me most of the time, and only changed after she signed her modeling contract. I believe her handlers instructed her to stay away from me so she wouldn't jeopardize her career," I said.

Wendy stood up and walked to the door that led to the patio. She parted the curtains. The early morning sun illuminated her face. She peered out into the distance as I walked over to her. I put my arms around her shoulders and she rubbed my forearm. It was hard to figure out which burden was weighing more on her at that moment, but I felt that addressing one of the possible burdens was necessary. I whispered in her ear, "I hope you still believe that I wasn't in love with Francesca. You are my first, and my only love, Wendy."

She turned around and hugged me. Tears flowed from her eyes as she spoke. "It was my fault, Joseph. I couldn't bear the thought of losing everything in my life because my father couldn't accept you, so I took the easy way out and ran to France. I was miserable without you, and you made it worse for me by running around with my friend."

"You claim that you love him, but your daddy hates him. I believe your daddy has all the aces, and will eventually tell you what to do about your annoying black boy. Or should I say 'Negro boy' as James Crane probably says when he talks about Joseph," Gina said. Even though I was angry, I could not help but laugh at Gina's wit.

"I'm not sure how my dad feels about Joseph now. He spends more time in Europe than the States expanding his business. Maybe being in Europe will help him be more accepting of cross-cultural relationships," Wendy said.

"Give me a break. He may accept mixed relationships of other people's kids, but his pride and joy is a different case. No mixed-race grandbabies for James Crane. When do you plan to tell daddy that you are back with your forbidden Negro love?" Gina giggled as she spoke.

"I don't need my father's approval to be in love, Gina. For someone whose parents are mutts, you're pretty critical of interracial relationships," Wendy said.

"Are you insulting my parents?" Gina asked.

"I meant that your parents are in a mixed race relationship, and probably proud of it," Wendy replied.

"As long as you don't hurt Joseph anymore, I don't have an issue with you. I'll assume you love him for now. But will you be able to withstand the scrutiny and prejudice you'll face in North Carolina?" Gina asked.

"I'm very grateful for your concern about our welfare, but we don't need your help or advice. I've grown a lot since I met Joseph. I know what I want," Wendy retorted.

"My father said it took selfless love and unwavering dedication to my mother to survive," Gina said.

I became more irritated with the endless bickering, so I stepped in, and said, "We made mistakes, but we can't change the past. I was a seventeen-year-old kid when I met Wendy. I didn't know how to express my feelings to her. How can you blame her for leaving me when I never asked her to stay? She was the one chasing after me, and I kept bumbling around like a fool. For all the gifts she gave me, and favors she did for me, I never showed any appreciation. Gina, it was mostly my fault things didn't work out for us, so let's end this hurtful discussion."

"So you really want me to butt out of your business," Gina said. "Only a fool would keep trying to get through to you when her opinion isn't appreciated. Fine. I'll back off from your love affair. Find out for yourself."

* * *

We walked to the nearby pancake house. Even from a distance, I could tell it was a ramshackle building. A partially cracked wooden sign that hung on the street side of the building had the name of the eatery and their service hours hand painted on it. Prolonged exposure to the hot, humid Florida weather had left cracks on the walls. I paced around as we waited for the restaurant to open at six a.m.

As the first customers, we had the opportunity to sit anywhere. Wendy walked to a booth next to the window and asked me to sit next to her. Gina sat across from me and picked up a worn out, one-page menu. She looked at the menu for a few minutes, before she placed it back on the table. "Greasy breakfast, plus the fat from a glass of milk earlier," Gina said.

"It's your city, and we're willing to go anywhere you want," I said.

"Speak for yourself, Joseph. I want to stay here and eat before I die of starvation," Wendy protested.

Our server came before Gina could make up her mind and made a long speech about what made their restaurant special. Wendy became impatient. "Can I have toast, eggs Benedict, and a small glass of orange juice?" The woman looked at her and frowned. Wendy, who appeared unperturbed, asked for a bowl of fresh fruit. The woman laughed and said, "We serve good old-fashioned American breakfast, like bacon, sausages, eggs, pancakes, and grits." I ordered pancakes and scrambled eggs. Wendy and Gina ordered the same breakfast as I did.

We sat in silence, out of fatigue and fear of argument. I looked at Wendy and wondered why the daughter of one of the richest men in North Carolina would lower her standards to be with me in a despicable greasy-spoon joint. But when Wendy smiled, I knew it was true. She was content being there with me.

Food finally came, not what we ordered. The waitress set fried sausages and stacks of waffles down on the table in front of us. I stared at the greasy sausage on my plate, and it took me back to my first year in college when I'd ventured into a local restaurant for a hamburger. The place must have used lard on their fries. When the French fries got cold, they stuck to the plate.

I picked up my fork and probed the sausage. Wendy and Gina looked on. "This one isn't an edible puck," I said as they laughed at me. 'Edible puck' was the nickname of the sausages served in our school cafeteria that could break dishes because of their hardness.

I avoided the sausage, and ate the three layers of waffles on my plate. If our server had given me the opportunity, I would have ordered more waffles. Instead, she came back and gave us separate checks. Gina picked up all three checks and walked to the cashier to pay them. We were too tired to protest against her generosity, but we thanked her.

*   *   *

Walking back to the apartment after a heavy breakfast was not an easy chore, but we made it, nonetheless. It was equally difficult climbing the steps to the second floor of Gina's apartment.

I undressed completely before walking into the bathroom. Wendy followed me into the shower stall, and asked, "Can you scrub my body. I'm too tired to wash myself." Gina's apartment was small, and I knew that she must have heard Wendy's request. There was no doubt in my mind that Gina, a devout Southern Baptist, would be unhappy with such a brazen display of what she probably would consider an immoral act.

The lukewarm shower did not revive me, as I expected. I fell asleep as soon as I lay on the bed with Wendy, and woke up six hours later. I tried to get out of bed, but could not. I was still exhausted after only six hours of sleep. However, when Gina called my name, I lifted Wendy's arm up from my body, and got out of bed. What a waste of a beautiful sunny day, I thought. We had partied all night, and slept all day, missing other interesting things to do in Florida.

Gina knocked at our bedroom door before I finished putting on my pants. I hurriedly zipped up before opening the door. I found Gina fully dressed, and I apologized to her for taking too long to answer the door.

"I have to run to the medical school for an end-of-the-year get together today. I'll only be gone for an hour," Gina said.

"We'll find something to do until you get back," I said.

"I'll bring back takeout dinner for you and your princess," Gina said.

"Thank you for everything you do for me," I said. She smiled and rubbed my neck.

"I enjoy doing things for you, because you're special, and one of the rare souls that have no vindictive tendencies. It's easy to be fond of you," Gina said. Wendy cleared her throat several times, but I ignored her. I looked behind me, relieved that she was not in too much distress. Gina ignored the distraction, and continued, "Oh! When I get back, we'll go to the mall. Maybe see a movie. Tomorrow, we're driving to Disney World to see Mickey. I'll see you later, Joseph," Gina said before she went down the steps, and out the front door.

Wendy had a grin on her face, but would not comment on what she found amusing. I slumped on the bed, and pulled her over to me. She looked at me, and said, "I heard your mommy give you instructions."

"She's four years older than me, so she can play mother if she wants," I said.

"Are you getting testy because I pointed out you're enjoying this big sister nonsense? Have you ever wondered if she's secretly in love with you? Maybe that's why she gets angry with me. Because you're my baby. I bet you she wants me out of your life so you'll be available for her. Next time she says something mean to me, I'm telling her to buzz off," Wendy passionately said.

"Where did you get that crazy idea?" I asked.

"I'm a woman, and I can tell," Wendy said.

"That's the best answer you can come up with?" I asked.

"You can be so naïve sometimes. That's why you fell for Francesca's antics," Wendy said.

"Not long ago, you defended your friend, and now you're criticizing her. How am I supposed to know how you really feel about anything, Wendy?"

"We're discussing a different issue now, Hon," she said.

"On our first vacation, we shouldn't argue about silly stuff. We should enjoy the short time we have together, since summer school starts next week," I said.

She lamented about the year wasted when she travelled to France and vowed never to leave me again. We promised each other that we would remain friends forever. "We're going to have the best wedding ever," Wendy said. She managed to sneak that statement in. I conveniently ignored the comment.

Gina returned from her medical school function, and as she promised, came back with several Styrofoam containers. We gathered in the living room and traded non-lethal banter with frequent breaks to stuff our mouths with slices of an oversized pastrami sandwich. Inadvertently, Wendy spoke with a mouthful, and Gina rebuked her. I could not help but ask, "Wendy, whose mom is she now?" She responded with a hearty laugh.

Before we finished eating, Wendy placed some money on the table, and said, "We came with enough money, so you don't have to pay for our meals. I'm paying you back for our lunch."

Gina's demeanor changed instantly, and she shouted at Wendy, "You always talk about money. I don't need it, and neither does Joseph." She lowered her voice midway and continued. "You're my guest, and it's my obligation to make sure you're cared for." She spoke with passion, and a great deal of control toward the end.

"You're a student like us, but you've been spending a lot of money since we arrived," Wendy said.

"Why don't we take you out tonight, Gina? Maybe that'll make you feel better," I said.

"It sounds like a good idea, but my stomach is already full. How about going to the mall to see a movie on us, if that's OK with you, Gina?" Wendy suggested.

"There's nothing wrong with trying to take care of my little brother. I'm the closest person to him," Gina said.

"You're wrong, Gina. I'm the closest person to Joseph," Wendy said.

"Girls, there's no need to always argue about petty issues. I'm close to the two of you, but our relationships are different. It's not fair to compare them. We should focus on having fun, and try to get along. My relative youth doesn't mean I'm helpless," I said.

"You're right, Joseph. I got used to your telephone calls, which stopped when she came back into your life. I want to always be a part of your daily life," Gina said in a solemn voice.

"I wouldn't have it any other way, Sis," I said. I hugged and held Gina.

Wendy looked at us, and walked away.

*   *   *

The girls had planned to shop for a few items in the mall before seeing a late movie, but instead of shopping in just a few stores, they walked aimlessly from one store to another. I got bored waiting for them, and decided to look around the mall. I stopped by a water fountain. Light reflected up the submerged coins.

Gazing at flowing water and the reflections was so mesmerizing that I dissociated from my surroundings. I was startled when someone touched my shoulder, and I heard, "I couldn't find a decent dress for church service tomorrow. I have given up searching for something decent, but not too expensive," Gina said.

Her mention of the church service made my stomach sink. Worrying about my queasy stomach, my heart took off as if it were trying to escape from my body, and I could feel pounding in my ears. I tried to alleviate my anxiety by breathing deep and slow, but cold sweat bathed my body.

"I wasn't aware we were going to a church in the morning," I said, my hands trembling.

"My devotion to God is something I take seriously," she replied.

"Well, I haven't been inside a church service since 1977. I told you about the unfortunate experience I had in a North Carolina church when we met. I was so incensed that I swore never to attend a church service again," I said. Gina looked at me vacuously. She didn't rememeber the sorry experience, so I recounted everything to her again.

"On the morning of my first Sunday in North Carolina in 1977, I had gone to a Catholic mass within walking distance of my dormitory. There were only a handful of people in the church when I arrived. I walked to the front pew and sat down. As more people arrived, the small church filled up. All of the available chairs were taken, but no one came to sit in my pew. Some of the parishioners stood at the back of the church, instead of filling the available spaces on my bench. The usher tried frantically to fill the available spaces in my row, but most of those standing declined the offer to sit near me. As the number of those standing grew, the usher approached me and asked me to leave. He stated that it was a private service and that I wasn't invited. I stood up, and he escorted me to the door. I went back to my dorm room and said my prayers privately. It took a few months before I got over that shameful experience."

"That was in North Carolina," Gina said. "Florida's different. My church is very progressive and there's no discrimination. It's a non-denominational congregation,"

"I don't mean to sound ignorant, but what's a non-denominational church? I was born a Catholic and will always be one," I said.

"Non-denominational simply means that all are welcome to give praise to God. We have Catholics and Protestants that attend the services," Gina said.

"I don't want to give up on Catholicism yet. In my country, things were different because we didn't have to deal with racial discrimination, but we have religious discrimination." I was still telling my story when I felt a pinch on my buttocks. I turned around and welcomed Wendy's smile.

"Have you missed me, Hon?" Wendy said.

I pulled her closer to me, and kissed her. "It's better to show you than to tell you how much I missed you," I said.

Gina looked away as we carried on. However, when Wendy said, "I found the cutest nightgown to wear tonight," Gina walked away from us, and sat on a nearby chair.

Gina demeanor had grown reserved.

Wendy put her hands under my shirt as she kissed me. Gina, who looked more dejected, rose from the chair, and walked toward the movie theater. We followed her until we came to the entrance. I rushed to the ticket booth, and bought tickets for the three of us.

"What's wrong Sis?" I asked after we sat down.

"Let's talk about it when we get home," Gina said. Wendy continued with her playful act, rubbing her hands all over my body, indifferent to Gina.

A few minutes after the movie started, Gina left, and never returned. I could not get out of my chair to look for her because Wendy was sitting on my lap. My whining failed to persuade Wendy to return to her own chair.

I barely saw the movie screen with Wendy sitting on me. Once the lights came on at the conclusion of the movie, we left the room and found Gina reading previews of future events on the wall. She gave us an unforced smile. "I hope you didn't make love in the theater," Gina said. I smiled without replying. Wendy acted as if she didn't hear what Gina said. Gina walked toward the exit.

We drove back to her apartment. Gina turned off the radio. Apart from the car's engine noise, we endured the eerie silence.

Gina excused herself, and retired for the night. Wendy and I watched a late movie.

* * *

On Sunday morning, this African Catholic boy, our Baptist woman of color hostess, and my Southern Lutheran white girlfriend, dressed for church service. We argued for almost thirty minutes about which denomination to patronize together. Since my last church service was more than twelve months, we decided to attend a Catholic church.

Once we pulled into the parking lot of the nearest Catholic Church, my anxiety became palpable. Getting out of the car, sweat dripped from my forehead. I was still anxious when I opened the heavy mahogany church door. The usher eagerly guided us to a row with three empty seats. I looked around the room, and found a cornucopia of different ethnicities. My sweating ceased, and without hesitation, I sat comfortably between my favorite girls.

Chapter 10

The next day, the girls got up early. Their boasts about their many trips to see Mickey Mouse did not impress me. I knew what it was to play, although not with Mickey Mouse

As a child in Nigeria, I had basked in the unforgiving equatorial sunshine with my friends. I left my childhood and all its captivating memories there, in my hometown, by the banks of the River Niger, where suffocating humidity was the norm. However, I could never forget the exhilarating tropical sun that baked our skins until it felt warm to the touch. Of all the fun we had, nothing was more rewarding than a street soccer game during a tropical rainstorm. Well, maybe a dangerous swim across the wide river. Or was it the other way around?

One April afternoon, in my twelfth year, some of my friends came to my house, and lured me outside with their new world-cup soccer balls. It started as back-and-forth soccer ball kicks, until enough boys joined in the fun. We grouped into two teams and played until it started to rain. Some boys ran home, but the stubborn ones played on. We ignored the thunder and lightning, until a bolt of lightning struck an electric pole and brought down live wire very close to us. The resultant electrical sparks, set a nearby car on fire, and it exploded. We ran in all directions in fear. Some of the boys soiled themselves according to the stories passed on by their parents. It was my last street soccer game, before I left home for boarding school. We lived dangerously in my youth. We were too ignorant to realize the risks.

* * *

The morning drive from Gainesville to Orlando started out good. Traffic was sparse on the road, and the weather was gorgeous. We rolled the windows down halfway. The crosswind cooled the car.

As the car wheels rolled along the highway, Gina and Wendy tried to outdo each other singing different songs from their childhood. Their early childhood was so different from mine that I could not relate to all their commotion. I sat quietly in the back seat, and drifted back to Nigeria.

On Christmas Eve of 1968, barely after midnight, missiles landed close to my house. A couple of missiles initially, then dozens, until we lost count. My father gathered the family in one room, and we prayed. As more missiles whistled past our house, our praying changed to crying. We were helpless. Out of frustration, my father picked up a spade, and went out despite the missile fire to dig a deep bunker in the back of our house as a hiding place for the family. He had blisters on the palms of his hands, after hours of digging alone. It was the night I learnt the true meaning of love. My father was ready to sacrifice his life for the safety of his family. We survived the night, and our love for each other grew stronger. I lived through the real fireworks of war, and I had no desire to experience Disney's pyrotechnic version.

I must have been half-asleep, because Wendy startled me with a tap on my shoulder.

"Did you fall asleep, Honey? I keep calling your name, but you don't answer." Wendy's gentle words sounded muffled initially, but eventually became clearer to me.

"I was daydreaming. Maybe a nightmare, depending on how you look at it," I said, yawning. It was so vivid, I could smell the warm bread in my mother's kitchen. The morning routine of cleaning her favorite teapot, scooping up the right amount of tealeaves, and boiling them until the light amber color darkened. Fresh cut tomatoes sautéed with red onions, mixed with scrambled eggs. We opened our warm bread to make breakfast sandwiches. I licked my lips. "Thank you mom, you're the best." I was not sure if I really said it in the car, or thought about it.

"Were you daydreaming about our wedding, and the beautiful house on the hill I want?" Wendy asked. The poor girl. I was dreaming about the first woman in my life, my mother.

Wendy said things that made me wonder if she was serious, or if she just wanted to elicit a reaction. I ignored her comment.

"You guys must be committed to each other to talk about marriage while you're still in school," Gina interjected.

"Of course, we're very serious," Wendy retorted.

"She's just messing with you, Gina. We're not ready to get married. I haven't proposed to her, as far as I know." I smiled as I spoke to avoid offending Wendy. When she smiled back, I felt confident enough to add, "How could I propose marriage when there's six years of the MD-PhD program ahead of me. Besides, where will I get the money to support a family at this stage in my life?"

"Joseph, you keep on forgetting that I'll turn twenty-one soon. My trust funds from my grandfather and father will become mine to control. We can live comfortably on those, until we finish medical school," Wendy said.

"Like I told you before, that's not what I want from you. I prefer to pay my own way, not depend on you. It's insulting when you talk about your trust funds and how you want to support me." I regretted my angry tone of voice as soon as I finished what I had to say. Wendy's face became a telltale of anger as she tried several times to speak, but nothing came out of her mouth.

"Children, if that's what you are today, we are going to Disney World. Stop all the bickering until we get to the playground," Gina said.

"Joseph is a knucklehead, and too proud to appreciate what I could do for him," Wendy said.

"I don't need any help from you. My own parents are helping me with my education. Even though we don't have corporate jets, we live comfortably." Once again, to my own disappointment, I delivered my statement with anger.

"I'll stop at the next rest area so you two can get out and make up. OK children?" Gina said, and then turned on the radio. She searched for a radio station with good reception and found a jazz station with clear transmission. The sequence of songs that the station played was like a roller-coaster-ride that progressed from mellow 'grooves' to thumping instrumentals, and back. Things were on a high note for us until the disc jockey stopped the music to announce a fatal motor vehicle accident that involved his former co-worker. He devoted the song 'A Remark You Made' from the group Weather Report to his friend. It became a somber moment for us as we stopped the finger popping and our rhythmic body movements. All the silly arguments, and inconsequential discussions we wasted our time on, came to a halt. We didn't say anything until we pulled into the Disney World parking lot.

*   *   *

Throngs of people meandered freely around the parking lot, which was already full of cars. Gina drove very slowly to avoid hitting other cars, as arriving families searched for available parking spaces. "How do you remember where you parked your car after the sun has baked your brain all day?" I asked Gina, but she did not answer.

We finally found an empty parking space, which was far away from the amusement park entrance. We got out of the car, and walked briskly to join the growing lines at the ticket counters. They extracted an exorbitant amount of money from us for the day's fun. We paid for our own tickets. To my surprise, Gina rebuffed my complaint about the expense. She was the person I had counted on to agree with me, but instead, she called me a cheapskate.

We did not pre-plan the day, so we stood by the entrance of the park for a while considering what to do next. In every direction I looked, people walked aimlessly as if they had no worries. No one seemed to be in a rush to get to any place.

It did not take long before I realized that we were laggards, as we looked in all directions without moving forward. While we considered various things to do, I reflected on the attributes of the amusement park, where children, and 'children-at-heart', indulged in fun-filled activities sprinkled with innocence.

"Are you impressed with what you've seen so far?" Wendy asked. I continued to look at the herds of people marching by.

"It depends. I'm impressed that grown people drive hundreds of miles to a playground and think it's for their children. Looking at how some of these adults are dressed, I wonder who's here to play." Wendy and Gina laughed.

"Gina, I have failed in my effort to teach Joseph how to relax, and have fun. The only time I saw him excited was in the chemistry lab when he synthesized a smelly compound." They laughed so hard that passersby stared at us. Their conviviality enthralled me because it was the first time they had expressed joy together. I had to laugh, too. Imagine the spectacle in Disney World in 1979 where a lily-white girl, a dark chocolate African boy, and a shade in-between girl, held on to each other to avoid rolling on the floor laughing. Fortunately, we ended our crass display before we earned a forced ride in a paddy wagon.

"Wendy, I always end up having fun with you," I finally said after we stopped laughing.

"I agree you have fun with me because I remember the first time I took my bathing suit off at the 'make out' lake. You stared at my breasts as if you were amazed. I still wonder what you found appealing about them," Wendy said to my surprise. Interestingly, Gina pretended as if she did not understand.

"I was probably worried about you being arrested for indecent exposure," I said.

"Do you mean that my body was indecent?" Wendy said.

"Taking your clothes off was the indecent part. You're not going to trick me again into making comments about your breasts," I said.

"Good choice of words, Joseph. You're a smart cookie," Gina said. I did not understand what she meant by being a 'smart cookie,' but I let her statement stand.

Wendy looked at me with a frown on her face, and walked away. We followed her to the merry-go-round where she climbed on for a spin. Gina and I climbed on, too. Wendy pouted when I sat close to her, but I ignored her. Before the merry-go-round's dizzying spin began, Gina turned to us and smirked. Wendy leaned forward, and said, "Why don't you mind your own damn business," but Gina continued to smile as the fulcrum started to turn.

"Girls, one minute ago we laughed together, and now you're back to your verbal war. Why do you guys constantly antagonize each other?" I asked them, but neither one answered me. As the speed of the merry-go-round picked up, and the accompanying music became more annoying, the girls held on to their private thoughts. We disembarked at the conclusion of the ride, and stood still to regain our balance. Wendy had beads of sweat on her face, which I wiped off with my hankie. She did not thank me.

Instead of acknowledging my gesture, Wendy turned her back on me. I walked in front of her and said, "I have never seen you sweat before, Wendy Sue. Why don't we drive back to Gainesville and leave this crazy place behind?" Fortunately, we did not leave the park as I suggested, instead, we spent the day having fun together.

*   *   *

It was completely dark by the time we left the amusement park. We sauntered into the parking lot fatigued and sleepy. Even though the area had adequate lighting, we struggled to find where Gina had parked her car. In the dark, all the parking rows looked the same and we had to walk down each one systematically until we found the right row.

Gina headed to the driver's side. Directly under a streetlight, her face appeared to have lost its luster, but she still looked beautiful. Trying to unlock her car door, she looked at me intently. She was tired. I walked over to her, as she fumbled with her keys, and took them away from her. She sighed, and without any protest, walked to the passenger side. Wendy watched us from afar.

Once I drove out of the parking lot, Gina and Wendy fell asleep. I turned on the radio to help keep me awake while I drove. A mellifluous female singer, and a gentle saxophone rendition, set me on a memorable jazz trip. Most of the selections that followed were heavy on saxophone, and their reverberations captivated me.

Halfway to Gainesville, my visual and auditory senses began to fade. I saw images of my mother. She asked angrily, "Joseph, how many times do I have to remind you to pay attention when you drive?" She was persistent with her scolding about my irresponsibility, when I briefly fell asleep at the wheel. I was lucky enough to pull off the road, and stepped out of the car. I walked along the gravel shoulder to clear the fog from my brain. After several trips to an overpass, fifty yards away from the car, I felt confident enough to continue driving.

We made it back to Gainesville without any mishap.

* * *

'I am going back home to my Carolina,' a song I heard before, resonated in my ears, and woke me up from sleep. What I heard, or imagined that I heard, during my sleep must not have come from Wendy because she lay next to me asleep. I concluded that it must have been Gina singing, but when I looked at the chair, she lay motionless.

The early morning sun peered through the sliding glass door and partially illuminated Wendy's body. Her perfectly tanned pair of legs was inviting, so I stroked them gently. She smiled, and said, "Good morning, Hon." Her sweet words sent shivers all over my body, and left me exhilarated. What a wonderful way to wake up that morning, next to someone I loved. I stroked her cheek, and then kissed her lips.

"I love you, Joseph," she said. She sighed, and ran the back of her hand all over my face.

"I love you too, Wendy." Words were not sufficient to express how I felt about her that morning. My thoughts veered to the simple fact that the same early morning sun shining in Florida was also shining in North Carolina. Two separate places that shared the same special gift of nature, which would be so until the end of time. Like the gift of love that I shared with Wendy, which would last for eternity. I looked at Wendy again, and she smiled as if she knew what was on my mind.

I stretched my hands and yawned. The rhythmic sound of the clock, counting the seconds at constant intervals, became louder. I looked at the clock, and noted that we had only a few hours left before our departure. We had to get to the airport.

"My dearest Gina, are you going to sleep all morning too?"
I said to her, slumped in the chair. Her eyes darted from side
to side, and tears trickled down her cheek. Looking at Gina,
my thoughts wandered endlessly.

Goodbye suggested the end, something permanently over.
Farewell sounded even worse. I wondered which one Gina
would use at the time of our departure. No words were suitable
as I fixed my eyes again on Gina. She wanted me to go to
Florida for med school, but North Carolina had Wendy, which
made the decision easy. Sudden sadness overcame me, as
Gina's tears flowed.

My eyes darted away from Gina as they swelled with tears.
I felt that there was no shame in crying, so I let my tears fall
too. I wiped my eyes, and crawled on my knees to where Gina
sat. "I love you, and I'll miss you terribly," I said. My voice
quavered. I wiped away my tears several times, and when I
tried to wipe her tears, she turned away from me. Weary silence
seized the room, when our desolate state of minds left us mute.

I kept watch over Gina from my kneeling position, and
after a while, I said, "You're coming home for the 4th of July
celebration?" It was a statement and a question, but she
ignored me.

Eventually, Gina said, "I don't know, Joseph. I thought
about going to Europe to be with my fiancé, but he'll be on a
training mission at that time."

"Why don't you come home to teach me how to ride a
horse?" I asked. Instead of answering my question directly, she
feigned a smile. Then, her smile broadened.

"The last time we rode horses you fell off my granddaddy's
stallion. You swore never to ride again," Gina said.

"Joseph, you never mentioned you rode a horse. I can't see you on a horse," Wendy interjected.

"We rode a lot last year until he rode Wild Bill, my gramp's horse. He took Joseph on a wild ride and threw him off at the edge of a field. Luckily, he didn't break any bones, but his ego was badly battered." Gina's voice was boisterous as she narrated the story. Her energy affected Wendy and me, as evidenced by our copious laughter reverberating across the room.

Some hurtful things in life are easy to forget. That shameful horse ride was one of them.

* * *

We had a memorable vacation in Florida. I felt separation anxiety set in before we even said goodbye to Gina. I knew that taking leave from Gina was temporary, but I still agonized over it.

We hurried through breakfast before we left for the airport. Gina and Wendy used up all the remaining time we had talking about my foibles. They engaged in a verbal dissection of my ethos as I sat helpless. Even though I was clothed, I felt naked when they finished their compilation of my flaws.

It felt like it took forever to get to the airport.

Men and women in shorts filled the departure lounge. Some passengers moved frantically to check in, while others ambled leisurely. Most of them had bronze skin, and many with the texture of seasoned leather. Wendy stood very close to one of the passengers, and my eyes instantly compared their skin. Wendy's skin was as smooth as alabaster, not like the dedicated sun worshipers' skin that sagged like leather bags. Wendy looked exotic with her light tan and golden hair. I walked up to her and whispered 'exquisite' in her ear. She poked her finger gently in my stomach and smiled. A bemused middle-aged woman watched our interaction.

Gina walked up to me and held my hand. She looked directly in my eyes, and said, "Don't forget about me this time." Wendy walked ahead of us, and as we approached the boarding area, Gina began to cry.

"I'll see you in North Carolina when you come home," I said calmly.

"You better be there waiting for me," she said, pointing her finger at me. She let go of my hand, turned around, and walked away. There was no goodbye or farewell.

Wendy initially ignored me as we queued with the rest of the passengers before we boarded the airplane. When she held my hand, I thought about the freedom we enjoyed in Florida, which would disappear once we returned to school. We would have to contend with whispered, ugly words, and the crassness of fellow students. All the racial taunting I had endured in my first two years in North Carolina lingered in my mind as I walked behind Wendy. She turned to me and put her arms around me as if she knew what was troubling me. Wendy's thoughtfulness made up for some of the unpleasant price I paid for her affection.

On the airplane, I pushed this thought aside. We would have many wonderful summer days ahead.

Chapter 11

THE SAME BLANK WALLS in the psychology office confronted me on the first day of summer school. Where were the photos and diplomas that had been there on my previous visits? Instead of mentally hanging framed pictures on the walls, I imagined the walls painted green. Not a bland green, but a vibrant color that welcomed everyone's provocative thoughts.

Staring at the taunting blank walls and foolishly analyzing them filled me with foreboding, as if threatening my sanity. Although my preoccupation with blank walls lingered on, I concluded that they were blank to occupy idle minds like mine.

My unpreparedness for Professor Crane's advanced psychology class lingered on in my thoughts.

I worried about my sanity, but I concluded that I did not need psychological counseling for obsessing over annoying blank walls. My interest in interventional psychoanalysis was academic, and I would have resisted such a probing psychological adventurism on the premise that my African heritage endowed me with an enviable stable mental state. My feeling was utterly jingoistic, but such an inclination helped me to face the rigors of my daily life.

Time slowly passed as my thoughts wandered from blank walls to the speech I had prepared for my first day of summer school. The hard oak chair I sat on made my continued wait unbearable. However, I had no other choice but to be patient. I closed my eyes, and an operetta intruded on my thoughts. It failed to stop me from wandering back to the speech I had planned to deliver to Professor Crane. Mastery of sheer concentration, as I had read, was the key to a successful mental channeling. As I battled to achieve that goal of cogitation, I mentally disconnected from my surroundings.

"Look at him. My new student is already in a trance before we even started our experiments," Professor Crane said. Her voice startled me. I looked up, and saw Wendy standing next to her aunt. I was excited to see Wendy, but could not express myself adequately. Instead, I smiled when she came over and sat next to me. "Wait for me here," Professor Crane said. She walked into her inner office without looking back.

I comported myself well after Professor Crane left the outer office, but Wendy started her effrontery, caressing the back of my neck with her right hand. My breathing became shallow and from the corner of my right eye, I saw the curious look on the secretary's face. I did not make any effort to stop Wendy's action because I felt that it would attract more attention from the secretary. Occasionally, I closed my eyes to avoid watching the secretary's reaction, but Wendy carried on without any regard to my uneasiness. It crossed my mind that her aunt may forgive her indiscretion, but may admonish me unduly. Since I could not do anything to help myself, I simply prayed.

"Have you missed me?" Wendy asked in a hushed voice after she stopped touching me. My eyes wandered to the secretary before I said, "Of course, I missed you terribly." I surveyed the secretary's area from the corner of my eye again. Fortunately, she was preoccupied with a telephone call.

"You could've come for me this morning, but you gave up that opportunity. I know you love me but you have to start showing me that you need me. A little gesture like a surprise visit makes a lot of difference to me," Wendy said with a raised voice, which worried me.

My sweaty palms and increased heart rate foretold the beads of sweat that soon rolled down my face. I had set out on the first day of summer school to impress Professor Crane, but Wendy's impudence threatened to rob me of that opportunity. As her hand travelled around my face again, I became more anxious. She rested her hand on my groin area. I involuntarily crossed my legs. She smiled and pretended to unzip my pants. I instinctively cupped my zipper with my two hands. My reactive measures stopped her from being impish. Professor Nancy Crane walked into the room, and Wendy removed her hand from my lap. I uncrossed my legs and crossed them again the other way. Wendy looked at me with a grin and whispered, "You're no fun to play with." I looked at her and frowned. She had never been this reckless.

Professor Crane, who was wearing a white laboratory coat over a long tan dress, was carrying a big stack of files. Her choice of a white lab coat for a psychology research class triggered unsavory thoughts. White laboratory coats were for 'tangible' researchers like Professor Ezir, whose experiments might splatter on them, and whose findings could be validated. I wished I had the power to knock the charts out of her hand by mind control. I was still wishing for bad things to happen when Wendy suddenly darted over to help carry the files.

It was my first day in the summer experimental psychology program. Instead of concentrating on how to be a good student, I focused on the Professor's files to test my imaginary power. Of course, I knew that I could not make the charts fall from her hands, but I still wished it would happen. I was subconsciously looking for an excuse to end my enrollment in experimental psychology out of fear that Wendy would top me in her Aunt's course.

"Let's go next door," Professor Crane said as she walked out of the office. I rushed over to offer my assistance with the remaining files, but she declined my offer and walked on.

The conference room was barren with only a long table and ten chairs. There were no windows for direct illumination from the sun, but the florescent lights overhead were bright enough for the room. I had imagined a special experimental room for psychological research. The tantalizing new craft of extrasensory perception—ESP—had a magical undertone, and I envisaged a special environment with appropriate paraphernalia for such a behavioral art.

Once Professor Crane sat down, I moved further away from her and sat down. Wendy placed the files she had on the table and sat next to me. Our professor read a small pamphlet for at least two minutes before she looked up. The room was silent until Professor Crane shuffled some papers in one of the files she had opened. She closed the files and set her eyes on us.

"Why don't you move closer to me? You're the only students I have for this summer session," Professor Crane said. She opened another file and then added, "I'll discuss what I expect you to get out of this summer project, but first, here are your reading assignments for the week. The theoretical aspect of what we're going to accomplish is the core knowledge that you need before we embark on the experimental aspect of the program."

Her long, disjointed sentences made it difficult to know what she wanted us to do. In chemistry and biochemistry, the experimental environment was different. We read and did things in a real laboratory environment. Our results were discernible and reproducible.

"Joseph, why don't you tell us about your background?" Professor Crane said. Her request saved me from drifting away from the conference room to my biochemistry research laboratory.

"I'm a senior biochemistry student . . . "

Professor Crane interrupted me before I could finish.

"I meant your family background, not your academic credentials. I already know about your academic exploits." Her voice was derisive, to my displeasure. I lifted my head and engaged her eyes. My eyes drifted to Wendy, who sat motionless next to me, and a fake smile enveloped my face as I re-engaged the Professor's eyes.

"There isn't much to tell about my family. I have an older brother and three older sisters. My father has done various things for the Catholic Church for more than four decades, and my mother owns various businesses. Compared to your American standard, we're an upper middle class family. Oh! I came to this country two years ago when I was seventeen years old. That's basically my story." I felt that I had covered everything she needed to know.

"Do you believe that what you just said about yourself is a sufficient biography? I don't mean to sound imperceptive, but your treatise lacks scholarship. I expected more from a *scholarly kid*, as the chairperson of your department defined you. Try not to be stingy with facts when you tell your story." She surprised me because I felt that the information I voluntarily gave was sufficient for a classroom setting. It conformed to my English teachers' emphasis on succinctness in academic-related speeches.

"I'm not sure what you would like to know about me." I said. My statement was genuine, and I hoped that she would not be offended.

She took her glasses off and looked at me absorbedly. Coincidentally, Wendy took off her silver headband and repositioned it.

As I pondered on what to say next, Professor Crane swung her chair around, and pulled it closer to me. "Maybe you prefer an interrogation instead of a simple academic exercise of narration?" she said with a chuckle.

Warm perspiration trickled down my face. I looked at Wendy for unspoken emotional support, but she looked away. She then focused her gaze on a piece of paper in front of her as if she had no stake in the unfolding academic exercise. What I needed was any sign of support from her, but none came. When I hesitated to respond to Professor Crane's question, she tapped on the table annoyingly.

"Professor Crane, I'm not sure what you need to know about my life." My voice quavered as I spoke. I did not want to come across as being intimidated. A slight anger over her tapping on the table was the only cause of my perspiration, and disengaged demeanor. Although I felt that her approach was reprehensible, I was determined to be respectful.

"Instead of talking about mundane things, let me guide you. Why did you leave your family at the age of seventeen and travel six thousand miles to a small college community like ours?"

"I was fascinated by American culture and its educational system from television programs at home," I said. As she deliberated on her next question, I looked at Wendy. She scribbled on a piece of paper in front of her, "I love you Joseph" and drew a smiley face. Wendy's gesture made me feel better.

"So your parents let you travel thousands of miles away from home because you loved American television shows?" Professor Crane's sarcasm hit me hard. I took her statement as an accusation of irresponsible behavior by my parents. It was an affront to the two people that meant everything to me. I thought about their weekly letter of encouragement to me, and some tears overwhelmed my determination to remain in control of myself.

"No, no, no, Professor Crane, that's not true. I was a good student in high school and my parents preferred that I attend a university in America. University education partially disintegrated in my country after the three-year Biafran war. Science education suffered the most, because the civil war destroyed most of the science labs." I became more confident as I spoke.

"So you were a war child? That's fascinating. How did the war affect you?" Her question was nonspecific, so I did not know where to start. However, I was determined not to let her get to me emotionally again.

"I was only eight years old when the war started, and it lasted three years. We were a minority Christian ethnic group that controlled most of the commerce in my country until 1967 when the majority Moslem ethnic group started a pogrom that caused a civil war. Our secession from the country was brief because the majority ethnic group, with their collaborators, violently reunited us with the rest of the country after three years of carnage. Most of the people who died were helpless women and children." Tears rolled down my face uncontrollably as I spoke. Professor Crane stood up and walked around the room. She returned to her chair, and asked me to stop my narration. I bowed my head down at the same time Wendy reached out to wipe my tears.

Silence reigned in the conference room as the three of us sat motionless. To help me escape from my desolate state, I continued my story. "I lost two of my cousins from the civil war, including my cousin Franco, who was like a brother to me. He came to live with my family after his mother died when he was only two years old. He had several failed attempts to live with his father during his teenage years, and he finally gave up trying. When the civil war started, he was one of the first boys to volunteer for the 'rebel army' against my mother's wish. He fought gallantly in several battles, until he sustained serious shrapnel wounds on his left knee, six months before the war ended. We became aware of his injury when his bloodstained letter arrived from a field hospital. The letter was apparently written after he received emergency surgical treatment." My tears continued to flow, and, embarrassingly, my nose began to run too. I excused myself from the room to attend to my runny nose in the bathroom.

I returned from the bathroom, and it was evident that neither Crane had moved in the room, while I was gone. I settled down and resumed my story. "Franco recovered from his wounds, which left him with a slight limp. He came home from the field hospital with a large healed scar on the inner side of his left knee. On Christmas Eve of 1970, he suddenly

became ill and incoherent. My parents took him to several
hospitals, but none of the places had antibiotics, or adequate
medical facilities to treat the presumed systemic tetanus
infection that afflicted him. The civil war destroyed most of
the hospital facilities, and an economic embargo during the
hostilities, rendered them unsuitable for acute medical care. His
doctors abandoned him when they realized that his medical
condition was grim, and he died in my mother's arms. Since his
death, I have dreaded Christmas holidays." I stopped my story
abruptly because I could not go on.

"Joseph, I didn't anticipate such a tragic story. From what
I heard about you, you are a mentally balanced person. I had
expected a story about your parents' success and its motivating
effect on you, rather than a tragedy. The first time we met, you
came across as a cocky kid, and I judged you unfairly. Who
could've imagined you dealt with such a tragedy at a very
tender age?" Professor Crane said.

"I'm very sorry for going too far with my story. Thank you
for giving me the opportunity to work with you this summer,"
I said with a subdued voice. I felt uncomfortable listening to
my professor apologize to me for an infraction she did not
commit. She exercised her right as an educator to learn about
my background, and her inquiry helped me to face one of the
most horrific experiences I had during my country's civil war.

"Excuse me, Aunt Nancy; I have something to say about
my life," Wendy said. I turned to her. She had a grim look on
her face.

"In my classroom, young lady, you call me Professor
Crane. I'm not your Aunt while you're in my class. Do you
understand me?" she said with a harsh tone, and waited for
Wendy to acknowledge her statement, but none came. "Is

there something you want to tell me about you that I don't already know?" she said.

Wendy turned to her and said, "I want you to know that I care about Joseph, and . . . ," she hesitated, then added. "I'm in love with him. You might as well know about us now, since we're the only students in your class." I fixed my eyes on the floor, embarrassed, as Wendy spoke. I had not expected such a blunt statement from her. My eyes closed involuntarily as I waited for a rejoinder from our professor.

Professor Crane was wearing a surprise look, which made the wrinkles on her face more noticeable. She shuffled her feet on the floor. "We have to devote another day to tease out your personal issues before we can proceed with the rest of our summer projects. I'll see the two of you later." She walked out of the room without directly addressing Wendy's statement. Her action confused me, and when I looked at Wendy, she had an incredulous stare on her face.

I lifted some of the files on the conference room table and handed them to Wendy. She accepted the files from me, and I picked up the remaining ones. We walked out of the room, in silence.

"Tease out your personal issues," lingered in my mind as I walked down the hall to deposit the files in my possession. My thoughts wandered endlessly without focusing on any plausible reason for the professor's comment. I placed the files on the secretary's desk, and turned to Wendy who looked cheerful. Her new demeanor confused me more than the Professor's action.

My disenchantment with psychology started after I read the mind-bending treatise, "The Stream of Consciousness"

(1890) by William James. The first time I read it, I did not
consider it a scholarly work, but suddenly it made sense to me.
I accepted, although with some reservation, that the lecture of
William James from 1890 about the 'absolute insulation' of
human thoughts was true. I wondered why I continued to
commit my summer months to advanced experimental
psychology with the desire to accomplish the impossible, when
there was no reliable way to validate any of the findings.

We were about to leave when Professor Crane came out of
her office, and asked Wendy to wait for her, but dismissed me
for the day. My wish for an intense discussion with Wendy
about our first day with her aunt had to wait, so disenchanted,
I walked out of the office. The sunshine that nearly blinded me
when I walked outside the psychology building could not
prevent me from drifting back to the concept of the
'irreducible pluralism' of thoughts. The obtuse psychological
concept that individual thoughts are, separate and unique,
became clearer as I walked from the psychology building to my
biochemistry research laboratory. Since there was
inaccessibility of human thoughts, as postulated years before
the new wave psychology, how could we justify the quest to
retrieve information completely shielded from external
meddling? My ambivalence about experimental psychology
made me question my blind loyalty to Wendy. After all, she
had led me to tread the path of pseudoscience.

*   *   *

My laboratory offered me solace. I became absorbed with
biochemical solutions, and instruments used for chemical

structural characterization that I'd taken for granted before then. I quickly immersed myself in measuring and quantifying things with certainty. Several hours into experimentation, I stepped outside for a break, but instead of enjoying the beautiful North Carolina weather, Wendy's confession to Professor Crane crept back to me.

As the sun soothed my skin, it reminded me that Wendy had not stopped by to see me. The thought of dropping the summer experimental psychology class occurred to me several times, but I felt that doing so would be the antithesis of admirable scholarly pursuit. A promulgation of academic unpreparedness. By the end of that day, I was still ambivalent about Professor Crane's summer program, but did not take any decisive action.

I stayed in the biochemistry laboratory until a few minutes after six that evening. Leaving the laboratory was the easy part, but deciding on whether to go to the cafeteria, or to Wendy's dorm, was very difficult. My greatest problem was my rigid logical thinking that did not always correlate with the behavior of people around me. I wasted valuable time wondering what Wendy would want me to do in such a situation.

There was still ample sunlight when I left the biochemistry laboratory. I took the scenic path that passed through the amphitheater. What compelled me to change my regular course that evening was not clear to me, but I felt disappointed when I found the amphitheater empty. I stood at the foot of the amphitheater, and envisioned being a part of the reigning play. I hoisted myself on the stage. Looking out at the empty seats, I paraded around reciting some of the words from *Romeo and Juliet* that I remembered. I exhausted all the lines that I could remember, before I lowered my body gently to the ground, adopted short, shallow breathing, and said, "Killing myself, to die upon a kiss." It sounded good at that moment, but as I fell to the floor, I realized it was a line from a different play. Othello.

Sometimes we may forget what role we are supposed to play.

Soft claps interrupted my performance, and before I could look up, I heard the sweetest word, "Bravo." It was unmistakably Doreen's voice. There was no escape route, so I looked up and found Doreen with a few of her friends clapping for me. She was wearing a loose orange dress that blended with the setting golden sun. A pair of sunglasses held her long black hair in place, and suspended beads of sweat were scattered all over her forehead. Even in her casual attire, she still looked exotic.

"I knew you would be good for the part of *Romeo*," Doreen said with the biggest smile I had ever seen on her face.

"I was passing by and couldn't resist the opportunity to make a fool of myself. It has been long since I read *Romeo and Juliet*. I only remembered a few lines," I said.

"You were very good with your unrehearsed line," Doreen said.

"Thank you for the compliment," I said.

"The stage is yours. We're not practicing today because our director had a baby yesterday. I stopped by to arrange things for tomorrow." Doreen's smile made her look more beautiful as she spoke. I prayed that she could not read my mind as I checked out her bosom.

"Are you performing or practicing tomorrow?" I asked as if I was interested in what she had to do.

"We have a meeting, and maybe a short rehearsal. An adjunct professor from a nearby college will start tomorrow with our production unit. You would have done a fantastic job playing the part of *Romeo*. You shouldn't have turned us down. I hope you can at least come see the play," Doreen said. Her friends cleaned the steps as we spoke, but one fellow hung around to listen to our conversation.

"Thank you again Doreen for the compliments but I have to go." I jumped down from the stage. She walked closer to where I landed.

"Let's get together sometime. I believe I gave you my telephone number last year," she said. Her affability made me uneasy, but I continued to look into her seductive eyes.

"We just got back from Florida, and I started my psychology research class today. I'm very busy, but I promise to call you soon," I said, even though I knew that I did not have her telephone number.

"Travelled alone?" she asked enthusiastically, thereby prolonging a conversation that I wanted to end.

"I went with a friend," I said, walking away.

"You went with your girlfriend? The one I met a few weeks ago with you, close to the cafeteria?" she asked without a smile.

"We went to visit my student mentor who's in medical school," I said.

"If you decide to stop by, I live close to the medical center. I make Portuguese food on weekends. Don't forget to come to the play tomorrow," she said. She shook my hand and held on to it. It felt awkward, but I did not complain. It puzzled me that she abandoned my Florida trip so quickly and reverted to something else, but before I could sort things out in my head, she said, "See you, Joseph."

"Take care, Doreen. I hope you have a successful production of *Romeo and Juliet*," I said as I walked away without looking back.

Walking briskly up the hill, I felt breathless. The previous summer, I had played soccer every day and I was in top physical shape. It appeared that spending most of my time in the classroom and laboratories had taken a toll on my body. It needed an urgent rehabilitation, but our soccer games dwindled when most of the players graduated the previous year. Lawn tennis was an option, but my ardent partner Gina was in Florida. Wendy was an avid dancer and she practiced every day. It seemed that all ballerinas were alike, and she was no exception. She was obsessed with her body weight, and kept in shape by dancing. She had no spare time for any other physical activity that could help me stay in shape. Preoccupied with my thoughts, I failed to notice Wendy, who was sitting in her car with the top down in front of my apartment.

"Where have you been? I have been waiting for the past hour," she inquired.

"I was waiting for you in the biochemistry lab too. I thought you would stop by so we could get something to eat," I said.

"But you came from the wrong direction. The biochemistry lab is on the other side of the campus," she said.

"I took a long walk because I was unhappy after you didn't show up," I said.

"You chose the woods, and the hilly part of the campus?" she asked.

"I just passed by the amphitheater," I said.

"What was going on there? I bet you were looking for your friend. I mean your Juliet," she said with biting sarcasm.

"It wasn't like that, Wendy. I did see her even though I wasn't looking for her," I said.

"You only make friends with beautiful girls, and it makes me uncomfortable. I don't want to share you with anyone," she said angrily.

"She's not my friend. As I told you before, we only took a class together. Why do we have to argue about stupid things all the time?" I said, and walked to my apartment. She got out of her car, and as I unlocked my apartment door, pushed me aside.

"I don't know why you act insecure. You're the most beautiful girl I have ever met. Look at your nice long legs and beautiful smile. *Ooh la la!*" I snickered.

"Wonders never cease. I thought you forgot conversational French. You used to try to speak French to me, but it seems you gave it up. Is it too painful for you to speak French because I ran away to France? *Tu es mon amour et mon coeur.*"

"What did you say?" I said.

"I said you're my love and my heart. You have to believe me because I miss you when I'm not with you. I want us to live together, but I already know what you'll say about it. I'll try to move in next door to you when the apartment becomes vacant in August."

"I don't mean to change the subject, but we have to eat and study before tomorrow. When we come back from studying, I want to know what your aunt said about me." Being with Wendy made me inefficient, and I was not willing to start any discussion about her Aunt that would take me away from my studies.

"We're driving to the restaurant because I'm tired of walking," she said.

"Let's get out of here. I'm starving to death." I had hunger shakes as I spoke. Wendy probably was not aware that I was hungry and tired because she jumped on my back as we walked to her car.

As soon as she drove off, she brought up the Doreen issue again. She did most of the talking. I listened. I rebuffed her complaint about my "wandering eyes" swiftly, but she continued to bring up more complaints against me. We drove to a nearby restaurant without resolving any of the issues she brought up.

Although the restaurant was crowded when we arrived, the maître'd offered us a place by the window and quickly assigned a waiter to us. He knew Wendy's father. We had limited time for dinner so I made sure that I thanked him profusely for expediting our service.

A clean cut young man in his early twenties came over to our table, and said, "Longest time." Without hesitation, he tried to hug Wendy. He did the hugging, whereas she looked disinterested.

"Hi Brad," Wendy said without enthusiasm.

"Haven't seen you at our frat parties lately," Brad said.

"I'm too busy studying and don't like stupid, immature boys' pranks anyway," Wendy said.

"I guess you have better things to do with your life now," Brad said.

It appeared that they knew each other well, but she did not introduce her friend to me. He asked her several personal questions in a hushed voice, but she ignored him initially. When she answered him, her answers were brief and sounded as if she was disconcerted. I ignored the annoying man, who ignored me too, and ate my meal. Before Brad walked away from our table, he gave me an unfriendly glance. I simply smiled.

Once I finished eating, Wendy threw her napkin on top of her food, left some money on the table, and walked out. I tried to catch up with her, but she was out of the restaurant.

"What was that all about?" I asked, as we drove away from the restaurant.

"Nothing, he's just a foolish boy who refuses to leave me alone," she said in a dismissive way.

"I guess you don't want to talk about it?" I asked.

"He was my boyfriend in high school and his father is a vice president in one of my father's subsidiary companies. Why are we talking about someone I dated in high school?" Wendy said.

"You should've introduced me as your boyfriend so he would leave you alone," I said.

"He's annoying, and I can't stand his arrogance sometimes. Let's not dwell on Brad," she said as she turned off the ignition.

"Now I know you dated a creep in high school," I joked.

"It's not funny. I don't want to talk about it," she requested.

We walked into the library and settled in our favorite corner. "I hope you still remember our study rule," I said.

"How could I forget your silly rule? It was not *our* rule. Study for at least two hours before you take a break, unless you have an urgent bathroom need. Silly rule," she said with a hint of sarcasm.

"You don't have to take out your anger on me, Wendy. I don't know why you let your ex-boyfriend get to you. Did he break your heart?" I asked calmly.

"He didn't break my heart. I was the one that ended the relationship," she snapped at me. Instead of saying anything else, I used the opportunity to leave our study desk.

I walked to the librarian's desk and asked for the psychology books reserved for Professor Crane's class. The receptionist lifted two big envelopes from a drawer and handed them over to me. "Return them when you're done. You may photocopy them, but you can't take them away from the library," she instructed.

I returned to our study table, and opened one of the envelopes. It contained research methods in social psychology with an emphasis on social perception and group behavior. The content was about experimental social psychology and not the assigned reading from earlier in the day. Wendy stared at me for a while before she asked, "Are you all right, Joseph?"

"The information is on experimental methods in social psychology, not extrasensory perception," I said.

Wendy smiled, and said, "My aunt changed her mind this morning about our research project. She felt that we need a better understanding of social psychology after your story, and my confession. I was to let you know about it, but you made me angry, so I forgot to tell you."

"What do you mean by social psychology?" I asked.

"She said we should focus on causes of ethnic prejudice, and its effect on society. Another aspect of our research is on how group behavior propagates misinformation and stereotyping." Wendy elucidated the project with great confidence and interest. It was funny how she enunciated her words without her southern drawl.

"How do we carry out such research?" I asked.

"Design questionnaires to be administered to our target groups, and afterward, analyze the results. The first thing she requested is to read up on the area," Wendy said with a professional tone of voice.

"I guess I have to thank you for clarifying things for me. It appears we're basically studying my plight in your country?" I said. Wendy ignored my comment as she pulled out papers from her envelope.

Professor Crane's assignment was a project on group behavior, and possible ways to improve inter-ethnic understanding. Her decision to assign such a daunting task during a short summer session surprised me, but since her decision was supreme, I accepted the project without resentment.

* * *

We labored for days to design a comprehensive questionnaire for our research project. Placing the emphasis on questions that addressed the origins of ethnic stereotypes and their propagation made our task more difficult. How stereotypical beliefs permeated institutions of higher learning without proof of their validity was particularly interesting to me. Since I was a victim of such ignorance, I wanted to understand why educated groups comfortably accepted irrational ideas and even participated in blatant mob actions. I recalled all the major racially motivated incidents from my first year in college and designed questions to address them. Discussing some of the incidents with Wendy created an emotional distance between us. In one instance, she curled up at the end of my sofa and sobbed. We were talking about a party we attended for the graduation of her first cousin Edward. Wendy had organized the party and invited me.

In most of those types of events with Wendy, I was the only non-Caucasian in attendance. We arrived at the event late. Standing in the entrance, I overheard a conversation.

"Hey John, what's going on?" a hairy guy, Frank, said to a youth, who was also late.

"Nothing much," he said as they shook hands and patted each other on the back. He shook hands with the rest of the boys, and stayed with the group.

"What are you guys drinking tonight?" One of the boys asked his friends.

"Whatever they offer us. I'm thirsty," Another boy replied.

"I know what I'm not drinking," Frank said with a smile. They laughed as if they knew what he meant. He then added, "Their malt liquor makes your head spin."

"That's not nice," John said.

"Yea," Two of the boys almost said in unison.

"Well, I won't drink that again," Frank said with seriousness, and the rest of the boys laughed.

"We're here for Edward. I'm sure he'll take care of us," John said as if to reassure them.

"Don't bet on it. Wendy is the one who organized the party. She's really into this Negro boy. I bet you her values have changed," Frank said while ruffling his bushy hair, which made his pudgy face look creepy.

"They're called blacks, not Negros," Another boy interjected. He then lowered his voice and added, "Please don't use the 'f' word."

"It doesn't matter, he's an African," John said, like he was teaching them something new.

"Which is worse?" Frank asked.

"What do you mean?" One of them inquired.

"Is the Negro better than the African?" Another boy asked. They chuckled at his question.

"They all look dumb to me," Frank said. They laughed more.

"I heard he plans to attend medical school. He must be smart," John said.

"I don't care if he's smart, or not. That'll be the day I let a Negro touch me," Frank said.

I paid attention to everything they said, but Wendy was oblivious to what was going on. She occupied herself with counting the number of guests.

I cleared my throat to get their attention.

"Lower your voices. He may hear us," John said.

"I don't care. Who gave him an American name in the first place?" Frank said. They rolled in laughter. Wendy walked closer to them and asked to be told the joke that made them laugh. They laughed harder after her request. I grabbed Wendy's hand, and led her away.

"What's wrong Joseph? My friends are having fun," Wendy said as I led her away from her 'friends.'

"Trust me, they're not your friends," I said. She gave me a bewildered look. I had no other option but to tell Wendy what the boys said about us. She sobbed, because she thought that they were her friends.

Reliving some of those events had the same emotional effect on Wendy, as it did when it happened.

We talked about her last note to me in 1978, which was one of the most painful experiences I had in my life. I brought out the note Wendy wrote to me and re-read it to her.

> *Hi!*
>
> *Not sure how this will go, but I need you to know how I am feeling ….. I sit in church nearly every Sunday and fight back the tears when I think about what I am doing to my family. I can't help but think that my father is miserable because of me. I feel that God will punish my father for being mean to you and the only way to stop it is for me to change. Then I look closely at you, and realize we are miserable most of the time because of the way you are treated in school. There just isn't a way for me to walk away from my family and be happy at the same time.*
>
> *I cannot imagine life without you, but lately, not with you either. I think it's time to be fair and honest with you, so I'm going to set you free once and for all. You need to forget about me and move on. I want happiness for you and I cannot give you that. So please, cherish our love and memories but let me go. I'm so sorry I had to do this in a letter, but I'm not strong enough to see, or talk to you. My heart is broken in pieces, and I will want you to pick them up and make me whole again. I promise to be your friend, but we both need time & space.*
>
> *Love forever,*
> *Wendy.*

Her written goodbye word hurt me deeply, but her callousness tore my heart apart. I felt that a handshake, or even a simple goodbye, could have been sufficient to end our friendship respectfully. She probably felt obligated to appease her bigot father, but in the process, trampled on my fragile ego. For more than one month after she left me, I merely existed.

* * *

Professor Crane approved the social psychology research questionnaire, after several revisions. We were eager to distribute the forms to willing participants, but the college press could not print the bi-leaflet forms within our stipulated time. We approached a local printer who accepted the printing job after an exhaustive interview with Wendy and me. He was initially concerned that we belonged to a left-wing radical group that was planning a scheme to promote racial disharmony in his small town. According to him, our project had the potential to incite ethnic protest, but when Wendy took out her purse, his greed alleviated any concern he had about his own culpability.

The questionnaires arrived at the psychology office two days before they were due, and we were pleased with the quality of the print job. We met with Professor Crane before distributing the forms, which I requested because of my concern about how Southern Caucasians would answer the questions if they received the forms directly from me.

Professor Crane pondered my concern, and for an unknown reason avoided looking at me directly. Waiting for her reply, I wondered again if she harbored any racial prejudice. She addressed Wendy instead of me, when she spoke, and it heightened my paranoia.

"The most important aspect of any sociological research is to educate the participants about their contribution to our society. They have to understand the importance of their participation, because without their involvement, the project would be a failure. Talk to them about how our project would contribute to better understanding of the participants' feelings toward people that are different from them. It's preferable to sound conciliatory and not judgmental in your presentation to potential participants. Try to respect their feelings and beliefs." At the end of her insightful speech, Professor Crane handed all the forms to Wendy. Handing all the forms to Wendy upset me, but I tried to keep my disappointment in check.

"Excuse me Professor Crane, but you didn't address my concern. I need to know what role I should play in this phase of our project," I said.

"You have to delve into it without a preconceived notion. Go out there and distribute your forms. They can turn you down, but don't give up." As Professor Crane spoke, she looked directly at me with a frown on her face.

"Thank you for the advice," I said, but she did not acknowledge my gratitude. Wendy tugged at the back of my shirt, probably to stop me from saying anything further. I felt that she knew something about her aunt that she had not shared with me.

"I'll be over on Saturday to help you set up for the tea party," Wendy said before we left her office.

"I hope we have a good turnout of younger members like you," Professor Crane said.

It was obvious to me that their conversation was personal, so I walked out of the room.

Wendy emerged from the office in a jovial mood, and did not talk about her Saturday event. Even though I did not ask her about the event, it lingered in my disturbed mind.

We deposited the questionnaires in my apartment because I had more space than Wendy had in the dormitory. Wendy excused herself and drove off to the mall.

I returned to my department to meet with Professor Ezir for about 15 minutes. I needed to discuss my class schedule for senior year, and officially request his approval for my early graduation. Although I would meet the requirements for graduation after spending only three years in college, he had the authority to reject my application.

"Your senior year is probably the most important one. It's a bridge to the next phase of your education," Professor Ezir said. He opened a folder and brought out my college transcript. "More biology classes will help you in the future," he added.

"I have taken all the biology classes required for graduation," I said.

"Your approach to learning is why I wanted you in my lab. You're among the rare students I have met over the years with the curiosity to find out how things are, and why. It's the simple question of why, which identifies a potential researcher," Professor Ezir said.

"Thank you Professor Ezir," I said.

"You go beyond the projects I assign to you, and do more because of your curiosity. Learning physiological functions will make you a better biochemist. Integration of biochemical and physiological functions is the future of medical research. That's why I proposed the combined degree program to our dean, to train people like you." His face beamed with a smile as he spoke. It was apparent that he was proud of his project.

"Thank you, sir, for having confidence in me," I said. What else could I have said to the genius I admired.

"You've had the required biology classes, but you need graduate level courses as a senior. I recommend 'Human Physiology' and 'Advanced Biophysical Chemistry,' Professor Ezir instructed me and I nodded in agreement.

Professor Ezir supported my ambitious plan for early graduation, and this did not surprise me.

Chapter 12

I WOKE UP EARLY on Friday morning in a pensive mood. As much as I yearned for the sun to brighten my spirit, I remained in bed and cursed my small apartment with its windowless bedroom. I was not sure what difference it would have made even if the morning sun illuminated the entire small partition. It was the last day of the summer session, which left me with mixed feelings about my summer accomplishments. The touted advanced experimental psychology research program was not what I expected, and Professor Crane was an emotionally detached academic cipher. Although we enrolled more than three thousand participants in our social psychology project by travelling to all the six universities in the surrounding area, Professor Crane deferred the statistical analyses for two weeks.

Before the end of the summer session, I had read several treatises on advanced psychology, but psychoanalysis fascinated me the most. My eagerness to discuss some of these areas with Professor Crane, and her detached responses to my questions, caused an unusual disquiet for me. I sensed I was failing her class. When my grades for the summer school arrived, I was afraid to open the envelope. My hands shook, and sweat poured down my face. I pulled the grade report out of the envelope and was shocked. Her glowing report about my academic promise, and an A+ grade for my effort surprised me since she did not embrace any of the ideas I presented.

On the final day of summer session, I felt empty, but did not know why. In search of answers, I took a long walk all over the east campus. It was an unusual day for many reasons, and, most importantly, it was the first time I had an early morning walk on campus. The fresh morning air had a rejuvenating effect on my tired psyche, and the unique musical sounds from birds hidden by thick foliage intrigued me. Occasionally, I stood under some of the trees and searched for the musical birds, but never found any.

But, you do not always have to identify the source of your inspiration, I thought, passing by the amphitheater. There was a note on the wall: after the night's program, the drama team would have a two-week hiatus before the audition for their fall play. I sat on a bench and watched two birds on the ground enthralled in a mating ritual. The birds seemed confused about what to do with each other. I walked to the school cafeteria

The once bustling place of social gathering for students was almost empty. I went through the breakfast line but could not find anything that pleased me. I yearned for my mother's *jollof* rice and plantain. After two years in North Carolina, I had not grown accustomed to grits, biscuits, and gravy for breakfast, so I passed on the opportunity to grease my stomach with semi-congealed lard. The fresh fruit basket was empty, so I paid for a glass of apple juice and left.

There was no doubt in my mind where I needed to be before I left the cafeteria. I found myself in the same familiar place. I called Wendy's room extension, and she unlocked the door to the lobby for me. I stood in front of the elevator and waited patiently for her to come down. The wait was longer than I had expected, so I sat down and picked up a magazine lying on top of a coffee table. "The Phil Donahue Show" was the featured article in the magazine, but I found a topic on the tributaries of the Amazon River more intriguing. Looking at the aerial pictures of the river tributaries, I thought about how one decides which tributary to follow on their journey. The journey of life is probably more complex than deciding on which tributary to take in a canoe, but there are similarities.

I was oblivious to the events around me until I heard a conversation between students passing through the lobby that brought me back to my reality.

"He's here again for Miss sorority queen," the first student said.

"Do you mean the ugly African sitting there in our lobby?" the second student asked.

"He's kind of cute," the first student said.

"I don't know what you guys see in him," the second student interjected.

"Are you blind not to see that he is tall and handsome? I like his physique too. I heard he's smart and a very nice guy," the first student said.

"Yea right," the second student said, before the elevator door closed.

They were aware that I heard everything they said, but carried on as if it did not matter how I felt. However, the entire exchange was amusing to me. The hostile college environment had changed me so much that I found such comments comical. In the process of analyzing their behavior and my feeling about their comments, I remembered that my advanced psychology reading called my reaction desensitization.

* * *

Wendy and I did not realize all our summer goals, but I had no regrets. We went dancing only twice after we returned from Florida, and she devoted the rest of her free time to her sorority activities. Occasionally, she attended tea parties organized by her Confederacy heritage group, but she rarely discussed the events with me. Conveniently, she avoided me every time they had a planned get together.

I even surprised myself with my indifference to her social connection to a group that was vocal about preservation of the 'Old South'. Only once did I wonder if she felt like a hypocrite cavorting with me, and then attending a meeting with a group that promoted racial purity.

I had expected that Wendy would come down wearing a casual rumpled frock, but she'd put on a dazzling two-tone pink and black dress. An oversized vintage black onyx ring that made an enviable fashion statement of its own, adorned her middle finger.

"Wow! You look dazzling, Wen," I said.

"Thank you for the compliment, Hon," she said with a smile.

"I just stopped by to see you. I didn't expect you to get dressed up for me," I said jokingly.

"Go on and flatter yourself. I'm going to spend the day with my grandmother. I should thank you for waking me up," she said.

"I guess you're going to be occupied all day? I wish we could see the play tonight since today is their last day," I said.

"You always find a way to see your hussy. Joseph, you've tried all kinds of schemes to justify hanging out at the amphitheater, so knock yourself out tonight. I won't be around to restrain you from flirting with Doreen," she said angrily.

"You lost me with all your North Carolina slang. What is a hussy, and why do I have to knock myself out?" I asked.

"Saint Joseph, please don't play innocent with me. You love to play mind games and I'm tired of falling for it."

"My interest is in *Romeo and Juliet*, not Doreen. I wish you could go with me tonight," I pleaded.

"I'll play Romeo and Juliet with you," she teased.

"Are you ready to leave?" I said, trying to change the subject.

"I probably should," she said.

Once we reached her car, I kissed her cheeks and tried to leave. She stood by the driver's door and looked at me intently without saying anything. I felt that she either knew what she wanted to say but could not find the courage to say it, or she was at a loss for words. I turned around and began to walk away. Unexpectedly, she said, "Don't flirt with Doreen, if you decide to go to the amphitheater without me." There was no other way to respond to her statement but to ignore it.

*   *   *

The big yellow sun suspended on the western horizon as dusk approached. I sat by the embankment opposite the amphitheater waiting for the first act. Once the curtains opened, I walked closer to the stage. The performance held me spellbound until the end. Only a small slice of the setting sun was still visible when Doreen came out, and asked, "Would you like to meet the cast?"

"It'd be an honor to meet your talented thespians," I said.

She gracefully introduced me to the slightly overweight boy who played the part of Romeo. Although I was impressed with his on-stage performance, I found his potbelly inconsistent with the young girl's obsessive love for him.

"You're the personification of Romeo," I said. I really did not know what possessed me to say it, but I smiled afterward.

"You don't say," he replied sarcastically.

"You were so good, that Doreen was falling for you on stage," I said. Although I was still trying to be jocular, I realized that I sounded rude. I held on to my apology, and turned to Doreen to congratulate her on a successful summer outing.

"Are you always so smug?" the angry *Romeo* boy asked me.

I turned around, and found him still standing where I last spoke to him. "I don't know what you mean," I said with a smile.

"You insult me, and turn your back on me as if you were superior," he retorted.

"I felt embarrassed about my choice of words, that's why I turned away from you. I'm really excited to meet you." I extended my hand, which he shook without much enthusiasm. Doreen watched our interaction with a smile.

"So Joseph, what plans do you have tonight?" Doreen inquired.

"Nothing for now. I'll probably stay home and listen to music."

"Music, what do you like?" she asked.

"I like all types, but how I feel influences what I listen to," I said.

"What would be your musical choice on the last day of summer school?" She persisted.

"I don't really know until I get back to my apartment," I replied. I felt that I had to turn the question and answer session around, so I asked her, "What type of music do you like?"

"I like any type of music that pulsates. Any song with good conga makes me feel like falling in love, and a good samba makes me . . ." She stopped before she finished her sentence, and smiled.

"It sounds like you're into music with African roots?" I asked with interest.

"I grew up in Brazil, where music was part of everything I did. I love to dance tango and meringue. Pure meringue, not what they dance here in America." She appeared excited talking about dancing. "Do you dance?" she asked.

"I dance, but not the formal type," I said.

"Then it's my job to teach you how to dance meringue. You will fall in love with the moves," she said.

"It's my last year in undergraduate school and my schedule is full. I doubt if I would be able to commit to dance lessons. Thank you anyway for being so kind," I said.

"If you change your mind, call me and let me know. I hope you still have my telephone number. You haven't called me since I gave it to you." she said.

"I have it on my desk at home, and I'll call you soon," I lied.

"I know your girlfriend doesn't like me. I'm not sure why she is insecure around me. Have you been unfaithful to her?"

The directness of her question surprised me, and I was not sure how to answer it.

"You don't seem to hide your feelings much," I said.

"Is that a compliment?" she asked.

"Of course, it's the best compliment you can get from me," I said emphatically.

"So you know how I feel now?" she teased.

"Not really. It's getting late. I hope we can finish this conversation some other time," I said, but Doreen did not appear to be in a hurry to leave. I added, "By the way, I have been faithful to my girlfriend."

"Why don't you ask her to dance meringue with you?" she asked.

"That sounds like a good idea. I'll ask her tonight. Thank you again, and I hope you have a good night." I took about ten steps and stopped. I remembered that all the female students were told to avoid walking alone in the dark on campus because of a rape incident. I ran back to her and offered to walk with her.

"I knew you were a gentleman, and I'm grateful you're attentive to my safety," Doreen said.

"I realized as soon as I left you that it's too late for you to walk home alone," I said.

"It's safer on campus now, even late at night, but I do appreciate your thoughtfulness," she said.

"Are you going home before the fall semester begins?" I asked.

"It depends on which home you mean. My father is a diplomat and he had served mostly in South America. He grew up in Northern Virginia, where we still have a house. My Mom was born in Sao Paulo, Brazil, but she went to school in

Washington, DC. My parents met in school and were married two days after their graduation from undergraduate school." She was telling an elaborate story when I interjected because I was not interested in her parents' biography. A simple answer would have been sufficient for me, but she was an art student and opted to elaborate on how it all came to be. It would have been an interesting conversation if I had the time.

"Where do you call home?" I asked to shorten her long tale.

"Alexandria in Northern Virginia," she said.

"Are your parents there now?" I asked as if I cared where they were. If she had the power to read minds, she would have known that I had mentally checked out with her when I first tried to say goodbye.

"My father is in Chile, but he's coming home in two months to work in the State Department. My grandmother lives in our house with my brother who's a sophomore in college." When my mind stopped wandering, I realized that Doreen was still telling me the elaborate story, but, fortunately, we had made it to her residence. "You're welcome to come in," she said, and waited for my answer, but I was a bit preoccupied with which direction to take after I left her.

"Thank you for the invitation, but it's getting late. Some other time." I said. I watched her walk to her door. "I promise to stop by before the fall semester starts," I added.

"Call me and we'll talk about it. Goodnight Joseph," she said, before she closed her door.

Wendy's whereabouts occupied my mind. It was getting late and I had not made any effort to find out if she had come back to school. Although Doreen appeared to be a good person, and I liked her simple approach to life problems, I had to look for Wendy. It had been more than twelve hours since I last saw her, and if she were in my position, I believed that she would have looked for me. When school was in session, we knew where to find each other, but since we were free until fall semester, her dormitory was the only reasonable place to look for her.

Hunger pains rattled my stomach as soon as I walked away from Doreen. How deceptive could my body be? While I was talking to a beautiful girl, I had no manifestation of hunger, but when she was no longer satiating my mind, it reminded my stomach that it had failed in its duty to provide nutrition.

The front parking space was empty when I arrived home, even though I had predicted that Wendy would be waiting for me. Nevertheless, I opened my front door and found a note on the floor.

> *Dearest Joseph:*
> *I thought you would miss me, but I was wrong. I came by several times, but you were not home. As much as I wanted to see you, I could not bear the thought of looking for you at the amphitheater. Since you do not need me, I may go home tomorrow to be with my family.*
> *Wendy.*
> *P.S. I love you regardless.*

Panic gripped me after I read Wendy's note. The fear of losing her again made my heart race. Lack of time from my busy research schedule had taken me back to that dreaded state of complacency, which was my norm during our first stint with each other. I could not wait until the following day to find out what she decided to do.

Instead of calling Wendy on the telephone, I felt that a face-to-face apology would work better. She had become such a part of my everyday life that losing her at that time would have been dangerous for me mentally. My desire for her had transcended a physical need, and had transformed into an emotional dependency. I felt lonely when we were apart, even if I was in the company of other friends.

Deliberating on what to do next, my hands trembled. I threw the note down on the floor and left my apartment. I ran so fast to Wendy's dormitory that I had to rest to catch my breath before I dialed her room intercom. The dash to her dormitory took away the remaining energy I had, and a band-like headache gripped my head like a vice. I waited for her response.

I dialed her room intercom several times without any response. I had given up when a sleepy voice came on, and asked, "Who's it?"

"It's me Joseph. I'm very sorry about today. I really messed things up. Can you come down to talk?" I rambled on until her voice came on again.

"Let me put on my gown and I'll be right down," she said. She unlocked the front door to let me into the lobby. A lone student was fiddling with a broken television antenna, while the receptionist watched a comedy show with hazy black and white pictures. I found a clean vacant chair and slumped down in it.

I had waited for more than 10 minutes, before the elevator door slowly squeaked open. Wendy emerged from it more ebullient than I had expected. Her pink hair scarf, which matched her long silk gown, amused me for an unknown reason, but she did not find my laughter funny. Apart from her fading Florida tan, she had no makeup on. Even in the poorly lighted lobby, her eyes glistened.

"I mess up a lot, but for some reason you always forgive me. I need you so much, I won't know what to do if I lose you." I said. I hugged her, and continued, "Do you mind staying with me until fall semester starts?" I did not know what compelled me to make such an outlandish request.

"Joseph, I have been waiting for you to ask me to move in with you. I'm yours whenever you're ready for me." She was more excited than I had expected. I watched her smile, and could not find the courage to tell her that I did not expect her to accept my offer so readily. With her bubbling excitement, she said, "Come up to my room and help me put some of my essential things together." We rode the elevator to her floor.

Her "essentials" barely fit in the small trunk of her convertible, which made the drive uncomfortable. On our way to my apartment, she suggested making breakfast for me in the morning, so we drove to a nearby convenience store to buy some food.

I had a shower, and whistled on my way into the bedroom. Wendy had turned on all the lights in the bedroom. She gently asked, "Where were you all day?"

"I did basically nothing. I just loafed around," I said.

"So you didn't see the play?" she asked.

"Yeah, I did. They did a good job putting it together. I was impressed." It was a candid answer, and I felt that I could not have done any better.

"What you meant to say was that your friend did a good job," she said.

"It took more than her effort to put the show together," I said.

"What else happened over there with her?" she asked.

"We talked about dance. She wants to teach me how to dance meringue." I hesitated before I continued. "I meant to say, she wants to teach us how to dance."

"I'm a dancer. I don't need her stinking lessons," she said angrily.

"I know you are, but I didn't know you could dance meringue. Forgive me for thinking you're a ballet dancer, and nothing else," I said.

"I didn't say I dance meringue. I'm a ballet dancer, not a fruitcake. Even if I want to dance with you, I don't have the time. I'm organizing my grandmother's eightieth birthday party at the country club," she said.

"You didn't tell me about it. Maybe we should dance for her to spice it up." I watched her face as I spoke.

"Do you really want to dance for my grandmother?" she asked.

"Of course I do," I replied immediately

"Do you mind if we change the dance to a tango? She loves tango, and would be thrilled if we could dance for her," Wendy said with a smile. "We may need your friend's help after all. My tango routine is a little stale," Wendy added.

"By the way, you looked good this morning. I liked that big ring on your finger," I said.

"Thank you Joseph, but why are you trying to change the subject now?" she asked.

I got out of bed and turned off the bedroom lights. "I guess it's too late to continue our conversation?" Wendy asked.

"We probably should go to sleep," I said.

"So Joseph, when are you going to propose to me?" she asked.

"Propose to you? I don't think I'm good enough for the daughter of the richest man in this part of Dixie," I drawled.

Wendy laughed at my attempt at a Southern drawl with a British-influenced accent. We lay in the dark and talked about mundane issues until we fell asleep.

* * *

I remained transfixed, watching Wendy cavort across the hardwood floor in the dance studio. Her deceptively dainty toes pivoted the rest of her body on an imaginary arc. At times, she appeared to be suspended in midair as she twisted and leaped up. She was a ballerina extraordinaire who even with her award-winning talent preferred practice to professional dancing.

Wendy used her muscles supporting her waist. With meringue, provocative movements of the hip and pelvis are the highlights of the dance steps. As the music pulsated, Doreen took off her shoes, and we did the same. She grabbed my hands and demonstrated the basic meringue steps. Her emphasis was on the mechanics of hip and pelvic motions, which, she said, were the essence of the dance.

After a few days of dedicated dancing lessons, and discernable progress in our dance steps, Doreen introduced the music of Tito Puente to blend salsa with meringue. We practiced passionately at the college dance hall until fall semester started. Thereafter, we reduced our practice to twice a week. It amazed me that Wendy's palpable mistrust of Doreen dissipated after we spent a few days dancing with her.

Even with her fulltime dedication to teaching meringue to neophytes, Doreen refused to accept any fee from us for the dance lessons. She said that it was a gift to her new friends, an exemplary behavior for a young college student.

My fall semester class schedule was awful, because I had to take graduate-level classes in chemistry and biology, but I made time for my dance lessons. We eventually delved into tango, but found the blend of meringue with salsa more appealing. For a dancer I initially felt was stiff, Wendy's pelvic thrust in due course became more limber than waddling jelly. Her transformation, and new style of dancing, evoked essence of erotic rapture.

*   *   *

For being a steadfast student, Professor Ezir rewarded me with the worst class schedule anyone could imagine for my final year in undergraduate school. I was the only undergraduate student in physical chemistry, applied mathematics in chemistry, and frontiers in biochemistry research. The only other class that I took in the fall semester was human physiology, which was a graduate-level class too. Physical chemistry, which was purported to be the hardest course, was more exciting to me than the rest. Only five students registered for the course initially, but one student dropped out after two weeks. The rest of us hung on until the end.

Our first examination in physical chemistry was on a Saturday, and we had eight hours to answer all the questions. It was the longest single subject exam I had during my school days.

My immersion in my classes created a social problem for me. Some of my friends, including Wendy, felt that I lived in the chemistry building. Wendy frequented the department looking for me because I skipped our routine lunch dates several times. Occasionally, she brought lunch trays to the chemistry department for us to share.

For all the effort she made to keep me fed, I did not express my appreciation adequately. Sometimes, I ignored her while solving physical chemistry problems, but the situation improved after I had mastered most of the concepts. I was able to solve the mathematical problems faster.

One sunny day, Wendy came to my late morning class and sat behind me. She rubbed my neck and shoulders, anytime the Professor turned his back to the class. Midway through the lecture, she leaned toward me and whispered, "I want you to feel what I can do for you." I ignored her and focused my attention on the blackboard. Once the lecture was over, I could not wait to get away with her.

The nearby lake was desolate when we arrived. It was a warm day, but the humidity was uncharacteristically tolerable, which made our picnic fun. It felt good lying next to Wendy without any worries about chemistry experiments. Instead of fumbling with hot beakers and Bunsen burners, I concentrated on the leisurely pursuit of fondling. The entrancing blue Carolina sky reflected on the calm lake. Out of mischievousness, I threw pebbles in the lake to disrupt the tranquil water. Consecutive ripples travelled circumferentially to the edge of the water. I continued with my silliness, until it dawned on me that my preoccupation with the formation and dissipation of ripples was probably a distraction to stop staring lustfully at Wendy's chest.

"Why can't you enjoy free time with me?" Wendy asked.

"I enjoy every moment I spend with you, but I'm restless sometimes, as you already know," I said.

"You have to show me how you feel, Joseph. I feel like I don't interest you anymore," she said. I wanted to play with her half-naked body to show her how I felt, but we were out in the open.

"You're so wrong, Wendy. I'm crazy about you, and I feel lost when you're not around. I'm just worried about my upcoming medical school interview," I said. Talking about academic issues at that moment was not my plan, but it came out.

"The interview is just a formality as you already know. Professor Ezir guaranteed a slot for you," she said.

"I know you're right, but it's still an interview," I said.

"My aunt will probably interview you, and she knows you well. You only have to worry about the others, who are strangers."

"That's not reassuring because I don't think that she likes me," I said.

"You're very wrong Joseph. She told me she admires your intellect," she said emphatically. She probably was defending her aunt. She then continued with a softer voice, "After our summer research project ended, she volunteered to speak to my father about you, but I would not let her get involved in my relationship with you."

"What would she have said to your dad about me?" I asked.

"He's her brother, I'm sure she knows what to say. She probably wants him to be tolerant and stay out of my relationship with you."

"I didn't know she cared about anything other than her warped social scientific nothingness," I said.

"That's a mean, classless statement. We should go back to the campus because you don't appreciate what I try to do for us," Wendy snapped.

Chapter 13

PROFESSOR EZIR WAS THE BEST academic adviser I had in undergraduate school. For an academically acclaimed older man, he was still ambitious when I met him. He spent more time in his research laboratory than any other faculty member I knew at that time, and his research publications graced the pages of all the notable biochemical journals. He was so beloved that most people ignored his glaring flaw, which was the ever-present, pungent stogy that dangled from the side of his mouth. The septuagenarian was physically nimble, and his mind was as sharp as his lashing tongue. His scientific mind never left anything he could control to an unpredictable outcome.

Professor Ezir called me into his office the day before my medical school admission interview to go over the master plan for my six-year MD-PhD program. In his proposed scheme, the basic medical science classes and research blocks covered most of the first four years of my training. I was not surprised that he made an exhaustive schedule for my initial four years in medical school even before I had my interview. He even gave me a copy of his suggested course outline for me to present to the admissions interviewers. The only thing he left out of my schedule was my bathroom privilege.

On the day of my interview, four clinical faculty members seated in a semicircle barely looked up when I walked into the interview room. My chair was equidistant from all the interviewers, a layout reminiscent of an inquisition. They pored over the papers in my folder, probably for the first time, after I walked into the interview room. From my standing position, I saw copies of my undergraduate transcript and letters of recommendation in their folders. I stood next to my chair for longer than a minute waiting for their instructions.

"Be seated, Joseph," the one member with a beard said. My hesitation prompted him to ask, "Are you not Joseph Fafa?"

"I am, sir," I said before I sat down.

"I'm Doctor Andrew Gray from the surgery department," he informed me.

"I'm very sorry for calling you a sir, instead of Doctor," I said, but he ignored me.

As the rest of the panelists introduced themselves, I tried to remember their various departments in case if I had any questions during the interview. The psychiatrist was the only female interviewer in the room, and I felt that she looked at me more intently than the rest. Her probing eyes were so intimidating that my palms began to sweat. She was not Professor Crane, as I had expected from Wendy's assertion that her aunt would interview me. Rubbing my palms under the table, I could not help but wonder why they needed a psychologist. I was not so sure about the differences between the two professions, but I knew that the two had to deal with the mind and behavioral assessments.

In the process of analyzing my surroundings and interviewers, it appeared that time stood still. The unsettling silence in the room became more sinister when my mind focused on the intermittent gentle tapping of Doctor Gray's pen on the table. The interviewers had no sense of time.

"Do you need to use the men's room?" Doctor Gray asked.

I feigned a smile and said, "I'm OK. Thank you for asking." I started deep breathing exercises to alleviate my worries.

"I was once in Rhodesia for a big game hunt. Did you travel much in Africa?" Doctor Gray said. I could not discern if his question was part of my interview, so I hesitated before I answered him.

"I'm from Nigeria, and I didn't travel much in Africa." It was the most honest answer I could give him. Doctor Gray retreated to studying my folder, while the rest of the interviewers looked at each other probably to decide who would interview me first. It was obvious that they had no preplanned sequence for the interview process.

The psychiatrist was the one I dreaded the most. "You have an impeccable academic record, but do you have any hobbies? I'm not sure how you were able to take all these courses in two years and be ready to graduate in May," Doctor Humbel said. She looked at my folder again before she continued. "Our medical school is looking for well-rounded students with good academic records. Tell me what else you do apart from studying." My fear had come true. I was not sure if she had disqualified me from the interview process.

"I'm a soccer player. I also love field hockey. Most of the students around here had not heard about field hockey until I made a fool of myself trying to sign up for a nonexistent team when I came here in 1977." I stopped talking because they laughed at my statement. I waited for the laughter to stop before I continued. "Two days after I arrived in 1977, I went to the athletic department to sign up for soccer, field hockey, and cricket teams but they laughed at me. They asked me to go back to Africa, or maybe try Europe. Their sarcasm did not stop me from trying out for the position of a kicker in our school's American football team. Unfortunately, I couldn't participate in all the practices because of my classes." In my mind, things were going well because they looked at me attentively until I said, "I took meringue dance lessons this fall, and ballroom dancing the year before." They smiled at the mention of my dance lessons. I stopped talking because I felt that I was making a fool of myself.

Scribbling on a piece of paper, Doctor Wood, the public health specialist asked, "Why do you want to become a physician?"

"I lost my cousin Franco after a civil war in my country, and I believe his doctors didn't provide adequate care for him. He died after he contracted tetanus through his inadequately treated shrapnel wounds. He could have been alive today if he had received appropriate medical care." My voice quavered, but I resisted crying. "Given the opportunity, I could become a good physician to help patients like my cousin Franco who was neglected."

"How do you plan to pay for your medical education?" Doctor Gray asked.

"My father has been my main sponsor, and he's willing to pay my way through medical school." I intentionally left out the fact that Professor Ezir had promised me an academic scholarship from the biochemistry department to avoid sounding arrogant.

"If you fail to gain admission to our medical school, do you have any backup academic plan?" the psychiatrist asked.

I lifted my face up, and looking at her, I said, "I haven't thought about any other profession because becoming a physician is the only thing I want to do with my life." Waiting for her follow up statement, I continued to engage her eyes. I was astonished when she shook her head in disbelief. What I said was how I felt, and I could not have answered her question any other way.

"So, what happens if we decide today not to extend an invitation to you? Are you applying to other medical schools?" the psychiatrist continued with her questions.

"I'm only applying to one medical school, because I love this school and want to work with my mentor, Professor Ezir. He's like a father to me, and has taught me a lot in research techniques. I would love to continue with the research work I'm currently doing with him during medical school," I said.

"What do you have to offer our medical school if admitted?" Again, the psychiatrist posed a challenging question. The rest of the interviewers smiled as she pelted me with disconcerting questions.

Her last question baffled me so much that I hesitated longer than usual before I answered it. However, to avoid stalling any further, I asked, "I'm not sure what you meant by what I have to offer the medical school." Instead of clarifying what she wanted to know, she said, "I already know your answer." My loud sigh that followed her statement elicited laughter from some of the interview panelists.

"After you finish your medical training in this country, how do you plan to establish a medical research lab in your country?" Doctor Gray asked. He stalled before he added, "From what I have read, your country can't provide basic amenities to its citizens, not to talk about setting up a decent medical research lab."

At that instant, the sweat that moistened my undershirt was from anger and not from anxiety. The surgeon's annoying statement made me so mad that I could not look at him when I gave my response. "Because it's difficult to establish a decent research lab doesn't mean that one should not try. I learned in science research to tackle difficult challenges I face systematically, and I intend to confront every problem I may have in the future that way." I said.

Even after my statement, an unsettling look of smugness lingered on his face.

"You're self-absorbed. To be a good physician, you have to be dedicated to your patients, not only yourself," Doctor Gray said.

"I make time to be involved in social issues, because I care about the welfare of suffering people all over the world. I'm involved in antiapartheid movement. It wasn't a popular cause on campus, but I persevered. I feel the same way about the health care of the less privileged," I said.

"You should broaden your education by taking more non-science classes. It's the best option for you to be competitive in the medical school admission process. Being a well-rounded person is a better qualification than being the best science student with no social outlet," Doctor Humbel said.

They criticized every decision I had made since I enrolled in college, as though their opinions were sacrosanct. I muttered under my breath several times, "Idiots." None of my interviewers sounded compassionate, and it appeared that my expectation of scholarly recompense for all the efforts I had made over the years with my education would not materialize.

From their comments, I concluded that they did not assign much value to my quest for academic excellence. I despised them.

To make things worse, Doctor Humbel said, "You're untested, and there is no documentation of altruism, which makes it difficult for me in this interview process." An indirect way of telling me that I was not qualified to contend for a slot in their medical school. Each time she spoke, she found a different way to convey that message.

"A developing country needs clinicians, not medical researchers. The new MD-PhD program is for American students. I doubt if it'll benefit you, and Nigeria," Doctor Wood said.

"Doctor Wood, I hate to disagree with you about what my country needs. I came to this country to acquire skills that are not readily available in Nigeria. My country has enough general clinicians, but has limited specialists and medical researchers. I need the opportunity to provide such skills in a developing country," I said. I had nothing left to lose, so I had to speak my mind.

I waited for compliments about my academic accomplishments, but none of them said anything about my transcript or academic awards. At the conclusion of the interview, I was unsure of the chances I had to gain admission into the medical school. I dreaded the idea of telling my parents that I had failed them. It was my father's desire to see me qualify as a physician.

The triumphant trip to Wendy's dormitory I had planned before the interview did not happen. It turned out that the interview was not the endorsement of my exemplary academic record that I had expected. Instead, they did a thorough interview, and made me feel inadequate. I walked away with my head bowed, and spent at least thirty minutes in my laboratory staring at the floor.

I tried to do some experiments, but could not focus, so I went back to my apartment. I wasted the rest of the day feeling sorry for myself, and at night, I could not go to sleep. The constant ringing of my telephone almost drove me insane. It did not matter to me what the caller wanted, because I was not ready to face the truth that I was not as special as I had thought.

I lay on my back and stared at the ceiling thinking about all the mistakes I had made during my interview. An idea about joining the Dominican priesthood crept into my mind and dissipated. I imagined conducting Sunday Mass as a priest, thinking about Wendy's breasts every time I raised the chalice. That made me sick. I had strong desires of the flesh that I could not suppress. Finally, I fell asleep.

In my dream, I stood in front of the hospital pavilion with other medical students during the lunch break. When the break was over, all the medical students walked through the revolving glass door without a glitch until it was my turn. I was stuck in the revolving door and no one could get me out. I woke up from sleep and sat up in my bed . Fortunately, I fell back asleep and avoided the agony of needless worrying.

The following day, I met with Wendy, but left out the sordid details of my interview. She simply said, "Congrats." She had the mindset that my admission to the medical was a cinch. I did not have the courage to dispel her false notion.

* * *

As weeks went by after the interview, I became more isolated from Wendy. I took refuge in my laboratory when I was not in the classroom. Wendy came by to see me several times but found me engrossed in laboratory experiments each time. It was physically evident that she became more despondent as time went on, and on a Friday afternoon, she finally confronted me after I refused to go out to dinner with her.

"This is not the way to end our relationship. If you've met someone else, tell me now so we can still be friends. You can't continue to avoid me, and pretend we don't have problems. I must have done something you're not willing to tell me," she said angrily.

It was evident as she spoke that my mental anguish had caused her physical pain. There was no doubt in my mind that she suffered equally due to my unwillingness to express my fear of getting a denial letter from the medical school admissions committee. Wendy had not known me to be vulnerable, but I was terrified of being an academic failure. Even when she'd left me to travel to France, I did not disclose my broken heart to her. After all, in my culture, men were not supposed to show overt emotions.

I looked into Wendy's eyes and found genuine tears. It affected me profoundly. I hugged and held on to her to conceal my own tears. My greatest fear was losing her because of my arrogance, which I'd displayed to the group that had the power to stop me from enrolling in medical school.

"Please tell me you love me. That's all I want to hear from you now," she said, sobbing.

"I love you, Wendy, but it's not about loving you. It's about losing you. I have been worried about my interview. My fear is that I may not be admitted to the medical school," I said.

"Is there something I can do to help you? You're the best science student in this school. It would be a travesty if you didn't get in," she said with a stern voice, and without a drawl.

"There's more to the process than grades. Apparently, I haven't shown commitment to helping others," I said.

"You've done so much to help a lot of people, like volunteering for Big Brother and Big Sister. You volunteer at the soup kitchen. Maybe you didn't present your best attributes well. Why not wait until you hear from them before you beat yourself up. If you want me to, I can talk to my daddy about you so that they treat you fairly," Wendy said.

"Wen, you seem to forget, your father doesn't like me. Why should he help me when he wants me to stay away from you?"

"He may not like you because of me, but he respects your academic promise. I believe my father is a decent man and would like you to be treated fairly," she said.

"Wen, what do you mean by academic promise? It sounds like the nonsense you complain about that comes out of my mouth," I said. I drawled when I added, "You're my best friend."

She could not help but laugh.

"Listen, knucklehead Joe, I'm not your friend. I'm your love, and don't you ever forget it." She was once again in a lighter mood and it felt good to see her happy. The main issue that consumed me seemed to be less important after our discussion.

* * *

We left the campus that evening because we could not find anything interesting to do and travelled east without a predetermined destination. When we reached Wilmington, North Carolina, it was too late to visit some of the historical places. Since we had no provisions for an overnight stay, we went to a small store and bought toiletries. Our fervent effort to get a room in a local bed and breakfast failed, so we drove to a local motel where Wendy secured a room for the night. It was not even a one star hotel, but the accommodation was sufficient for two desperate college students. Before Wendy fell asleep, she looked at me, and said, "Even a manger would be good enough for me as long as I'm with you."

I laughed at her comment, and said, "I'm not as pious as Joseph."

"So you take me as your wife?" Wendy asked.

"You always manage to set me up. I meant that figuratively," I said.

"Am I not good enough to be your wife?" Wendy asked.

"You insist on talking about marriage when we still have a lot of schooling ahead of us," I said.

"Look at this irony. You want me to be with you, but you don't want me to be yours," Wendy said.

I held her hand and said, "I belong to you Wendy but don't take that to mean the Old South way of belonging to someone." We both laughed. Even though it was a joke about slavery, I was serious. I did not want her to be the one making decisions about our relationship and my future. If I wanted to undress the truth, I would accept that I was afraid of Wendy dominating me. Blame it on my outdated upbringing, because in my culture men made most of the decisions.

"Belonging to someone is different from owning someone, Joseph. So, I belong to you too," she said.

She held on to me and brooded until tender sleep finally took her away from me.

*　*　*

The City of Wilmington had beautiful historical sites, including the partially destroyed Bellamy Mansion, which was a grandiose architectural masterpiece, built in 1859 by Dr. Bellamy, and equipped with a slave quarter. The imposing mansion did not convey any image of altruism on the part of the owner, which made me question if Dr. Bellamy's quest for wealth and power was the norm for physicians of his era. Was the hunger for money and power an acceptable quality in physicians of the nineteenth century? I posed that question to myself several times. I compared myself to Dr. Bellamy, and I could not find anything about him that highlighted his dedication to selfless service to humanity. I believed that I had done more for humanity at my tender age, than he did in his entire life.

Touring the slave quarter part of the estate, I looked at Wendy and said, "This would have been my place, and the main house yours, in the Old South."

"I would have been lusting after you from my window, and baring my breasts to you," Wendy said.

"An offence punishable by lynching," I said.

"You would have protected me from such an awful death," she said.

"Not you silly. They would have lynched me for looking at your breasts as a slave of the household," I said.

"I would've asked to be lynched with you," Wendy said.

"The same way you stood up for me when you ran away to France, just for ordinary racial taunting on campus," I said.

"Why do you have to spoil the good time we're having?" she asked.

"I apologize. We shouldn't dwell on our past mistakes. I made many of them too," I said.

We left the manicured grounds of Bellamy mansion as Wendy pouted. I tried to hold her hand, but she rejected my gesture. Passersby looked at us curiously, as I attempted to alleviate the tension between us.

We sat in the car for a long time looking at each other. Sometimes I could not believe that such a privileged, beautiful girl wanted to be with me. "Where do we go next?" I asked. She ignored me and drove on. I sat back and closed my eyes.

The checkered history of North Carolina was more evident on our visit to the Sadgwar family home. The available family history revealed a cornucopia of information on how a wealthy family handled the birth of an illegitimate child from an unflattering sexual liaison. David Elias Sadgwar was born in Wilmington in 1817 and handed over to two slaves to raise as their own because his father, a French sea captain, did not accept a 'mulatto' as his son. His mother was apparently a black slave.

"How could an enlightened Frenchman give away his son because the child was of mixed race?" I asked. It took Wendy a while to reply to my comment cum question. Having children was one issue we had never discussed, and she probably was unsure of what to say.

"Things were different in 1817, so it's unfair to judge what he did at that time," Wendy replied. We argued about the philosophical meaning of parental love for longer than ten minutes until she angrily said, "Quit arguing." My quixotic view on the Sadgwar family baffled Wendy because it was not common for me to share such inner feelings.

We left the Sadgwar estate and opted to visit some of the famed Wilmington gardens before we drove back to school.

Chapter 14

THERE WAS LESS HUMIDITY, and a gentle wind even availed itself to desperate souls like me on Monday evening. I picked up my mail and riffled through the letters. An envelope from the medical school admissions office. An unprecedented fear gripped me. The light envelope looked ominous because it was common knowledge at that time that accepted candidates received bigger envelopes. I had expected a large envelope with a letter to announce the offer of admission and pertinent information leaflets. My hands trembled uncontrollably. The envelope in my hand terrified me so much that I felt nauseated, and could not find the courage to open it.

I walked around aimlessly in my apartment before I placed the envelope on the coffee table. For a moment, it felt like an end to my academic pursuits. I should have applied to other schools. I imagined saying goodbye to Wendy and my heart breaking. The more I stared at my coffee table, the more ominous the envelope became. An illogical decision to delay the inevitable by leaving the envelope unopened was an act of immaturity, but I chose that path. Therefore, the envelope lay on the table.

Fear of failing to gain admission to the medical school had tortured me enough since my interview, but I had been set free after coming back from Wilmington. However, what lay on my coffee table that evening, set me back emotionally.

I returned from my classes on Tuesday to confront the mystery envelope, I still could not find the courage to open it.

Since I could not shake my fear, I explored the musical option to find solace. The best selection of songs I had that dealt with heartbreak was my compilation from the time Wendy left for France. My reel-to-reel player delivered in a crisp stereo sound, a heart-wrenching musical journey to hopelessness, not my original intention.

As the reels slowly turned, I took an inward trip to a blissful solitude. At times, I drifted into a dreamlike state where I faced the wrath of my parents. I was losing my mind, so I took my books from the coffee table, and ran to the library. My escape to the library ended at 11 p.m. when it closed. Five minutes afterwards, I was at Wendy's deserted residential tower calling her room intercom.

"Why are you here so late on a school day? Are you OK?" Her questions would have continued if I did not respond immediately.

"I'm fine Wendy, but I need you tonight. Bring your things for tomorrow's classes and come down." My demand surprised me since her stay with me in the past failed because I was not home to be with her as much as she expected.

"If you want me to go with you, I'm spending more than one night. You want me to stay with you one minute, then you change your mind the next minute. I don't even know why we still live apart," she said.

"Just come down first, then we can talk about our future later," I said. At that moment, I was unsure of what my future would be.

Even in the tranquil night outside Wendy's residence hall, I could not find solace. I paced up and down the sidewalk waiting for her. Things were looking so grim for me that I did not pay attention to what Wendy was wearing when she finally came down to meet me. We walked to her car barely exchanging any words. I could tell that she was tired, so I drove. She fell asleep before we arrived at my apartment.

"Are we home yet, Hon?" she asked, when she woke up,

"We're home finally," I said, as I played along with her.

Once inside my apartment, she proceeded to the coffee table to set her books down. She found the letter from the admissions office and excitedly picked it up. "You've been hiding your good news from me," she said, before she realized that the mail was unopened. "What are you waiting for? Open it, let's see what it says," she continued.

I tried to hide my trembling hands from her as I said, "Open it, since you're so eager." Before I could finish what I was saying, she tore the envelope open and read it aloud.

"Congratulations on your admission into the Medical Scholar program and your selection as the first recipient of the college Regent Medical Scholarship . . ." Her words became inaudible to my ears as she continued. It was fear, happiness, and everything else that I felt, but could not describe, which made me temporarily deaf. Although I was physically sound, the interview had battered my psyche, and deprived me of the pleasure of deep slumber for many weeks. Inner peace slowly crept over me as I stood there and wept.

Exhilaration extinguished any traces of sleep that had taken hold of Wendy before we arrived at my apartment. It appeared that she was more excited than I had expected. We held on to each other and rejoiced.

The rest of the night, we talked about her upcoming medical school interview and the powerful medical couple we would become. Yes! During that brief moment of ecstasy, I probably accepted a marriage proposal from Wendy.

*   *   *

Our favorable class schedule on Wednesday morning offered us a reprieve, but we barely had enough time to shower and make it to the cafeteria before my afternoon laboratory classes. I was in a hurry to leave, but Wendy found time to search for a spare key to my apartment. The frenzy with which she looked for the key made me apprehensive. "This is permanently mine," she said after she found the spare key. "I'll leave my clothes in your closet," she continued without any comment from me.

The late morning sun was a welcome sight. It felt as though I had died while I waited for a decision from the admissions committee, and revivified only the night before. Everything looked brighter and more appealing to me. I took a deep breath to express my new zest for life and smiled as wide as I could.

"Your good news deserves a celebration. I'll throw a party for you this weekend," Wendy said, as we walked to the cafeteria.

"Why do I need a party?" I inquired.

"Your hard work and dedication should be celebrated," she stated.

"It's only an admission to a medical school," I protested.

"How about a small party in your apartment with some of our friends?" she asked.

"Which friends? I don't have any. You and my books are the only friends I have," I said with a subdued laugh.

"You do have friends. How about the boys you played soccer with last year?" she asked.

"I don't consider them my friends. Anyway, most of them graduated and left the country," I said.

"How about Doreen? She likes you, and I think she is a good friend," Wendy said.

"If you seem to know my friends, why don't you invite them, and spare me the rejections," I joked.

"OK. I'll write an official invitation to all our friends. Trust me, I'll surprise you, my love," she said with a smile.

"It sounds scary to me," I said.

"Nothing to worry about," she said.

We met some of her friends in the cafeteria and sat with them during lunch. When one of the girls, Angelica, asked Wendy, "What are you guys up to?"

"We're having a big party for Joseph, and you're invited," Wendy said.

"He's having a birthday party?" Angelica asked.

I was afraid of what Angelica would ask next. I remembered one question she asked me when Wendy introduced us a week earlier, which stuck in my mind, "Do you feel you're better than the rest of your people because you are going out with Wendy?" I did not ask her to explain what she meant at that time, but I saw an opportunity to go back to her question. However, I waited for Wendy to finish what she had to say.

"It's a welcome to the medical school party," Wendy said.

"Welcome to the medical school party?" another girl asked Wendy.

"Well, my smart boyfriend here received his admissions letter to our medical school with a full scholarship recently," Wendy said, pointing at me.

"Congratulations, Joseph," the girls said.

"Thank you very much," I replied.

Apart from Angelica, the rest of the girls left for their various classes. I was surprised that Angelica asked Wendy for details about the party because it was obvious from our previous encounter that she did not like me.

"Sorry to bring up an old issue, but Angelica, do you remember what you asked me a week ago about dating Wendy?" I asked.

"I don't even remember yesterday, not to mention a week ago," Angelica said.

"I can refresh your memory if you want me to," I said.

"Joseph, would you mind not bringing up the past? I'm sure Angelica didn't intend to offend you then," Wendy said.

"Did I say anything offensive to you?" Angelica asked.

"No, Angelica, you didn't. I believe that Joseph isn't going to rehash an unfortunate event from a week ago," Wendy said.

"Wendy is probably right. Let's forget about it," I said.

Angelica left us after the exchange and did not commit to Wendy about attending my party. Before we left the cafeteria, Wendy said, "You always drive people away with your unforgiving attitude on everything. The poor girl was trying to get to know you, but you rubbed her past mistake all over her face." It was obvious that Wendy was angry, so I did not respond to her comment. We dined quietly afterward. However, I occasionally looked at Wendy and smiled. She reciprocated gracefully with her own smile.

* * *

The comprehensive list of the attendees to the impromptu party Wendy organized barely filled half a page of a small piece of paper. As I anticipated, she invited only a limited number of her sorority sisters, since most believed that her relationship with me had diminished their revered sisterhood. In my first year in college, only two of her sorority sisters tolerated our friendship, but fortunately, the number increased to only five after two years.

It was difficult to find fellow students I considered close friends. Even though I met many students in college, I did not form strong bonds with any of them, except for Wendy. Therefore, she invited all the four international students I knew, and gave them the option to come with their friends. Apart from her sorority sisters, she invited some boys she knew from high school. I knew the girls well, but Wendy did not really introduce the boys. I only knew their first names.

I expected a dance party since it was the disco era, but Wendy organized a cocktail type of gathering with animated discussions about intercultural hitches in our citadel of learning. Even amongst the enlightened senior students who attended, some still had reservations about according everyone the same liberty that they enjoyed. I was not surprised when two distinct groups emerged during the party: an American-born group of students, and a group of foreigners. The two groups avoided each other.

Wendy walked from the living room of my apartment to the kitchen several times to ask the two groups to, "Please mingle, and talk to each other." She looked weary after no one responded positively to her request.

I watched Wendy's frantic effort with aloofness that surprised even me. Eventually, I walked to the kitchen and asked my friends to interact more with the loud boys in the living room. Without much persuasion, they obliged my request. For a moment, I saw a smile on Wendy's face.

There were uneasy smiles, on both sides, when the foreigners approached the Americans, until Eric said, "I remember you, we took English composition together," to the Iranian boy, Jay.

Jay was an engineering student whose father was an oil minister in the Iranian government. He was one of the kindest students I met in college, and an avid soccer player.

Jay looked at Eric briefly, and then smiled genuinely. "Yes, yes, I remember you," Jay said. They hugged as though they were long lost friends. The rest of the American boys frowned.

"So, what are you up to?" Eric asked.

"Finishing my classes, and going home," Jay replied.

One of the American boys, Frank, turned to Jay and said, "How many of our girls have you used?" His husky frame shadowed Jay in such a way that I felt he expected an immediate answer to his question. Jay looked at him with visible anger.

Eric cut in, and said, "That's stupid Frank."

"Which girls are you talking about," Jay asked.

The exchange of words between Frank and Jay attracted more attention than I wanted at my own party. "We're here to have fun not fight," I said. Frank ignored me.

"You know what I mean. You come over here, deceive our girls, then go home," Frank said, as he engaged Jay's eyes with a cold stare. He turned to me, pointed his finger in my face, and said, "Look at this one, deceiving a beautiful girl like Wendy. What do you think will happen to her after you're gone? No one will want her."

"Listen to this fool run his mouth," Jay said angrily.

Frank laughed at Jay's comment, and then looked at him from head to toe. His demeanor instantly changed from a pathetic laughter to a sinister look, and I could feel the palpable tension in the room. "Call me a fool again, and you'll regret being born," Frank said.

"Frank, watch what you're saying," Eric said.

Frank continued with his belligerence, mumbling incomprehensible trash.

"Haven't you said enough?" Eric asked Frank, who continued his wanton bellicosity.

"Ragheaded Arab," Frank said.

"I'm Persian, but you're probably too ignorant to know the difference," Jay said.

I walked closer to Frank and said, "I have listened to your crap all night. I'm really tired of it. You need to go home now." I was so angry that my hands were shaking as I spoke.

"Go ahead, make me," Frank said. He taunted me with a wry smile, which made me angrier.

"Get out of here," I yelled at him.

He yelled back at me, "Useless Nig... can't control himself." Whether he deliberately did not complete the word, or that I did not hear it well, it was obvious what he meant to say.

"Say what? What did you say fool? I hope you meant 'Nigerian'." I reached out to grab Frank's shirt collar, but Eric grabbed my hand. Everyone joined Eric to separate us. By the time Eric let go of my hand, Frank had left my apartment. Things happened so fast, but it felt like eternity for me. The shame of losing my composure was overwhelming, but I tried to hide it.

I found Wendy with swollen red eyes. Tears rolled down my face. She sobbed and ran into my bedroom, before I could reach her. I ran after her, but she locked the door. After several knocks on the locked door without a response, I returned to the living room, and dismissed everyone. I sat down and wept for the simple reason that I let a fool make me lose my composure.

There were two different groups of thought out of the attendees, and the two sides were as far apart in their beliefs as they were before the party started. Some of the prejudiced opinions they expressed shocked me, even after weathering stinging disparaging comments from fellow students for two years. The party was a monumental failure, whichever way you analyzed it.

Chapter 15

THE LONG, DREARY WINTER DAYS fostered feelings of despair, but the sprouting of green leaves, beautiful flowers, and the effusive birds' songs heralded spring's revival of botanical life. I was not sure how time had passed so fast, but it was a big relief when spring arrived early. The rigors of the medical school admission process made me insecure initially, but eventually it reassured me that a meritocracy was the best reward system in our civilized world. Wendy's admission process was quite different from mine because she opted for the four-year program and received her acceptance letter in less than two weeks from the date of her interview. Of course, she was a Crane coupled with her high academic honors. She was confident after her interview because, unlike my interview process, her interviewers praised her academic record. Although we ignored the fact that her father was in charge of the college board of trustees and the highest donor to the college, I felt that such details mattered to the admission officers. Irrespective of all the unnecessary details, we were ready for our undergraduate school days to be over, as we embraced the beautiful spring days with vigor.

On a sunny spring afternoon, Wendy and I walked the trails in a captivating garden of butterfly-daffodils. We had gone to the garden to escape from some of the vagaries of her stressful schedule, but her grandmother's eightieth birthday party still loomed large. Student fun seekers thronged the expansive nature trails, which had enclaves of flower gardens.

Exotic flowers lined the promenade, which had us walking with short steps to appreciate their myriad of beautiful colors. At times, we even stopped completely, to admire unusual blossoms. The *Halesia carolina* flowers were so beautiful that I involuntarily plucked one and placed it on Wendy's hair. "Wendy Crane, this is your flower and on your wedding day you will be festooned with its petals," I said as she beamed with a smile.

"You foreigner, are you proposing to me?" she asked with seriousness.

"Not yet, but eventually I will, when I have the money to buy a decent ring," I said.

Some of the students who saw me pluck the flower whispered that I was violating the botanical garden rule, but I ignored them. Wendy's radiant beauty so controlled most of my actions that I embraced her with ardor and kissed her lips with unmitigated intensity. "Control yourself and let me breathe," she said with a smile.

"We're in paradise, and you ask me to behave. It would be unnatural if I failed to express my feelings for you," I said.

Wendy looked at me and said with seriousness, "You broke the garden's rule, and we may be banned from this ground for life."

"Get used to it, because as long as I'm alive, I'll never stop breaking rules for you," I replied.

"Stop being so fresh. I'm already yours," she said and giggled. I felt that she liked the gesture but was too modest to thank me.

"I may be fresh, but I have good eyes for beautiful things. You're beautiful, Doctor Wendy Crane," I said.

"Doctor Crane? We don't start medical school until August, and I have four years before I earn my degree. You, Hon, have six long years to go. We're a long way from becoming Doctor Fafa and Doctor Crane," she said.

"You're going to earn your degree before me, so I'm practicing how to address you as Doctor Crane before I join the club. By the way, since MD degree means 'My Darling' does that mean that you will dump me when you get your new darling?" She laughed so uncontrollably that I could not finish.

"I'll never leave you, Joseph Fafa. Not even after my death. You're stuck with me for eternity," she said in a somber tone.

"Your commitment to me was never in doubt. Just that, sometimes I still wonder why you chose me from all the schmucks around here," I said.

"Well, I'll give you some of the reasons again. You're tall, handsome, intelligent, a good dancer, and the rest of the stuff I forget," she giggled.

"Thank you for the compliment, but we need to leave this place, and find an ice cream parlor," I said.

"We still have to plan my grandmother's birthday party," she said.

I reasoned that some time away from the issues at hand would clear the fog from her brain, but I was wrong. By the time we arrived at the local ice cream parlor, she was irritable and distant. She was worried about the "logistics of the party" as she put it, but was not specific. It was difficult for me to help her when she could not state what the problem was.

How fast things changed between us as soon as we got to the ice cream parlor worried me. However, I had to appreciate the enormity of the coming event. Who would not have been anxious when the governor of the state and many state politicians were invited? It was a Crane party, and most of the state politicians had benefited from Mr. Crane's political largesse. It was therefore their duty to honor their benefactor.

* * *

On the last Saturday of March, 1980, the biggest social event in our small college town kicked off with a morning service at a local church. Only immediate family members and their closest friends were invited to attend the service, while the rest of us prepared for the evening grand finale at the country club.

Doreen hired a musical group from the Dominican Republic to play meringue and salsa. Due to the number of musicians in the group, it was a logistical nightmare for the exclusive country club, which had never hosted a live band before then. We used a long landing just off the dining area overlooking the golf course as the stage for the band.

The evening program kickoff drew closer, we dressed up in our outfits and practiced our dance steps. Doreen guided us intensely and made a few last-minute changes that helped our coordination tremendously. Lisa showed up late. She was the designated photographer, but forgot her camera..

We were ready mentally and physically to give the Crane family a big surprise. The band was the last act in a slew of fervent activities. All that waiting sent shivers throughout my body.

The birthday matriarch with her ornate gown and dazzling jewelry finally walked out and sat in a chair provided by the country club manager. The band quickly gathered behind her, and to her surprise, started their opening number. The folks in the dining room trooped outside to listen to the music.

The large setting sun illuminated the venue on the west side of the expansive country club grounds, as the musical group heralded the closing phase of the party with the rhythm of the conga. The beat was so riveting that even the bodies buried in the nearby cemetery must have felt it. The unmistakable pulsating energy from the confluence of meringue and salsa resonated all over. As the audience looked on in disbelief, Wendy and I wowed them with the Cuban version of Meringue. With my right hand placed on her haunch, our exaggerated hip movements, and coordinated pelvic thrusts, were so suggestive that we probably caused some of the older gentlemen to have their first erections in decades. Some even joined in the dancing despite unforgiving stiff knee joints from decades of inactivity. Only one man appeared annoyed by our antics. His face turned red instantly, and his anger was so evident that I thought I saw smoke seeping out of his pores.

Right in front of everyone, the business mogul stood up waving his arms. Suddenly, the toast of the political class, clutched his chest. As he crashed into his chair, some of the doctors in the audience rushed to his side. One of them activated the emergency system. The music stopped. The guests stood still. A somber look descended on everyone present. Wendy pushed me aside and rushed to her father.

"I'm very sorry, Daddy," I heard Wendy repeat many times as she stood by his side.

I stood there, lost in the middle of the large crowd. I broke away from the crowd and tried to comfort Wendy, but Professor Nancy Crane towered over me. "I think you'd better go back to your apartment."

"I'm needed here."

"I said, go home, and wait for Wendy to call you," Professor Crane said.

A country club manager escorted me off the premises.

I ran after the ambulance that conveyed Mr. Crane to the University Medical Center, and waited in the Emergency room for Wendy to arrive with her family. Wendy came in with her mother and Professor Nancy Crane. They looked somber.

"I'm very sorry about your husband," I said. Mrs. Crane was crying uncontrollably.

She looked at me and said, "It's not your fault, Joseph. He has been feeling tired lately because of his frequent trips to Europe." From her statement, I deduced that she probably felt that I blamed myself for her husband's medical problem. Either way, I was happy that she spoke to me. Wendy stood there staring into space. I tried to hug her, but she turned away from me.

"Leave her alone. Can't you see she's in shock?" Professor Crane barked at me.

"That's why I'm here. To offer her my support," I retorted.

"We're here to support each other. The Cranes are tough. She doesn't need your support right now," Professor Crane said.

"Do you want me to stay with you?" I asked Wendy, but she ignored me.

One of the doctors came from the emergency room to inform the family that Mr. Crane's chest pain had gone away. However, he told them that Mr. Crane would spend the night in the intensive care unit for observation. The three women left me in the waiting area and followed the doctor to the emergency room. I could not muster the courage to follow them, so I sat down in one of the empty chairs. I cupped my forehead with my hands and reflected on the events leading up to the hospital.

It took a lot of soul searching to convince myself that I was not culpable for Mr. Crane's heart attack. I lifted my head up, and beheld a shocking display on the wall in front of me. A spectacular oil painting of the patriarch of the family, Joseph Crane, hung on a magnificent marble wall facing the entrance to the waiting area. Beneath the painting was an inscription that read, "Hospital Wing Donated in Memory of Joseph Crane." Wendy loved me because her grandfather was named Joseph? I sighed.

I shifted my eyes away from the painting and watched the clock until it was midnight. The massive swinging doors of the emergency room remained shut. No one came back for me. It grew late, and the hospital security guard came by several times to ask more questions about my prolonged stay in the waiting area.

* * *

Days passed before I finally tracked Wendy down in her biology class. I hugged her, but she did not reciprocate.

"I have missed you so much, but that's not important right now. I understand you have to be with your family. How's your dad doing? I'm worried about him," I said, trying to hold her.

"He's back home and doing well. The doctor said he needs a rest from his travels," she said in a monotone voice. I loosened my grip because she sounded uncomfortable.

"How about you? Are you OK? I have been worried sick about you," I said anxiously.

"I'm doing well, but I have to spend more time at home to support my father emotionally," she said in the same monotone voice.

"Are we OK, Wendy? I mean us, like you and me," I asked.

She avoided looking at me, and ignored my question.

"I have another class to get to in less than five minutes," she said, before she walked away.

I could not discern if Wendy felt responsible for her father's mishap, but I was not willing to accept culpability. Her immediate dissociation from me made me question her resilience. In 1978, she chose to run to France rather than stick around and support me when racial tension nearly claimed my life on campus. "How deep is your love?" was the simple question I asked Wendy when she accused me of separating her from her family.

"I'll die for you, but I can't give up my family," Wendy said. I did not expect her to give up her family for me. Interestingly, the best way Wendy chose to die for me was to run away.

Even with all my doubts about the viability of our relationship, I felt that I should not give up on her.

I waited for her outside the biology building before the end of her genetics laboratory session at five p.m.. She emerged from her class still looking unhappy, but she managed to hug me. She stared at me for a long time without uttering a word.

"Joseph, I've missed you so much, but let's face it. I'm no good for you," she said with tears flowing down her face. "I told my father how good you are to me and how dedicated you are to education. I even bragged about your acceptance into the Medical Scholar's program, and your scholarship award. All he said was, you tarnished the Crane's name. My father was so angry when I said your name that I was worried about his health. Aunt Nancy tried to mediate, but he wouldn't talk to her." Wendy sighed deeply.

"I told you before. Your father never liked me. He hated me from the first day we met. He can't overcome his prejudice," I said.

"He's not that bad, Joseph. It may be hard for you to accept, but my father isn't a bigot," she said, attracting the attention of other students walking by.

I turned my face away from her to hide my disbelief.

"If you don't mind, let's go to your apartment and talk. We shouldn't argue out here," Wendy said.

"Should we get dinner first?" I asked her.

"I'm not hungry, but I can go to the cafeteria with you. Since Daddy's heart attack, I've lost my appetite," she said.

"You have to eat to remain healthy. I don't want my girlfriend to get anorexia. That's, if you're still my girlfriend?" I teased, but she did not smile. She was expressively vacuous, sitting with me in a half-empty cafeteria. I was surprised that she followed me back to my apartment.

*   *   *

Wendy spent the night with me. We did not discuss a strategy to mitigate our shared burden, or what I called the 'Cranes' burden'. Her father was the last person she wanted to talk about. I understood her dilemma. There was no easy way to approach a weighty family problem, even if we agreed that her father's prejudice could eventually unravel the gains we had made in our relationship since she came back from France. I settled for the fire brigade approach, which was to quench the fire when it ignited rather than concentrate on preventive measures. Predicting human behavior was as hard as predicting the time of birth, or the time of death. So, we inadvertently left our future together to the uncontrollable forces in our lives.

Chapter 16

BY EARLY APRIL OF 1980, spring had lost its mystique. Senior students grew wary, anticipating graduation in May. As for me, I could no longer tolerate the dreary clouds and daily rainfall. I missed my parents more each day, and yearned for my mother's home cooking. On rainy days, memories of childhood escapades during tropical thunderstorms flooded my mind. I remembered vividly that we hid under my parents' bed, which gave us a false sense of protection from lightning. We were young and naïve. Unfortunately, no such place existed for me to seek mental refuge in North Carolina.

It would be exhilarating if 'Pappy' and 'Mama' could attend my graduation, but educating their children in foreign countries was taking a mental toll on my father. He suffered from insomnia, and I had to protect him from further stress of six thousand mile journey. I lied to them about the unimportance of the graduation ceremony to me. My father sent me a one-line telegram, "You are a good son." He was a man of few words, and that suited me just fine.

With secured admission and a scholarship to one of the most prestigious medical schools in the country, I was eager to conclude my undergraduate education. Even though I might win major awards from the college during the graduation ceremony, they did not elicit as much excitement as the previous awards I had received from various science departments. One major thing that was important to me, my relationship with Wendy, had waned so much that I could not count on her emotional support. Our once promising love affair withered, our burning passion dowsed by local mores. Regardless of how Wendy felt about our precarious situation, she found solace at home with her parents and left me to sort out sundry things alone. Although her house was not too far from school, she might as well have been a million miles away from me. To get to Wendy outside the school premises meant that I had to go through her father, or his cohorts who were like impregnable walls separating us. She was virtually a prisoner in her parents' home.

During the day, Wendy had an assigned driver who was also her security detail. He waited for her outside the classrooms, and made it difficult for me to talk to her. As much as I tried, I could not find a way to have a private conversation with her. One day, I followed her into the women's restroom to steal a kiss. Once I locked the bathroom door, she held on to me and would not let go. Making out in a women's bathroom was not the respectable romantic adventure I had envisioned, but it was the only opportunity available.

Holding each other, she said, "I have died without you, Joseph. Most of the time, I forget what I'm doing. I'm a useless fool now," she sobbed as she spoke.

"I'm glad you still need me as much as I need you," I said. Those were the only words that came to my mind because of my agony, and they sounded hollow. Words could not adequately convey how lost I felt without her.

"If we care about each other as much as we say we do, we should run away and get married. That's probably the only way they would leave us alone," she said angrily. Her defiant tone made me worry about her mental state.

"There's no reason to act impulsively. It could complicate things for us. We should wait until after graduation, to talk about marriage," I reassured her.

I exited the bathroom first, and was lucky not to run into anyone in the hallway. Wendy left the bathroom, and handed a piece of paper to me with her private telephone number at home. She wrote below her telephone number, "Call me after midnight on Mondays and Fridays."

*   *   *

On a Tuesday afternoon, in mid-April, Professor Ezir was outside the physical chemistry laboratory puffing on his stogy, waiting for me. His rumpled tweed jacket gave him the air of a living fossil. For him to be waiting for me outside a laboratory was so unusual that my mind raced to the many things that I could have done wrong. Earlier that day, I had left a biochemistry research report on his desk, and when I remembered it, I felt that I must have made a major mistake. However, his stone face made things seem worse.

"I need to talk to you. Let's go into the conference room," Professor Ezir said. I felt that I probably had lost a relative, and he had to break the bad news to me privately. We walked to the conference room in silence, and he barely puffed on his stogy.

He pulled out a wrinkled envelope from his pocket and observed it for a while. My heart raced as I waited for the terrible thing he had to tell me. However, I remembered my bathroom exploit with Wendy, and concluded that he had found out about it. My heart pounded intensely.

I waited anxiously until he put the envelope back in his coat pocket, and said, "Son, I'm very sorry to let you know that they cancelled your medical scholar admission and scholarship. I spoke to the medical school dean earlier today on your behalf, but they could not admit you to the regular class for the upcoming school year. Apparently, the board of trustees rescinded the funding for the MD-PhD program for one year, pending reorganization of the curriculum. I'm not sure what your options are since the changes affect my laboratory grants too, making it impossible for me to offer you a place in the graduate school."

I rubbed my head, then my face. I covered my eyes with the palms of my hands. It was less than four weeks before my graduation, and all the medical schools in the country had concluded their admission processes. Crying would have been the easiest thing for me to do, but no tears came. I wanted Professor Ezir to say something reassuring, but he remained silent.

"Thank you Professor Ezir for everything you've done for me since I came to your department. I was looking forward to working with you for the next four years." I sighed, and then continued. "Since I can't stay and work with you, what should I do now? I'm lost. Should I go and talk to the medical school dean?"

"I already spoke to him. Since you're not a medical student yet, the dean may not offer you an appointment. Worry about your classes for now, and let me talk to more people around here. I hope to find some answers for you soon," he said in a reassuring way.

"Professor Ezir, what have I done wrong?" I asked, and then sobbed uncontrollably.

"It's OK, Joseph. You have not done anything wrong. That's all I'm allowed to say for now," he said, wiping his eyes. He stood up and walked out of the room like a man on an urgent mission. I stayed behind to collect my thoughts and paced around the conference room. I was happy that it was not a death in my family, but what a loss!

The only thing I could remember about the rest of that day was the worst frontal headache of my life. The once-coveted Carolina sunshine made my headache worse. I could not keep my eyes open walking back to my apartment. I collected my mail before I retreated to my bedroom and slumped on the bed. For hours, I sobbed alone in the darkness. The more I thought about my dire situation, the more I realized I had no viable long-term plan. After years of hard work. It made me cry more. Eventually, sleep intervened, mercifully.

I woke up to the sound of the phone. I couldn't answer it. My twilight state of mind had robbed me of the strength to lift my heavy arms. I went back to sleep. Close to midnight, hunger woke me up. I staggered to the kitchen and found my refrigerator empty. Out of desperation, I settled for a slice of stale bread that I found on the counter.

A few minutes after midnight, I called Wendy. Her telephone rang twice, before I hung up. I did not know what I would have said to her. I picked up the telephone receiver again and called her back. My hands shook as I waited for her to answer. All sorts of silly platitudes went through my head as I searched for a catchy phrase to open the conversation with Wendy. Whatever I said, it wouldn't solve my problem.

"Hello," came Wendy's sleepy voice.

"I'm very sorry, Wendy, but I have to talk to you about a big problem."

"What's wrong Joseph? Are you sick?" she asked.

"It's worse than that, Wendy."

"Stop torturing me and tell me what's wrong," she said.

"The college cancelled my admission and scholarship. I've been crying all day," I said as tears flowed from my eyes again.

"Oh no! How could they do that? I can't believe it. Listen, Joseph, I'll be over there as soon as I can. You need me. I'm coming."

"Thank you, but you don't have to come over. I'll be fine," I said.

"I'll be there soon," she said, and hung up.

Waiting for her, I wondered how she would escape from her house without attracting her parents' attention. My biggest worry was her father trailing her to my apartment. The possibility of a physical confrontation with Mr. Crane terrified me more than my sudden loss of academic identity. Fear gripped me as I thought about the ugly outcome of a confrontation with Mr. Crane.

To alleviate my anxiety, I changed my thoughts to Wendy's body, and went down an exhaustive mental list of her physical attributes. Apart from my impious feelings, the emotional excitement from the realization that she would risk everything to see me was almost orgasmic.

Wendy leapt out of her car and ran into my arms. She kissed every part of my face before I was able to close my apartment front door. We held each other and wept. Sorrowful wailing overwhelmed us, and every attempt we made to regain our composure failed. We took turns wiping each other's tears.

She came inside. Wendy looked at me mournfully before she took off her nightgown.

"I want more than kisses tonight. Take me. I'm yours. Make love to me," she said, as she took my hand and placed it on her left breast. "You're mine, and I want to surrender my virginity to you. I promised to give it to the man that would be mine forever. You're all I want. We can make tonight a special one, for us, and may the rest of our nights be special for eternity." She pressed the palm of her right hand firmly on my hand that rested on her left breast until I could feel the rapid pulsation of her heart. "Please, Joseph, let's pretend that only the two of us exist. Forget this hateful world." Her crying became uncontrollable as she rambled on to incoherence.

"Wendy! Wendy! Listen to me." I felt like a hypocrite with the speech I was about to make because of my yearning for her. "This isn't the right situation to break your pledge. We're not getting married tonight, and I'm not going to let you break the promise you made to yourself to wait because of my plight. You may hate me in the morning after coitus, and that's not what I want for us. Whatever happens after tonight, let's maintain our dignity and respect for each other." Wendy suddenly stopped crying.

I felt relieved until she said, "You're really stupid, Joseph. What do you mean by coitus? Why couldn't you say that I would regret things in the morning after you fucked me? There, I said it for you, Saint Joseph." In an acerbic tone, she added, "Maybe you don't find me as attractive as you claim."

"I thought you came here to talk about my medical school admission mess, but it seems you've managed to turn it into an exercise in seduction," I said.

"I'm guilty as accused, but I want you to remember one thing tonight. I can't live in this town without you. We can move to France and go to school there. After all, there's too much hatred and intolerance in this small town." She held my face very close to hers and continued. "Please, come with me to France, where we can live peacefully."

To run away with Wendy. When all I had left was my pride. "Before you arrived here tonight, I thought about joining the French Foreign Legion. Stupidly, I felt that you may not want me anymore because I lost my place in your medical school entering class. But seriously, why should you run away with me? You have a guaranteed position in medical school this fall. I won't let you give it away just to be with me. I'll find something to do until I can apply to other medical schools next year." I kissed her lips, her nose, and her cheeks.

"You're crazy, Joseph. I remember the time you threatened to join the legion and move to France to be with me," she said, and snickered, before she added, "It sounded romantic then, but now it sounds dumb. Why are you fascinated with the French Foreign Legion, anyway?"

"In my current state of mind, a stint in the military might be just what I need," I said.

"Forget about the Foreign Legion and talk about reality. Tell me what you plan to do that includes me?" she demanded.

"I'm meeting with Professor Ezir tomorrow. I hope he has some ideas. Can you stay with me until we graduate?" I said.

"Stay with you? My father would have you arrested for kidnapping," she said.

"You're an adult. You can make your own decisions," I said.

"If you marry me then we can live together," she retorted.

"That would be an easy path to suicide. Your father would have me hung from a tree," I said.

"That's a provocative statement Joseph. My father may even be a bigot, but saying he would have you hanged is cold," she said angrily.

"I didn't mean to imply he would have me hung for a racial reason," I lied, and moved slightly away from her.

"Like I offered to you before, I'll discuss your admission problem with Daddy and see if there's anything he could do for you," she said as she moved closer to me.

Yes, surely her father could talk to the admissions board. Exert some influence. But would he do it? "Since he doesn't want me near you, he might just applaud the medical school's decision," I stated.

"How could you say such a thing, Joseph! Are you insinuating that he has something to do with the decision?" she retorted.

"I didn't say that. I was only stating the facts as I know them. He doesn't like me and doesn't want me around you. That's all I said."

"Forget it. I'll approach Daddy and demand that he tell me what he knows about your predicament," she said. Wagging her finger in my face, she added, "I'll prove you're wrong about my Daddy." She stormed out of my apartment.

Chapter 17

I STOOD IN MY LIVING ROOM reliving the previous night with Wendy. Even the enticing aroma of her perfume, which usually lingered on for days after her visit, had deserted my lonely apartment. I folded her last pair of slacks in my closet and placed it in a box. How would things have turned out if I had proposed to her, as she had requested so many times? I found the silver bracelet she'd given me, and put it in the box.

I slept for only two hours before the early morning sun peeped through an opening in my curtains and dotted the worn carpet in my living room.

Two days of waiting in vain for proof from Wendy forced me to accept the inevitable. I decided to chart my life without her. Her relegation of our love hurt me more than the college board of trustees' abrogation of my medical school admission. Without Wendy's help or any legal recourse, I had to accept my fate.

Class attendance was never an issue for me, but I spent the rest of my time in my apartment. What difference would it make? Everyone knew about my predicament. I avoided going to places where I would run into people who knew me. I had no appetite. Occasionally, I walked through the cafeteria without ordering any food.

I wanted to stay in North Carolina, but Professor Ezir advised me to apply to out-of-state universities. He guessed that I must have incurred the wrath of powerful people there, but would not elaborate. For days, Professor Ezir made frantic telephone calls to find a university that would accept me for the upcoming academic year. Eventually, he found a program willing to consider my late application. He spoke with one of his former protégés on my behalf before he handed the telephone over to me.

"Hello Joe. Congrats on your upcoming graduation," Professor Mohr said. He was one of my formers teacher at North Carolina before he became the chairman of the biophysics department in Michigan.

"Thanks, Professor Mohr. I feel good about graduating, but I suddenly have nowhere to go in the fall," I said.

Professor Ezir left the room, giving me some privacy and preserving his deniability.

"We're offering you a place in my department with paid tuition and a monthly stipend in return for some teaching," Professor Mohr said.

"Are you serious?" I yelled. I calmed down quickly, and added, "Thank you for helping me, Professor Mohr!"

"We're offering you what you deserve. Not a charity. I'm sure you'll contribute immensely to the department," Professor Mohr said.

It felt good to be wanted, even though it was not a medical school admission offer.

"Thank you, thank you, Professor Mohr," I wasn't sure what else to say. I could have gone on forever thanking him for the offer.

Three days before my graduation from college, I signed a letter of acceptance to the Biophysics doctoral program in Michigan.

*   *   *

Our campus was abuzz with festivities the week of graduation. Old and young found common ground in the endless merriment. My soul yearned for inner peace. I skipped all the pre-graduation ceremonies. The confines of my apartment offered me solitude, and I used the time for introspection.

Two days before graduation, I received my graduation clearance letter from the registrar's office. I went to see Professor Ezir. He was sitting in his chair with the squeaking wheels and rolling around his office doing his filing. As he puffed on his stogy, the smoke rose to the ceiling tiles and scattered. I looked at him more keenly. He must have enjoyed smoking. For the first time, the pungent tobacco odor did not bother me as much as it had in the past.

Professor Ezir took the last puff of his cigar and asked, "My boy, are you ready for cap and gown day?"

"Yes, I am. I'm here to thank you for everything you've done for me over the past three years," I said.

"There is no reason to thank me. You've been a good student, and it'll be my pleasure to present the school honors gold medal to you on Saturday. I'm very proud of you. I hope you continue to do well in the future." He shook my hand and hesitated before he continued. "I don't really know all the details about what happened to your medical school admission, but it almost ended my career at this institution." He sighed repeatedly as he spoke. "No one is willing to talk about it, but it seems someone wants you gone from this school and the state of North Carolina."

"I'm very sorry, Professor Ezir, but whatever I did, I wasn't aware of it."

"Wherever you go, try to be careful, and stay away from rich girls."

So that was it. The resurgence of his jocular mood helped alleviate some of the tension. "You're like my father in so many ways. He lets me figure things out by myself. I'll always be grateful for all you've done for me, and I'll try to avoid girls from rich families, like the Crane's," I said with a smile. Professor Ezir's face beamed with the widest smile I had ever seen on his face.

"I recommend you take some time off after graduation." He lit another fat cigar. "I'll see you during the graduation ceremony."

I left his office and walked out into the breezy sunny day. I would have considered it a perfect day, if not for my travails.

* * *

Wendy's absence from my daily activities created a void in my life. As graduating seniors perambulated around campus with their family and friends, I watched them from a small bench on a ridge I called 'Wendy's Crest.' I thought about her birthday when Wendy and I tipped the bench backward trying to kiss. I could not help but smile for the first time in days. The irony of my situation was that the same love that had nurtured me had also left me vulnerable.

I took a long walk across the east and west campuses after I left the crest. On reaching the medical school section, the memory of my dash to the basic science building for my interview was so vivid that I panted. I walked up to one of the limestone pillars of the building and embraced it, a symbolic goodbye to Wendy. I quickly looked around to make sure that no one had seen me embrace a pillar. The steps on the long walkway were no match for my legs as I ascended with long strides. Peering into one of the lecture halls adorned with mahogany paneling and semicircular desks, I picked out the desk that I wanted to share with Wendy. A sudden sensation of emptiness came over me as tears trickled down my face.

Instead of walking away, I ran from the basic medical science building until I was more than one hundred yards away. I looked back at the building and broke down. It dawned on me that my fantasy about studying with Wendy would never come true. I sat on the grass and supported my chin with my hands. Academic excellence alone was not enough for me.

* * *

The airport was desolate when I arrived. The amber street lights came on. I waited in the arrival section for more than an hour before Gina's flight touched down at eight p.m. She stepped out of the airplane wearing a yellow sundress and flip-flops. Florida had changed her style so much that I worried she wouldn't fit in anymore in my conservative college town. We ran toward each other and embraced for a long time.

"My, my, my, you look more handsome than the last time I saw you," she said.

"You're the one who looks smoking, my dearest sister," I said in a halting voice.

"So, this is what you've become since I left you here, a local Joe," she said with a mocking laugh.

"I'm trying my best to fit in," I replied.

"Before you continue the fake jive talk, if that's what you're trying to do, where's Wendy? I thought she would come with you."

"I haven't seen Wendy lately, but there are more pressing issues for me than her. I'll tell you everything later," I said.

"What happened between you two?" she asked.

"I don't think it's anything serious, because she has not told me about it yet," I joked.

"You don't seem to manage relationships well. Wendy was the first, then Francesca, and then Wendy again. Now Wendy is gone. What the heck is going on with you, Joseph?" she said angrily.

"My problem with Wendy has to do with her father, and he'll never get over his bigotry. She's actually the victim, because she's forced to choose between her family and me." I was vague because I didn't want to tell her about my medical school predicament until after the graduation ceremony.

We retrieved her luggage and walked to my car holding hands like two small children. I turned the radio on and reminisced about my trip to Florida. Halfway to her parents' house, she grew quiet and rarely looked my way. She fell asleep. I turned the volume down and hummed out of sync. Gina woke up when I stopped the car in front of her parents' house. She looked at me and said, "Why did you let me fall asleep in the car?"

"You were tired, so I left you alone. I assumed you'd studied a lot this past semester and needed a nap before you met your parents," I said.

"Oh!" was the only thing she said as she walked to the front door. She searched for her house key for a long time before she gave up, and rang the doorbell.

Gina's mother screamed when she opened the door. She hugged and held on to her daughter while I stood holding Gina's luggage. "I'm sorry, Joseph, but I haven't seen my daughter since Christmas," she said. She gave me a quick hug.

"I guess I deserve only a leftover hug," I said. Gina's mother pulled me by the shirt and gave me another hug. We walked into their living room where I set Gina's suitcase down. The hugging continued when the rest of the family assembled in the living room. It appeared that nothing had changed in the household since I'd last visited. Predictably, they all settled into their favorite chairs. I sat down on one of the unclaimed chairs and watched the matriarch's ardent effort to provide snacks to anyone who was willing to eat that late. Every time Gina's mother came back to the living room with a different plate of food, she went over to her daughter and hugged her. It was amusing watching Gina, usually an unapologetic firebrand, become placid as her mother showered her with attention. I felt jealous of the maternal fellowship Gina had with her mother. Even amidst all the people in the living room, I felt lonesome.

My mother would have been there for me, if I had not chosen loneliness to prove that I could make it on my own. Right then, I needed my own mother to pamper me.

I was not sure if it was maternal instinct or coincidence, but Gina's mother came over to me and placed her hand on my shoulder. My body vibrated as though electrical energy passed through it, and when I looked up, she kissed my cheek. Instinctively, I stood up and hugged her. As she patted my hair, I closed my eyes and imagined that she was my own mother. She held my hand and led me into her kitchen. "Everything OK with you?" Gina's mother asked me once we were alone in the kitchen.

"Yes, ma'am. Except, I'm probably overwhelmed with the upcoming graduation ceremony," I said. My answer even confused me. Was it an affirmative answer, or a negative one?

"It's unfortunate your parents won't be able to attend your graduation," she said.

"It was partly my fault. I didn't inform them about it in time. I didn't see the need for them to travel six thousand miles to attend a graduation ceremony," I said.

"We'll be there tomorrow for you. You're a part of our family," she said and hugged me tight. She handed me a piece of cake, and said, "Make sure you eat your cake with a full glass of milk." It was her usual instruction, and I couldn't find the courage to ask the revered matriarch why a full glass of milk was necessary with her scrumptious cake.

Gina had fallen asleep when we returned to their living room. Since I did not want to keep Gina from going to bed, I announced to the family that I had to leave to be ready for graduation day. I walked over to Gina's father, shook his hand, and said, "Thank you sir for having me in your home."

"Think of us as your family. You can come by any time you want. You don't always have to wait until Gina comes home before you visit," he said.

I walked over to Gina, who was still asleep, and woke her up. "Sleepyhead, I'll pick you up in the morning for the 'honors graduates' breakfast with the school president," I said as I pulled her up from the chair.

"Why don't I go with you tonight so you don't have to drive over here in the morning?" she asked.

"I don't mind coming by to pick you up in the morning. I'm sure your parents want you home with them tonight," I said. She staggered, trying to walk with me to the door.

"I can drive my mother's car to the event. Don't worry about picking me up," Gina said.

I said to Gina's father, "Remember to be at the school at least an hour before the ceremony starts so you can get good seats."

"Don't worry, Joseph," Gina's mother said reassuringly. "I'll drag his butt over there early tomorrow."

Gina closed the door behind me. I walked into the dark humid night alone, and wished that I had stayed with them longer. I closed my squeaky car door, and drove off. My mind wandered to the graduation ceremony. What if I didn't see Wendy graduate? I would receive a biochemistry degree and Wendy a biology degree, so I reasoned that they should seat us close to each other during the ceremony. The thought pacified me temporarily.

Instead of driving directly to my apartment, I went by the Medical Center to catch a last glimpse of the place before going on to my uncertain future. I reached the traffic light in front of the medical center and stepped on the brake. I stared at the lighted bold letters on the wall, which should have read, 'Crane-University Medical Center.'

I was in a battle of hegemony with a behemoth who had immense financial and political power. Even if I had known how rich the Cranes were, it would not have changed my feelings toward Wendy.

But it did change the way I felt about myself: I felt inadequate and conquered as I drove away from the medical center. In my new state of mind, all the songs from every radio station irritated me, so I turned the radio off. I wallowed in reflective silence, unaware whether my car was standing still or rolling along. Somehow, I managed to reach my apartment without any mishap. I parked my car, and looked around to see if Wendy was waiting for me to come home, but she was not there.

On the eve of my graduation, I dreaded going inside my lonely apartment.

Chapter 18

THERE WAS NOTHING SPECIAL about the morning of the commencement day. The sun rose at the expected time, and the early morning humidity was typical for a North Carolina summer. My warm morning shower did not last longer than the usual fifteen minutes, and sweat poured down my face after I dried my body.

The pervasive blend of happiness and desolation confused me. I tried to concentrate on happy events, but my thoughts wandered back to my rescinded medical school admission. I knew that only direct intervention from a supreme power could change my lot, but none came to my rescue.

I stepped out of my car, composed myself, and smiled at anyone who acknowledged me. It was my alter ego, the honors graduate, who walked into the festooned school cafeteria. I took a deep breath, and looked around at the walls decorated with colorful banners. Abundant balloons lined the ceiling, while others tethered to small heavy objects rose to the height of their strings. Appropriately. In life, we only soar to our own level.

Dr. Everly, the smiling president of the college, and some members of the school board occupied seats on a temporary dais, while subdued classical music punctuated the noise made by the guests. More honor students and their parents filtered in. I watched for my Wendy in their midst. Instead, I saw Gina and hurried to her table, but my eyes continued to wander around the expanse of the cafeteria.

"My you're restless this morning," Gina said.

I shifted my chair closer to her to avoid yelling over the background noise. "I'm not restless. I just want this stupid program to start on time," I said.

"You contradict yourself," she said.

As my eyes darted around the hall again, I saw Wendy walk in with her family. Her father went up to the podium to sit with the president of the college, while her mother and brother looked around for empty seats. I stood up, and beckoned to Wendy to come to my table. Her mother saw me first and waved. She whispered to Wendy as they walked over to my table.

"Hello Mrs. Crane. You look younger every day," I said as I shook her hand. To my surprise, Wendy hugged Gina before she came to me. It was obvious that Gina was surprised, because before she sat down, I read her lips, "What's going on?" when Wendy turned away.

"Hello Joseph," Wendy said, as she sat down. She did not shake my hand or hug me. Her mother watched our interaction very closely and smiled.

"You look smashing today, Wendy," I said.

"Thank you," Wendy said.

After a brief moment, I moved my chair closer to Wendy. Somehow, we stood up at the same time and hugged very tightly. Surprisingly, she whispered, "I love you Joseph." I closed my eyes and took a big whiff of her perfume. It must have overpowered my sense of reasoning because I kissed her lips and unfortunately smudged her red lipstick. She tried to wipe my lips with her fingers, but I reached out and grabbed her wrist. Her mother observed us with a frown. Gina rolled her eyes. I lowered my hand and led Wendy away to the back of the cafeteria. We paused in front of the wall that separated the two restrooms, and I kissed her passionately.

We were still kissing when I heard, "You're worse than an ape. Look at your disgusting behavior in public. No sense of decency even after all the years we tried to civilize you." The voice sounded familiar, and I knew that I was the one he was referring to.

Wendy stopped kissing me and pushed me away.

It was a big mistake to turn around, because he slapped my face so hard that it dazed me. I saw traces of sparkling lights.

"Stop it, Daddy," I heard Wendy scream, as I rubbed my eyes.

"Stay away from my daughter. Find your own kind. I want you gone from this institution as soon as possible. If I see you around my daughter again, I'll call the police." He grabbed my shirt collars and added, "It's obvious that you are not ready for civilized society."

Wendy intervened and held him back.

"Mr. Crane, maybe you forgot that Wendy is an adult, and she can make her own decisions. The only reason I would let you get away with slapping me is that I love your daughter, and I refuse to embarrass her in public place in the uncivilized way that you just did." I forced a smiled, and added, "You must really feel big, slapping me because your daughter can't stay away from me. What else are you going to do to me? Maybe you should arrange to have me lynched tonight?"

"Joseph. Stop saying foolish things," Wendy said, standing between her father and me.

"Listen boy, I want you out of this place today after you get your diploma. Don't ever come back to this town, if you know what's good for you." He pointed his finger in my face as Wendy yanked his other arm.

"Sorry sir. I forgot you own this town. Wendy, remind me to send your papa a thank you note for letting me stay in his town for three years," I said. If it were not for Wendy, I would have punched him. "By the way, Mr. Big, I have nothing left to lose since I lost your daughter to your bigotry. So be careful how you approach me," I added.

"Joseph, why don't you leave and let me talk to my father alone," Wendy said. Her makeup was running down her cheeks, and her eyes were red. I felt sorry for the trouble I had caused her.

"I need to use the bathroom, if your father would permit me to take a leak," I said.

"In the jungle where you came from, boy, did you need a bathroom to do your business?" he said.

"Thank you my master for teaching me your civilized way," I said, as I walked into the men's room.

"I'm glad the medical school terminated your admission and kicked your ass out of this institution," he said, after I closed the bathroom doors. When I heard what he said, I opened the bathroom door and came out to challenge him again.

"I knew you were responsible for that. To keep me away from your daughter, you found it more expedient to change the medical school rules after I had already signed the letter of acceptance. I hope you receive your punishment in hell." I was so angry that I kept pacing around hoping that Wendy would step aside to allow me to punch his face.

Mr. Crane merely looked at me and grinned. Wendy questioned her father, and he sighed. "Daddy! You didn't!" But she kept shielding her father.

It was one of life's ironies. Wendy was five foot three, protecting husky Mr. Crane, who was probably six foot four. I was barely six foot, and my English teacher in high school once called me a "lanky boy."

Mr. Crane's smug smile riled me so much that I gave up on using the bathroom. I went back to my table and sat next to Gina. She looked at me, and asked, "What happened to you?"

"I was accosted by Mr. Crane in front of the bathroom while kissing his daughter," I whispered to Gina.

"We should leave this table and go somewhere else to sit. They own this town. You should avoid antagonizing them since you're going to be here for medical school," Gina said.

"They rescinded my admission to the medical school because of late changes in the school policy," I said. Gina cupped her wide-open mouth with her hand. She looked at me with solemn eyes, and could not speak.

She leaned her head toward me, and whispered, "I knew you would get yourself into trouble with Wendy. Rich people don't like people like us coming into their families and stirring things up. They're afraid you want to take their money away." Gina stopped whispering when Mrs. Crane turned around and looked in our direction. When Mrs. Crane looked away, Gina continued, "Is it safe to stay here for the program?"

"Tell me, what crime have I committed that makes my presence here unsafe?" I asked Gina, as she rubbed my knees.

"I agree, you haven't done anything wrong by being here to celebrate your graduation, but we should think about your safety first," Gina said.

Wendy came back to our table with a drawn face. She tapped her mother on the shoulder and then whispered in her ear. Mother and daughter left the dining room together.

A few minutes before the program started, Wendy and her mother rejoined us. Wendy's mother looked distraught, but she managed to feign a smile.

As though a mischievous spirit possessed me, I pulled my chair closer to Wendy, and put my arms around her. She gave me a cold stare, and then turned her head away.

Mrs. Crane lowered her head and whispered. "I apologize for my husband's behavior. Wendy told me what happened in front of the restroom."

"You don't have to apologize, Mrs. Crane. You've always been supportive. I sincerely appreciate your goodwill," I said. I tried to fake a smile, but tears flowed instead. Mrs. Crane began to shed tears too, and reached out to hold my hand.

"Thank you, Mom, for being nice to Joseph," Wendy said, after initially ignoring the exchange between her mother and me.

*   *   *

I watched the school president leave the podium, after the breakfast ended. I decided to talk to Mr. Crane. As I approached him, he wiped the sweat off his forehead.

"I'm very sorry for the anguish I caused you during your mother's birthday party. Your daughter wanted to impress her, but didn't know you found meringue offensive." His damp forehead and trembling hands gave me joy as I spoke to him, because I felt that he was afraid of me in front of everyone watching us on the podium. "About the incident earlier today, you owe me an apology. I hope you'll desist from ruining other peoples' lives with your wealth and power." Just then, Mrs. Crane joined us. She appeared anxious.

"John, I heard about the incident in front of the bathroom from Wendy. Sometimes you forget about your position in this town, and act as if you're still in college. I'm not going to be a part of this. You deliberately undermined a young man's quest to better himself."

Mr. Crane interrupted her speech. "I want him out of our lives. As far as I'm concerned, he can go back to his jungle in Africa and leave my daughter alone. That's all I have to say." But it was Mr. Crane who left the dining hall first. His wife went after him.

I rejoined Gina, who had watched us from a distance. She informed me that Wendy left as soon as I walked to the podium. I sat in the empty dining hall with Gina.

"Tell me what you said to that pig," Gina said.

"Let's get out of here, sis. I'll tell you about it later." We headed to the botanical garden trails.

"Why not tell me what's going on, before I go crazy," Gina said, and stopped walking. "Tell me, or I'll stand here until you do," her voice quavered as she spoke.

"I came to a country I thought was enlightened, but discovered that humans are the same everywhere. In my country, it was the Muslims attacking Christians because of ignorance and religious prejudice. In your country, it is racial prejudice. It wasn't my goal to fall in love, but my heart betrayed me. How do I move on from here? I mean, will I ever fall in love again? I don't think so, Gina," I said.

Gina held my hand and wept. I tried to console her, but she walked to a bench and sat down. Without any prodding from her, I told her all the sundry details of my misfortunes.

On the surface, the beautiful botanical garden looked unchanged since the first day I'd walked through it with Wendy. Even after all the seasonal changes, birds still remembered how to intersperse their tweets with songs, and the stream continued to carry fallen leaves to their final destinations. Squirrels darted from one side of the road to the other, and occasionally displayed their skills in scaling trees of varying sizes. The natural events in the garden were mostly the same, but the participants had changed over time because of attrition. In the microcosm of the North Carolina college campus, my role had ended, but others would take my place. As I walked with Gina back through the ornate garden entrance, I reflected on the things that I had done wrong in my life.

To love someone is to give of yourself, knowing that you'll never get that part of yourself back. I left a part of me in that beautiful garden in Central North Carolina. I had no desire to return to reclaim it. It was in the spring of my life, my North Carolina, where I began my new life, and where my lost youth would remain eternally young. As the end drew near, I implored the heavens to cleanse me with their rainfall, and the sun to rejuvenate me perpetually.

* * *

The end of my quest in North Carolina finally came that evening. I graduated with the highest honors, and received three commemorative honor gold medals. Wendy graduated with honors and received a gold medal. As she walked down from the podium, I went to her and ran the back of my hand on her cheeks. She kissed my hand gently, lifted it up, and placed it on her shoulder. "You know I'm yours, if you would only ask me. If you leave without me, never claim that my father kept us apart. Joseph, it's your reluctance to fully commit your love to me that separates us," she said as we hugged.

"I can't ask you to be mine and give up your family. It's better to keep what you already have, than to take a chance on me. You'll always be with me, wherever I am, as long as the sun still shines, and there's air I can breathe freely. When you think of me, remember that the two of us own the beautiful Carolina sun. Our love and friendship will last until the end of time." I was barely done when her parents came to congratulate her. Her father expressed his ongoing displeasure with me, but I ignored him.

I walked away, and the proud parents took over. Their right to be with her, as dutiful parents, superseded my right as her undefined companion. Since I knew that my time with her had ended, I never looked back. There would not be a tomorrow for us; instead, the memories of our past would sustain me for as long as I could remember the love we had.

Chapter 19

MY UNCEREMONIOUS DEPARTURE from North Carolina, and midnight arrival in Detroit airport added the curse of a migraine headache to my worries. The bright sunshine I once cherished became my greatest hindrance. For days, I could not go outside of my apartment during the day because of the propensity for my throbbing frontal headache to worsen. Worst of all, I could not see well in the sun. Defensively, I spent most of my time indoors until graduate school started in early August.

On the first day of graduate school, I sat in the quietness of the general chemistry laboratory alone and read the handbook given to me as a graduate teaching assistant. It was a position that paid my tuition, and included a meager monthly allowance.

I only had thirty minutes before my first group of freshmen showed up for their first lab. When I looked around the room, all the chemicals and experimental wares for the session were in place, but my mind was far away in North Carolina. I wondered where Wendy sat in the main medical school lecture hall, though I knew that it would not change my beleaguered life.

As my freshmen chemistry students walked into the laboratory, some of them came up to me to introduce themselves. The introductions were brief until a tall, scrawny student with a self-haircut asked me, "Where do you come from, teach?" Before I could answer his question, he asked another one. "Why did you choose our drab city for graduate school?"

Instead of providing him with an honest answer, I conveniently smiled, and carried on with other issues of academic importance. Once all the students were at their workstations, I started the session. I introduced myself to the class, and laid out the laboratory rules. Most of my rules were revised versions of Professor Ezir's laboratory guidelines.

Surprisingly, my headache eased when the laboratory session started, but my mind would not stop wandering back to North Carolina. At times, I closed my eyes and imagined sitting next to Wendy in her classroom at the medical school. Sudden sadness overwhelmed me, as I recited my liberation mantra inaudibly, "I'm only in this exile for one year," several times. That was what I had decided about Michigan when I first arrived there. How could I love a place that was a stopgap for an inadvertent academic sabbatical? However, I took my assignment as a graduate teaching assistant seriously.

Regardless of my predicament, I was eager to share my knowledge of chemistry with my freshman class. I went from one bench to the next and helped students with their experiments. As I made my way through the room, I stopped at the counter of a quiet black girl who was working alone. Her virtuous face looked too young to be in college. She fumbled with her papers, and almost spilled the contents of her beaker when I stood beside her.

"How's your experiment going?" I asked.

She avoided looking at me. "Good, sir." I smiled and wondered when I became a sir to college students. I left her side and went back to my desk.

At the conclusion of the laboratory session, the black girl stayed behind and played with her laboratory notebook. I watched her for more than five minutes before I walked over to her workstation, and asked, "Do you need more time with your experiments?"

"I have finished my experiments, but I don't want to go home," she said.

"So you live off campus?" I asked.

"Yes, sir. I live at home with my mother and her new husband," she said with a sardonic voice.

A lot of things went through my mind, but I felt that it was not my responsibility to inquire about what was obviously not an academic issue.

"I hope you sort things out with your parents, if you have issues at home," I said as I left her workstation and walked toward the door. "I have to lock the lab. We can finish our discussion in the hallway," I continued, opening the door. She walked out of the laboratory and stood in the hallway. I locked the door and walked down the hall. She followed me.

"Mr. Fafa. I have a terrible secret. My stepfather touches me at night when I go to sleep. My mother works the midnight shift, and I don't know how to tell her about it."

I felt angry about her tribulation, and my heart fluttered, as she continued.

"What he did to me last night scared me the most, but I acted as if I was sleeping." She shivered and jerked her shoulders. I sighed as I watched her actions.

"Why don't you go home and tell your mother about your stepfather before she goes to work tonight," I said. She looked at me and smiled. I tried not to smile back, but I could not help myself. Afterwards, I felt stupid about my smile when I felt anger inside.

"You don't know my mother. She'll side with him. She warned me not to cause trouble when I moved in with them, after my real father died in a car accident two months ago. She loves her new husband more than me," she said.

"What do you want me to do for you, Miss George?" I asked. She didn't say anything, so I continued, "You can always move into the dorm, or find your own place. You're probably older than eighteen?"

"I thought you knew my name, Mr. Fafa. I'm Mavenka, but my Mom calls me Mave," she said.

"You have a beautiful name, Mavenka," I said.

She smiled and blushed. "Sir, could you please come to my house and tell my mother about my stepfather because I have no money to live on my own," she asked with a sad look .

"Are you serious? It would be inappropriate for me to get involved in a domestic issue involving a student," I said.

"So you don't want to help me," she said. Tears rolled down her face.

"Tell your mother what your stepfather did to you, and let me know what she says. You may also consider filing a report with the police after you tell your mother about it." Before I finished what I had to say, I felt that I should do more for Mave but I did not know how to help her. Mave walked away, leaving me feeling guilty. I stood where she left me and deliberated on what I might have done to help her.

* * *

Mavenka did not show up for class after her first day. Her absence from my laboratory group tore me apart. I wondered what happened to her. Despite the fact that no one appointed me as her guardian, I felt that it was my obligation to protect her.

My life partially returned to its baseline until one Friday afternoon. The department secretary brought a brown paper bag to the laboratory and left it on my desk. I peeled off the note that was attached to it and read it. "Listen to Brainy Smurf and you will know what happened to me, Mave." My heart sunk as I read the note several times. I could not decipher what she meant. The "Smurfs" cartoon program was popular in 1980 and I had occasionally watched the Saturday morning babble. However, the familiar fluffy doll with white hat and blue body in the brown bag did not offer any clues about Mavenka's physical condition, or her state of mind. I stopped torturing myself and pushed the brown bag to the side of the desk. The mystery that the brown bag held remained unsolved.

Mavenka was my first major failure as a graduate student, and it made me question my preparedness to mentor undergraduates. For too long, I had felt victimized, but now the victim was a hapless student who could not find succor, not in her own home, not from her laboratory graduate assistant. Rather than continuing to wallow in self-pity, I immersed myself in the education and mental growth of my students.

It was my turn to nurture young, impressionable students, and that task required fortitude.

*   *   *

The harsh Michigan winter seemed to conspire with my negative opinion of the state, and kept me indoors apart from the walk from my apartment to the biochemistry department. I enjoyed the time I spent outside the state travelling for my medical school admission interviews.

After visiting different parts of the country, and even Toronto, Canada for interviews, I settled on a school that offered me a full academic scholarship. To keep my mind engaged while I waited for medical school enrollment the following fall, I resorted to spending long hours in the public library after my studies, listening to classical music. I had no interest in any type of social life on campus because of my reprehensible attitude that Michigan was my prison. I was also in love with Wendy and could not bear the thought of going out with anyone else.

The awful winter weather eventually abated. The spring season that followed was not as momentous as the ones I had experienced in North Carolina.

On a lonely Friday night, I succumbed to a yearning for social interaction and attended a biochemistry graduate student's birthday party. She was a girl I passed in the hallway several times, and I was surprised that she invited me to her party.

There was barely an empty space when I arrived, and meandering through the crowded room to find the host was a futile exercise. I became tired of searching for Monica and leaned against the wall.

Most students who arrived late couldn't get into Monica's apartment, and at one point, it appeared that there were more people in the hallway than in the apartment. Out of frustration, I headed to the kitchen for some refreshment, but couldn't find anything to drink. Trying to get out of the kitchen, I stepped on the foot of a beautiful young woman. Her scream blotted out the noise from the ragged loudspeakers shrieking disco sounds. She was tall, and athletically built. Her luscious neckline revealed an elegant gold necklace with sparkling gems, and her clothes conveyed an image of a privileged life. Professor Ezir's warning flashed through my mind.

"I'm sorry for stepping on your foot," I yelled out to her.

"It wasn't your fault. I should've kept my foot away from the floor," she joked. For someone that screamed when I stepped on her foot, her response surprised me.

"You don't look like one of us. I mean, you don't look like a poor graduate student," I said, staring at her necklace.

"Why don't you look at my face instead of staring at my chest?" she asked.

"I was admiring your necklace. That was the only thing I was checking out," I said. She rubbed her necklace with her right fingers.

"I'm Joseph Fafa, a graduate student in biophysics and biochemistry," I said.

"It's nice to meet you, Joseph. I'm Elaine." She paused, adding, "I'm a forensic psychiatry fellow at the University Medical Center."

"Forensic Psychiatry? What do you do?" I asked.

"Not the right place or situation to discuss what I do," she said with a restrained smile. It appeared that Elaine had no interest in talking to me.

"I hope you recover from the damage done by my big foot," I said.

I tried to find my way out of the apartment. I stopped to say hello to a fellow graduate student and noticed that Elaine was behind me.

Once we made it to the hallway, away from the noise, Elaine said, "Thank you for your concern about my foot, but I'm fine."

I smiled at her, and said, "I could've done major damage to your foot, but I'm glad you're OK."

"Biophysics and biochemistry, how many years will it take you to complete the PhD program?" Elaine asked.

"I'm only here for a few more months before I start medical school," I said.

"Neat," she said. I had no clue what she meant by *neat*. She walked on without saying anything further.

Elaine was close to thirty feet away from me when I said loudly, "I forgot to tell you. You look very nice tonight, Doctor Elaine." She stopped and turned around. I walked up to her, and added, "I really mean what I said about how good you look." She looked at me keenly from head to toe, and for a brief moment, she bore an uncanny resemblance to someone I left behind in North Carolina.

"Thank you for the compliment. It's Elaine." Her delivery was acerbic, not like Wendy's, to my delight. There would always be one Wendy in my life.

"I would like to ask you out, but I'm leaving Michigan soon. So, you're justified if you say no to me." My words came out wrong, but I could not take them back.

"You still have a few months here. Go ahead, ask me out," she said.

"Would you like to see a movie tomorrow with me?" I asked.

"Tomorrow's not a good day for me. I'll be in Mount Holly with some people. We have a cabin there, and I love the tranquil environment after a long week dealing with psychopaths. You're welcome to join us, if you want," she said.

"It sounds like fun, but how do I find the place?" I asked.

"You don't have to worry about getting hold of me. I'll ask Monica about you. If she says you're a good guy, I'll find a way to reach you," she said.

"If Monica doesn't know where I live, how will you find me?" I asked.

"Give me your telephone number," she said.

"I don't have a pen or a piece of paper to write my telephone number, but my apartment is in Canfield Towers, number 413. I guess you'd have to come over tomorrow and buzz my apartment," I said.

"Expect me at your place around 10 a.m., if I don't change my mind," she said and walked away.

*   *   *

I was sure Elaine would come for me that Saturday morning because of how she smiled. My foolish male ego. Excited, I got ready earlier than necessary. It was a sunny, cold day, but that did not diminish my anticipation. Waiting for Elaine, I imagined a serene cabin tucked inside a wooded mountainside with a crackling fireplace. My eyes fixated on my clock as I paced around my apartment. After a while, my apartment felt too constricting, so I went down to the lobby to wait for her.

It was around 10:15 a.m. when Elaine showed up. She was wearing a tight pair of blue jeans and a thick blue sweater.

"Good morning, Elaine. I'm glad you didn't change your mind," I said.

"Let's get out of here. We have a long drive ahead of us," she said. Once we reached her car, she said, "Please forgive me for my bad manners. I was so eager to get to Mount Holly that I forgot to say hello to you."

"Thank you for inviting me to Mount Holly," I said.

"I'll drive since you don't know your way around here," she said.

"I'm glad you plan to drive. I sold my car before I left North Carolina," I said.

"So you came from North Carolina? I thought you probably came from one of the Islands," she said.

"I came from Nigeria originally, but I did my undergraduate studies in North Carolina," I said.

"Your life sounds very fascinating. If you don't mind me asking, why are you wasting a year in Michigan before medical school?" she asked. When I hesitated, she glanced at me and smiled.

"It's a long story, Elaine, and I'm not sure if you have time to hear it all."

"We have an hour of driving ahead of us. I'm sure it's enough time to hear your story," she said.

"It's nothing profound. I mistakenly fell in love with the wrong girl, and her father didn't want me around. That's basically it," I said. She barely kept her eyes on the road as I spoke, and occasionally veered into the shoulder. I was nervous about her erratic driving, but I maintained my composure.

"Something tells me you're a better storyteller than that. Come on Joseph, I want the smut. Talk to me. You're killing me with your foolish suspense." Her voice rose to a crescendo as she spoke.

"I promise to fill in the details when we get to Mount Holly. You have to concentrate on your driving," I said. To my surprise, she agreed with my recommendation without any argument.

We talked about central Michigan and the lakes in the area until we made it to their cabin. It was not the shack I had imagined. The wooded cabin was an expansive lodge surrounded by more than twenty acres of prime land. Apart from a small lake by the side of the cabin, the rest of the land was a dense forest.

We walked inside, and I was awe stricken by the exquisite furnishings. The walls displayed stuffed animal trophies from successful hunting expeditions. In the inner part of the sitting room, two couples were drinking hard liquor by the fireplace. They rose to their feet when they saw us.

"Elaine, I thought you were coming alone," one of the women said.

"I was coming alone until I found this guy on my way here. He was lost in our state and needed my help," Elaine joked.

"Come on, Elaine, stop the comedy and introduce us to your friend," one of the men said.

"Well, my dear sisters, and not so dear brothers-in-law, this is Joseph. I met him last night at Monica's party. He wants to be a doctor like you alcoholics," Elaine said.

"So you met him last night and you travelled across the state with him today? Tell us a better story," one of her sisters said.

"Joseph, meet my sister India," Elaine said.

"She's telling the truth. We met last night when I stepped on her foot during the party," I said, as we shook hands.

"That's the new way to pick up women? Step on their feet, and then lasso them?" One of the brother-in-laws said.

"Meet Fred, my alcoholic brother-in-law. The other two clowns over there are my sister April and her husband Tom," Elaine said.

"You're drunk, Fred. Please try not to disgrace me in front of Joseph," Elaine requested as Fred staggered close to me.

"Welcome to our lodge, Joseph," India said, but April interjected, saying, "Welcome to our daddy's lodge." I shook their hands and they resumed their drinking.

Elaine walked into a side room and motioned to me to join her. It was a well-decorated den with all the amenities of modern living, including a telephone. The room was big enough to contain a couch, two chairs, and a desk. Photographs of a middle-aged man wearing a pith helmet hung neatly on all the walls. In some of the photographs, he rested his left foot and the butt of his rifle on his kill. Elaine watched me closely as I observed the photographs. They reminded me of my father. He was an avid hunter, and had a similar helmet.

"Interesting photographs?" Elaine asked.

"Sorry for being preoccupied. I'm just curious about the pith helmet proclivity with big game hunters, which as you may already know started during the European misadventure into Asia and Africa," I said.

"I have no idea what you're talking about. Who cares about pith helmets? Well, whatever turns you on," Elaine said.

I settled into the comfortable couch to give her the opportunity to sit next to me, but she did not fall for my scheme. She opted for a chair next to me.

"Those are the pictures my father took on one of his safaris in Africa," she said. With a taunting voice she asked, "Do you hunt, Joseph?"

"I don't kill animals unless it's for food," I whispered to her sarcastically. It was difficult to ascertain if I gave the answer she wanted from me. Regardless, she did not pursue that line of questioning.

"Tell me about your life in North Carolina. I'm eager to hear about the South," she said.

"There's nothing much to tell. I studied most of the time," I said.

"What types of girls do you like?" she asked.

"I never thought about the type I like. Well, I like beautiful girls. Is that a type?" I asked.

She smiled mischievously, and asked, "You have an aversion to ugly girls?"

"I don't know what you mean," I said with honesty. I did not know where she was headed with her questions.

"Do you value beauty more than character?" she asked. I was exasperated, but I tried to hide my true feelings. She looked at me, and added, "Some cultures value beauty in women more than any other qualities. Just curious about your culture."

I managed to smile and ignored her question.

"Are you upset with me?" she asked. She had waited for a while for an answer from me, but none came.

"I have no reason to be. You have the right to know stuff," I said.

"So, I can ask one more question? Do you prefer black girls to white girls?" she asked.

I sighed louder than I had ever done before out of frustration. A few 'unprintable' words came to mind, but I restrained myself. I looked straight at her, and said, "It's not the race that matters to me, but the individual. After all, we don't control who we meet in our lives." I wanted to say more, but decided that it would not be nice to curse at a beautiful woman.

She watched my reaction to her last question, and changed her approach to direct questions that required extensive answers. I protested after an hour of what I finally realized was an intrusive psychoanalysis. She watched me leave the den without any comment but her last question worried me. "So you think you can heal with your hands? Interesting." I could not remember telling her that I could heal with my hands. Was I hypnotized by Elaine?

I returned to the den and found her still sitting in the same spot. She was ready to complete her interrogation. She smiled, and asked, "You don't have any male friends?" I refused to answer any more questions. We did not have a friendly chat as I had wished. Instead, I became her clinical exercise. She finally gave up with her inquest and escorted me back to the living room. She whispered to her sisters and giggled. Watching them laugh, I felt violated.

April walked up to me and said, "I hope you don't take your friendship with Elaine seriously because she's utterly paranoid of men taking advantage of her. We knew what she was doing to you in the den. She's the one who's a psycho, not her patients."

"Some of her questions were okay," I said, trying to salvage the situation, as Elaine joined us.

"Don't listen to my sister. She tends to exaggerate a bit," Elaine said.

"You hate to face the truth about yourself, but you try to dig up dirt on other people," April said.

"When do we drive back to the city?" I said with a smirk.

"We're not going back yet. You have to see the area first. The best way is by ATV," Elaine said.

"I'll ride with you," I said.

We rode around the wooded area surrounding their property. Occasionally, I glanced at her and smiled. She had failed to uncover the fact that I wished it were Wendy sitting next to me.

As beautiful as Elaine was, and with all her desirable physical assets, I could not bring myself to desire her in any other way than as a casual acquaintance. It was too soon to get involved with anyone else after my debacle with Wendy.

* * *

At the end of spring semester, before the start of my chemistry laboratory session, Mavenka showed up. It was the first time I had seen her since she dropped her chemistry class. She would have looked as young as she did the first time she walked into my class were it not for her pink lipstick.

"Mavenka!"

"Hello Mr. Fafa. I hope I didn't disappoint you when I dropped chemistry," she said.

"I was more concerned about your safety than my chemistry class. Can't you tell I'm happy to see you again?" I said.

"I survived my home situation the best way I could," she said as she shook my hand.

"I'm very sorry about my aloofness," I said. "I had no experience with handling such matters, and I was going through a difficult time myself."

"It's all in the past, Mr. Fafa. My life is going to change for the better. I'm moving to Alabama to live with my grandma," she said. She opened a brown paper bag and retrieved a doll. The doll had long blond hair, a fluffy blue body, and was wearing a white dress. "Here's 'Smurfette' to keep 'Brainy Smurf' from getting lonely at your place. This ends my secret fantasy about you," she added.

I began to suspect that I'd done the right thing not to get involved. "You shouldn't have fantasies about your teachers," I said. "My name is Joseph, and not Mr. Fafa," I added.

"You're boring me, Mr. Fafa," she said jokingly.

"It's better to be boring than a pervert," I said.

"You're right, Mr. Fafa. I like you either way," she said, and then quickly added, "I mean, boring or not boring." She left the laboratory without saying goodbye as more students walked in.

*   *   *

I never saw Mavenka again, but floundered through my friendship with Elaine until I left Michigan. Even with the inordinate amount of time we spent together, I resisted all temptation to bond with Elaine.

That year was the most formative period in my life. Alone, in Michigan, I made the transition from teenager to man.

Twenty-nine years later

ON DECEMBER 25, 2009, I tended to patients in the intensive care unit of my local hospital very early in the morning. The first patient I visited was an elderly man who presented to the emergency department on Christmas Eve because of loss of consciousness while eating dinner with his family. He was a wiry fellow with frontal baldness and unpleasant disposition. Without a flicker of a smile, he looked me over as I walked into his room. His hospital demographic information stated that his name was John Smith, Sr.

"Mr. Smith, I'm Doctor Fafa. I heard you passed out last night," I said as I extended my hand to him. He ignored my hand, which I held out for a long time. Although it was Christmas day, I avoided saying happy holidays to him since I did not know his religious affiliation. I'd had a previous unpleasant experience with a Jehovah's Witness patient.

I turned his monitor screen to face me. He watched every move I made, and said, "What type of name is Fafa? You damn foreigners are everywhere. I want a good white, American doctor." He then turned around and looked away from me.

I checked the display of his blood pressure and heart rhythm before I walked to the opposite side of his bed to engage his eyes. "Mr. Smith, I am the doctor assigned to you from the emergency room last night, but you do have the right to request another doctor. Let your nurse know that you want a white, American doctor instead of me," I said. "I hope you get better soon," I added before I left his room.

After seeing other patients in the ICU, I walked by Mr. Smith's room and waved at him. "Come in, Doc," he said. I reluctantly walked into his room and extended my hand again. He shook my hand this time without any hesitation.

"What can I do for you?" I asked.

"Sit down, Doc. My nurse said you're the best specialist to see for my problem. Can you check me out?" he requested. "I'm a country boy, and sometimes I say the wrong thing," he added.

"I don't mind at all, but my skin color has not changed since you asked for a white doctor earlier," I said with a smile.

"I like you, Doc. You are a straight shooter," he said as he sat up on his bed. "Sit close to me, Doc, I have a secret to tell you," he added.

"I'm not a priest, in case you are looking for a confessor," I said jokingly.

"You're better than the priest we have here in the hospital. I have to talk to you. My mind has been troubled since I dropped bombs on German kids playing in front of their house on Christmas Eve of 1943. When I passed out last night, I heard those children's voices cursing me. They said I would go to hell soon. Doc, you look like a special man who can help me get over my nightmare," he pleaded while holding my two hands.

"I'm neither a psychiatrist nor a priest. We have priests on call who can help you. Are you a Catholic or a Protestant?" I asked.

"I belong to neither of the two. I just go to church, but I haven't been to one in a long time," he said as he let go of my hands.

"What do you think I could do for you, apart from finding out what caused you to pass out?" I asked.

"Heal me, Doc. I felt your power when I held your hands. I'm feeling good already," he said with seriousness.

"You probably felt my warm hands. I washed my hands with warm water before I came into your room." He looked at me attentively as I spoke. I could sense the fear in his eyes. I had seen that look in other patients' eyes before they died. After a thorough physical examination, I discussed my findings with him and reassured him that his medical condition shouldn't be life threatening.

"Stay with me, Doc, until my son gets here from North Carolina. He was only two hours away the last time he called." His nurse walked in as he spoke. I looked at the old man again and thought about my experiences with bigotry in North Carolina. His face and accent reminded me of an old barber in North Carolina who asked me to find a different place to "mow that kinky hair." It was not funny then, but I smiled as I thought about it now.

Years had passed and my wounded soul had healed. My responsibility had changed to that of a healer.

"I'm very sorry, Doctor Fafa, but my patient hasn't slept all night. He may need a sedative to calm him down."

"He sounds reasonable to me and only has a few concerns he needs addressed." I was about to go on break anyway. "I'll stay with him until his son gets here," I said. Mr. Smith let out a loud sigh and thereafter drifted into a deep sleep with loud snoring.

As I watched him sleep, my mind drifted to my parents, who had died in my absence many years before. I read the Christmas-day newspaper on his side table while he slept. After sitting by his bedside for an hour, I called and apologized to my wife for being late.

Due to my father's apparent depression after my mother died, I resorted to calling him every Sunday morning to talk about all the fun things we did as a family. The loud laughs that emanated from the telephone receiver during those Sunday morning chats resonated in my ears as I thought about my father. I closed my eyes, and the tears I had suppressed for fifteen years dropped in my lap. I wept for my inadequacy as a son. I was not with my parents when they needed me the most because of my hospital responsibilities. Although years had passed since their deaths, my guilty feeling had persisted.

My patient's son finally made it to the hospital. I left his father's bedside without waking him up. I felt that I had fulfilled my duty to him, as a good son should do, for he needed me that morning, not as his doctor, but as his son. Although he needed forgiveness for his moral lapse during a war he did not start, I only offered him the support I had the power to give.

* * *

On my way home from the hospital, I turned on the radio and my thoughts drifted to something more tangible. Pervasive health care reform was sweeping the country. People were debating about how to deal with the lack of adequate health care for all the citizens. Even in an advanced country like the US, adequate health care was a luxury. How could that be? A luxury is something one can forgo, but reliable medical care is a necessity. I prayed that we would find the courage to strive for universal coverage for the country as we reformed our broken health care system.

I relegated my encounter with Mr. Smith to the level of other unusual hospital experiences I had had until a few weeks after he left the hospital when I received a long letter from him about his spiritual journey with me. In his letter, he narrated his dreamlike state where he tried to leave his hospital room, but I stood by his door and stopped him from leaving. He said that I prevented every attempt he made to leave his hospital room and that he even fought me. Although his assertions were bizarre, his vivid narration of his experiences interested me enough that it rekindled my previous interest in spiritual medicine.

Due to my enormous clinical responsibilities, I neglected the research papers I gathered on spiritual healing in a box unattended to for many months. In 2010, I finally found the time to write a grant proposal for a new 'Spiritual Medicine Program' for our university hospital under my leadership, in collaboration with a colleague, Elisha Gold. She was a gifted physician and a scholar, the best ever trained by the premier New England Ivy League medical school. At various major academic conferences, Elisha held intellectuals and pseudo-intellectuals spellbound with her witty interviews. Although she was vulgar most of the time during those events, they worshiped her academic superstardom and savored her acid tongue. Her occasional charm and disarming smile left one wondering if she had a dual personality. Even with all her dubious qualities, she was my cherished friend and a trusted confidant. Moreover, her patients' testaments that she had special healing powers sealed the covenant for her as the proposed associate program director.

My secretary sent the grant applications to several foundations requesting funding. My goal was to secure reliable multi-year funding for the unique program that would incorporate evidence-based spiritual healing techniques in every aspect of medical care.

Six months passed before I heard from a foundation that requested extensive personal information on the proposed director of the program. I supplied all the information requested promptly and waited impatiently for another month.

On the same day that I received a telephone call from the foundation secretary about the approval of my funding request, I received another call to notify me of my nomination as a member of the board of directors of a major real estate holding company. I assumed that the second telephone call was a hoax, so I ignored it.

Two weeks after the telephone call from the grant foundation, I received an official notification letter titled, "Five-Year Funding Notification and Acceptance Letter." I hurriedly read the entire letter as my heart pounded uncontrollably. At the bottom of the letter was the signature of the foundation President: Wendy Crane-Smith. Scribbled below her signature was the following line, "Doctor Fafa, congratulations for conceiving such an incisive clinical program. You are still as innovative as you were many years ago."

My initial jubilation immediately turned into despair. In my desperation to secure funding for my program, I did not pay attention to the names behind the foundation before my secretary applied for their grant money. In my defense, the foundation was named after Wendy Crane maternal grandmother. Moreover, years had passed since I left North Carolina and Wendy Crane had not crossed my mind for a long time. I had forgotten her maternal grandmother's name.

I placed the letter back in the envelope and left it on my desk for more than a week. Eventually, I received a telephone call from the foundation secretary during my lunch break.

"Doctor Fafa, we haven't received your signed acceptance letter. I need the signed copy of the award letter returned to me as soon as possible. Our foundation president Doctor Wendy Crane-Smith also wants to talk to you. I'll get her on the line." She placed me on hold before I could object to speaking to Wendy Crane. I listened to an annoying country-western song about heartbreak while I was on hold. To say that I was anxious would be an understatement. I was petrified.

"Hello, this is Doctor Crane-Smith. I hope I haven't kept you holding for long?" she said.

"Not for too long, but thank you for being considerate," I said.

"Joseph, it's me, Wendy. After all these years, a worthy proposal for funding came from no other than you, wonderful prodigy that you are. I was flabbergasted and bemused. Your program is just the type of innovative proposal that we look for. To reassure you, in case if you have any worries, you're being funded on your merit and not because of my past with you," Wendy said.

"Thank you, Doctor Smith, but I can't accept your offer. It's best that I seek funding elsewhere," I said.

"It was your overblown pride that troubled me when I knew you in school and it appears you haven't changed much since then. I guess you're going to turn down your nomination to the board of our real estate holding too. You're an egotistical fanatic willing to lose it all because of foolish pride. Listen to me, Joseph; you're one of the most honest people I have met in my life, and you deserve to serve on our corporate board as a voice of reason against some of the prevalent excesses," she said.

"You don't owe me anything. Basically, things didn't work out between us, so I moved on," I said.

"Let's not go there because I remember the day you left me," she said.

"What did you expect me to do after your father sabotaged my medical school admission and nearly ruined my future?" I asked.

"You should accept my offer in our real estate holding as a compensation for your suffering," she said.

"I don't need your money, Wendy. I'm happy with my life," I said.

"I take it you're married and have a family?" she asked.

"I do have a wonderful family," I said.

"How is Gina? Is she the person you married?" she asked.

I laughed at her question.

"I haven't heard from her in twenty-seven years," I said.

"Really! What happened between the two of you?" she asked.

Wendy hadn't changed. "Gina confessed to me when I was in medical school that she had been in love with me since we met. She probably felt embarrassed because I didn't feel the same way about her. After that, she stopped calling me and stopped accepting my calls," I said.

"I knew she was a fake with all that big-sister garbage," Wendy said.

"Going back to the reason why we're on the telephone, I won't turn down the grant for my program. However, we had a history that neither of us will ever forget. I'll resign as the director of the program to let another physician shepherd it during the five years that your foundation will fund it. Goodbye, Wendy, and thank you for everything," I said.

"Resign? That's awful. It's your program. Please, reconsider your resignation. Don't resign because of me," she said. She would have continued, but I interrupted her.

"To maintain the integrity of the program, I have to resign. Thank you for your concern," I said.

Thank you too, Joseph, for the joy you brought to my life, and for making me a better person."

After further consideration, I placed a call to my colleague Elisha Gold to inform her about my decision to resign from the spiritual medicine program that I'd started. I felt that my resignation from the program would pave the way for its unimpeded growth.

*   *   *

Even after hearing Wendy's voice on the telephone twenty-nine years later, I responded to some of her questions as though we were still in college. I regretted that we carried on as two immature adults, instead of treating each other as professionals. I must have changed over time, since what I said during the phone conversation would not have been important to me twenty-nine years ago. My life then was about academic excellence and nothing else. Without Wendy, I probably would have gone through college and medical school without experiencing any type of failure in my life. It was because of our relationship that I enrolled in the psychology research project, which indirectly helped my personal growth. More importantly, losing my admission to medical school in North Carolina humbled me and probably made me a better person than I would have become.

Why we love or hate has a lot to do with the types of people that influence our lives. In North Carolina, I experienced both love and hate, but I left that paradise with only love, because of Wendy. She was a progressive thinker that tried her best to accommodate our differences and offered me the gift of love.

*   *   *

I had no regrets about Elisha Gold taking over my position. Her self-assuredness reminded me of my younger days. My only wish was that she would find her path to humility as she helped her patients through spiritual healing.

I received a large envelope from Wendy two weeks after we spoke on the telephone. 'Personal,' in red ink, stamped on the envelope attracted my attention, but it sat on my desk for two days. I picked up the envelope several times wondering what Wendy felt was personal between us after many years of living our separate lives.

I finally opened the envelope and read her note. *"Thank you for helping me to become a better person. I know that things could have been different between us if we'd had the will to commit to our goals. However, there are no regrets about the beautiful outcome, since you became the renowned Dr. Joseph Fafa."* In addition to the note, she enclosed my photographs from our college days and the donation check made payable to our spiritual medicine program.

I handed the check over to Elisha and realized that I had become her mentor.

Wendy's influence indirectly continued to affect my life positively.

More books from Harvard Square Editions

People and Peppers, Kelvin Christopher James
Gates of Eden, Charles Degelman
Living Treasures, Yang Huang
Close, Erika Raskin
Anomie, Jeff Lockwood
Transoceanic Lights, S. Li
Nature's Confession, J.L. Morin
A Little Something, Richard Haddaway
Dark Lady of Hollywood, Diane Haithman
Fugue for the Right Hand, Michele Tolela Myers
Growing Up White, James P. Stobaugh
Calling the Dead, R.K. Marfurt
Parallel, Sharon Erby